A SAM PRICHARD MYSTERY

FACT OR FICTION

DAVID ARCHER

USA TODAY BESTSELLING AUTHOR

FACT OR
FICTION

1

Grace Prichard liked to sleep in on Sundays. She'd started that habit many years ago, partly because she was angry at God over the death of her husband, and partly because she was just naturally lazy. It didn't really matter why she got into the habit; the fact was that she never intended to get out of it. Sunday mornings were for sleeping, as far as she was concerned, and absolutely nobody on earth was going to be able to tell her differently.

Unfortunately, that left room for someone who was not on earth to express an opinion, and that was the reason Grace was so irritable as she rolled over and yelled at her bedroom door, "Leave me alone, it's Sunday!"

"Grace?" Kim called through the door. Kim was Grace's tenant, because she rented a room in her house. Grace referred to her as her roommate, but they didn't actually room together. "Grace, I'm sorry to wake you, but Beauregard says..."

Grace's eyes popped open. "Beauregard? Beauregard? Beauregard doesn't even exist, you mental lunatic. He's a figment of your imagination, and everybody around you knows it except you."

As soon as she uttered the words, Grace regretted them. Kim was not only her tenant, but they were best friends too. They were also what Grace referred to as "joint grandmas." That was because Grace's son, Sam, was married to Kim's daughter, Indiana, and Indiana's daughter, Mackenzie, loved her grandmothers to pieces. Grace rolled her eyes and rubbed her face with her hands, then sat up on the bed. She couldn't say things like that to Kim and just leave them hanging. She needed to go and apologize immediately.

"Grace?" Kim said weakly through the door. "I think that's the problem. Beauregard says he's beginning to think the same thing."

Grace put on a light robe over her nightgown and shoved her feet into a pair of bunny slippers. It only took her three steps to reach the door, and she yanked it open to see Kim standing there looking frail and frightened. Instinctively, she wrapped her arms around the smaller woman and pulled her into a hug.

"What do you mean?" Grace asked. "I didn't mean to get you so upset, Kim, I really didn't. Everything will be okay, it really will."

"I know," Kim said. "I'm just worried about Beauregard. Something's happened, and he's beginning to doubt his own existence. Even he is beginning to wonder if I just made him up."

Grace turned and, keeping an arm around Kim, started toward the kitchen and the coffee she could already smell brewing. "Kim, just about everyone thinks you did, you know. Even Sam and Indie, they think so, too."

"I know, but why would I do that? Why would everybody think I would make him up? I mean, he's been a pain in my butt since almost the first day I had to deal with him, and the looks I get, the people always acting like I'm crazy—why would I make up something that would cause me that kind of problem?"

Grace parked Kim at the table and reached up to the cabinet to pull out a pair of coffee cups, then poured one for each of them. She set them on the table and pushed the sugar bowl close to Kim. She took her own coffee black, but Kim used enough sugar for a fair-sized cake.

"Okay, now," Grace said, "what brought all this on?"

Kim shook her head sadly, then slowly raised her eyes to meet Grace's. "Beauregard woke me up this morning," she said. "He said he'd learned something important and he was going to need to talk to Sam. I asked him if it was something about Sam being in danger and he said no, that it wasn't about Sam at all, so I asked him what it was about." She spread her hands helplessly.

"He said it was about his great-great-great-great-however-many-greats-grandchildren, that they were in some kind of trouble, but he didn't know how to find them."

Grace stared at her friend for a moment, then shook her head as if to clear the cobwebs. "He wants Sam to track down his descendants? I mean, does he know their names?"

Kim shook her head again, even more sadly than before. "That's why he's beginning to doubt himself," she said. "He says he knows they're in trouble, but he doesn't know who they are. I said, 'well, maybe you just need to think about it,' and he said, 'maybe the reason I don't know who they are is because I'm not real, maybe I really am just part of your imagination, maybe you really do see the future and use me to cover it up like Sam thinks.' So I said..."

Grace reached out and put a hand on Kim's arm. "Wait, wait, wait," she said. "He actually told you he's not sure if he's real?"

Kim nodded. "Yeah, that's what he said. He said maybe he's just a figment, and maybe Sam is right. You know Sam thinks I'm a split personality, right?"

"Yeah, yeah, we'll worry about that later," Grace said. "Did Beauregard say how Sam could find his great-great-whatever-grandchildren?"

"He doesn't know," Kim said, "but I think there has to be a way."

Grace stared at her friend for a couple of minutes,

then picked up her cup and took a sip of the hot coffee. She held the cup in both hands, bracing her elbows on the table, and mentally steeled herself for what she knew was coming. "Drink your coffee," she said. "We've got to go see Sam and Indie. Sounds to me like Sam has a case he has to solve once and for all."

"Grace, do you really think we should?" Kim asked. "I mean, you know Sam is going to get all pissed off when we tell him it's Beauregard who needs help, right?"

Grace grinned, but there was a bit of grimace in it. "He might," she allowed, "but he's Sam Prichard. To be honest, I don't think he could turn the case down to save his life. I mean, think about it; he'll either prove that Beauregard is all in your head, which is what he's always believed, or he'll find proof that we don't just come to an end when we die. Considering how many times he's come close to death, I think either one of those answers would be enough to make him want to take the case."

The two ladies finished their coffees and then went to their respective rooms to get dressed for the day. It was still early on a Sunday, but Grace had decided that this situation offered so many opportunities for her personal entertainment that there was no way she was going to miss it. She hurried up and put on a pair of designer jeans and a frilly shirt with a light jacket, slipped her feet into her leather boots, and walked out into the living room. Kim showed up there a couple of minutes later, and the two of them walked out to Grace's car. A moment later, they were on the way to Sam's house, and to what would turn out to be one of the greatest adventures any of them had ever seen.

* * * * *

Sam also enjoyed sleeping in, but things had changed lately. As Indie's belly grew along with the baby inside it, Sam found himself taking over more of the day-to-day chores around the house. This included, naturally, getting little Kenzie up and ready for school every day, but her early-morning energy didn't understand about weekends. The last three weeks, Sam had been up with her at six a.m. on both Saturday and Sunday, because the child simply could not sleep in the way her parents wanted to.

She'd also developed an annoying reluctance to go to sleep at a proper time. She could no longer simply enjoy the bedtime story Sam always climbed the stairs to read to her and drift off to sleep. Instead, Kenzie would often call out for a drink of water or another kiss good night just as Sam and his wife were settling into bed and thinking about having some private time for themselves. This would soon be followed by a "bad dream" and a heart-touching request to crawl in between them.

"It's normal," Indie had told him. "She's been the only child for six years, now. A new baby on the way means less attention for her, and she's smart enough to figure that out. She wants to get all that she can now, while she still has us to herself."

Sam understood, he really did, but he often found

himself longing for just an hour completely alone with the woman he loved. One hour, he often said to himself, that's all. Just one measly hour.

On that particular October Sunday, however, Sam had gotten up as soon as Kenzie peeked through the bedroom door. He leaned over and kissed his wife on the cheek, smiled at her, and mumbled, "Love you," and then put on his slippers and limped his way to the kitchen to make Kenzie and himself some breakfast. He would make some for Indie, as well, but not for at least a couple more hours.

Breakfast finished, the two of them made their way into the living room and sat down together on the big sofa. Kenzie grabbed the remote and searched through the DVR listings, looking for a movie she had recorded sometime in the past month. As Bill Gates had once discovered, however, icons are easier to recognize than titles; when she spotted the cartoon image of a Polynesian girl, she knew she had found the right movie. She hit the Select button, and it began to play.

This particular movie had become one of her favorites, so by this time, both she and Sam could recite almost the entire script. When the young heroine found herself facing the man who was supposed to help her but chickened out, they actually played out the parts. Sam recited the guy's lines while Kenzie delivered the girl's lines perfectly.

They were almost to the end of the movie when Sam

heard a car pull up, and he got up and walked over to peek through the windows on the front door. As soon as he did so, his eyes went wide; his mother and mother-in-law were sitting in the driveway, and it seemed that they were having an animated discussion of some sort. Sam opened the door and leaned out, and the two women got out of the car and started toward the house.

"Mom? Kim?" Sam said questioningly. "What are you doing here on a Sunday morning?"

"Chasing a ghost," Grace said. "No, wait, that's your job."

Sam stepped back and held the door for them as they entered, then invited them to sit down. Indie came into the living room at the same time, and the expression on her face showed as much surprise as Sam's.

"Mom? What's going on?"

Kim sat primly on the couch and looked like she was trying to gather her thoughts for a moment, but Grace was impatient. "It's Beauregard again," she said. "He wants to hire you, Sam."

Sam was about to sit down in his recliner and suddenly fell backward into it. "What?"

"It's true, I'm telling you," Grace said. "He suddenly wants to know if he's real or not, because now he's had a premonition that his great-great-forever-great-grandkids are in some kind of trouble."

Sam stared at his mother for a moment, then turned to Kim. "What is she talking about?"

Kim sighed and finally raised her eyes to meet Sam's. "She's mostly right," she said. "Beauregard woke me up this morning and said his grandchildren, several times removed, are in some kind of trouble. The problem is that he doesn't know who they are or where to find them, so he wants you to track them down. The only problem with that is that it means you have to first prove whether or not he even exists."

San shook his head for a moment, then looked at his mother-in-law again. "Kim—look, I don't know how to say this, but..."

"You don't believe in Beauregard," Kim said. "It's obvious, Sam—you don't need to apologize for it. In fact, Beauregard is beginning to believe you may be right. He actually told me this morning that he's not sure himself whether he's real or just some psychological mix-up in my head."

Sam sat still and stared at her for ten seconds, then shook his head again. "Wait, you're telling me that Beauregard doesn't believe in himself anymore? Then how in the hell is he even talking to you?"

"Sam," Indie said, "language."

Sam winced. "Sorry, babe," he said. "But still, if he doesn't believe in himself, then how could he even exist?"

"Well, if he really is just—just a figment of my imagination, some psychological construct I whipped together to hide my own ability to see the future, which is how you described him on more than one occasion, then I would imagine he's really just me trying to talk to myself, right? Whether he's real or not, I sure am."

Sam looked at her for a moment, then turned to look at his wife. Indie shrugged at him with her eyes wide, so he turned back to Kim. "I wouldn't have the slightest idea how to track down his great-whatevers, assuming they even exist. I mean, how would I go about it?"

Kim looked at him, but then suddenly her eyelids sagged and she seemed to wobble back and forth for a moment. When she suddenly sat up again and opened her eyes, Sam felt a frisson of fear run down his spine. "Beauregard?" Sam asked cautiously.

"Hello, Samuel," Kim said in a voice that sounded like a gentleman from the Deep South. "I do apologize for troubling you this way, but as you can imagine, there is no other that I can turn to. I need your help, Samuel, and there is no time to waste."

Sam rolled his eyes but then looked back at Kim's somewhat distorted face. "But what can I do, Beauregard? How do I find your grandkids if you don't even know who they are?"

"I have thought about this all the night," Kim said, "and I have some idea of a plan of action that might have some chance at success. If you were to go back to the places where I lived before I left the mortal plane, you might find some evidence of what happened to my children. As I recall, I had lost track of them some years

10

before my demise, but there should be some sort of record that might lead you to them, and to a record of their children, and so on. It is my hope that you can then determine which of my descendants might be they of whom I have had this premonition."

Sam stared at Kim's face, amazed at the fact that he could actually imagine that he was talking to an elderly gentleman, rather than a woman who was not yet quite forty-five years old. "I—I don't know. I wouldn't know where to begin. How do you track down somebody who's been dead for what, a hundred and fifty years?"

"It's been somewhat less than that, but I understand your concern. While I do not pretend to understand the workings of the device with which Miss Indiana learns so many things, I thought it might perhaps be able to provide some information?"

Sam looked at Indie and raised his eyebrows. She stared back for a second, then shrugged.

"I guess we could try ancestry.com," she said. "I know they have a lot of records of Civil War soldiers and people from that time." She rose from where she was sitting beside her mother and left the room but came back moments later with her laptop. She set it on the coffee table and powered it up, then began tapping on the keys. "Beauregard, what's your last name?"

"Beauregard," Kim said. "That was my surname. My Christian name is Henry. Henry Thomas Beauregard was my full name."

Indie tapped on the keys for a few moments, and then her own eyebrows went up. "I have an H. Beauregard from Virginia and three H. T. Beauregards. Two of them are from South Carolina, but the other one just says Confederate troops. Can you tell me what year you were born?"

Kim smiled. "That was in 1826," she said. "July the twenty ninth, in Johnson City, Tennessee."

"And the year you died? Do you remember that?"

"Yes," Kim said. "That would have been 1875, and it was springtime. May, I believe."

Sam did the math and looked at Kim. "You were only forty-nine? Somehow I thought you would have been quite a bit older than that."

"Ah, but the war did make old men of us. I was not quite to my forty-ninth birthday, but I had lost a leg to a cannonball and I had taken a bullet that had damaged my liver. I was fortunate to have lived so long, Samuel."

"May of 1875," Indie repeated back. "And you died in Hazard, Kentucky, right? In that house where Mom first heard you?"

Kim smiled, but again the smile looked like it belonged on a gray-haired man. "Yes, the one on Pikeville Road."

Indie nodded. "How many children did you have, and what were their names?"

"There were three," Kim said, "one from each of my three wives. In those days, I'm sorry to say, it was not

12

uncommon for young women to die in childbirth. Both of my first two wives did so. There were Henry Junior, Horace, and my only daughter, Winnifred."

Indie turned and looked at Sam. "Well," she said softly, "I found him, I think." She turned to her mother. "Beauregard, I've got a Henry Thomas Beauregard, born in Johnson City, Tennessee, on July 29, 1826. The only problem is that according to the information I see here, he died at fifty-one years old in Franklin, Tennessee, not Hazard, Kentucky."

"My goodness," Kim said. "If that is correct, then I am concerned. Is there any possibility that that information could be faulty?"

She shrugged. "That kind of information is often contributed by people using the system, so I suppose it could be wrong. Do you know what happened to your children? Anything at all?"

"I fear that I do not," Kim said. "As I said, I had lost track of them during the war. We had been living in Tennessee, in Greenville, but the family had to flee when it was under attack while I was gone. I was never able to find them after the war."

Indie bit her bottom lip for a second, then let out a sigh. "Well, Henry Junior, who was born in 1849, apparently joined the Army sometime after you did. He died on November 29, 1864, at the battle of Spring Hill, Tennessee."

Kim's face, already bearing the visage of age and

weariness, sank. She looked at the floor for a moment and then closed her eyes. "And Horace? Does your information machine tell you anything about him?"

"Yes," Indie said. "Horace was born in 1853, and never enlisted. He was married in 1870, in Franklin, Tennessee. He and his wife had one child, a girl named Annabelle, but she died of pneumonia when she was seven years old. Horace died in 1884, still in Franklin. According to this, he had lost his mind and was in some kind of an asylum at the time." She cleared her throat. "And that brings us to Winnifred. Winnifred was born in 1857, and she married a man named Arthur Chase in 1871. They had settled in Murfreesboro, Tennessee, and had three children, two boys and a girl. Their names were Andrew, Henry, and Martha. Arthur is listed as having died of consumption in 1889. Andrew married in 1890 but never had any children. He also seemed to have had mental issues, and he died in 1896 while in a hospital for people with dementia. Henry apparently never married, but he died in 1892 at the age of eighteen, in a horse race. Martha was married in 1895, to a man named Charles Wellington, a lawyer who was quite a bit older than she was. She had two daughters, Clara and Beatrice, but apparently Charles died in 1901. There is a reference that says she and her children then moved back in with her mother. She married again in 1906 but had no more children. She remained in Murfreesboro until 1939, when Winnifred passed away, and then moved to Nashville. Martha died at the age of seventy in 1956." She looked up at him. "I'm afraid there's no record of Clara or Beatrice ever getting married."

Kim kept her gaze on the floor for a moment but then looked up at her daughter. "And yet, at least one of them must have done so, if I am correct about having living descendants. Is there no other avenue you might explore, to find out what happened to them?"

Sam let out a sigh. "Look," he said, "this is—well, it's pretty spooky is what it is, but it could be just pure coincidence that he got so many details right."

"I agree with you, Samuel," said Beauregard's voice through Kim's lips. "This is my great worry, that although I feel myself to be genuine, you could be correct about me. Perhaps I am nothing more than some part of Miss Kimberly's imagination. I know that you believe me to be none else than that, and if you are right, then it may well be that my concerns about my distant offspring may be all for naught." Kim slowly turned her face to look into Sam's eyes. "Miss Kimberly has read many books about the workings of the mind and talked with me about them, so I am familiar with the concept of multiple personalities. I know that it is not uncommon for an individual to create a new personality, complete with its own sense of identity, to protect the individual from something it fears. In this case, it would appear that what she might fear is her own ability to predict some aspects of the future."

Indie nodded. "That's what I've always wondered," she said. "Mom was raised by strict Catholic parents, and then she was in Catholic foster homes until she got pregnant with me. Naturally, anything to do with the supernatural was considered an absolute taboo. Anyone who could see the future was considered to be involved in evil, maybe even possessed. I could see why she might be afraid if she suddenly developed a gift like that. To her, it would probably seem like something from the devil."

"But then how could Kim know all these things about this Henry Beauregard you found?" Sam asked. "How could she possibly know so accurately what the names of his children were? As much as I hate to admit it, this is making me consider the possibility, for the first time, that Beauregard is exactly who he claims to be."

Kim's eyes, already focused on Sam, crinkled as her face broke into a smile. "I am so relieved, Samuel, to hear those words come from you. For the time has come when I must know whether I am truly Henry Thomas Beauregard, or that part of him which remains upon the earth after his passing—or merely a simple construct of the imagination of this good lady. There is none other on this earth to whom I can turn, Samuel, but if I am correct, then there are those who are descended from Mr. Beauregard who need your help, and so it seems to me that by finding them you will also find the answer we both seek."

Sam stared at his mother-in-law for a moment, then

slowly nodded. "Beauregard, I'm willing to concede the possibility that you really are that old soldier. Tracking down your descendants is going to mean taking a trip to Tennessee, I'm sure, and who knows where after that. I'll get started on it immediately."

"Thank you, Samuel," Kim said. "If I might add only a bit more, it is that I do not sense any danger to yourself in this. If it would be possible, I would like Miss Kimberly to accompany you. I believe that I may be of assistance in this endeavor."

Sam's eyebrows rose a half inch, but Indie was nodding. "We can make it a family trip," she said. "Kenzie's way ahead on her schoolwork, so that's not a problem. Her teachers won't mind if she's gone for a few days. How about it, Sam?"

Sam rolled his eyes, but there was a hint of a smile on his face. "Sure, why not? The more the merrier. Let's all get packed, and we can head out today."

2

Beauregard had relinquished control to Kim only a moment later, and she was quickly brought up to date, but it only left her looking more confused. Grace came to her rescue.

"Oh, for goodness' sake," she said, "let's just go home and pack. We are all going on a trip, did you get that much?"

The two grandmothers left to go home, while Sam and Indie began preparing themselves for the journey. "I guess this can work," Sam said. "Sort of like a working vacation, right?"

Indie looked up at him with a grin. "Sam Prichard, if I didn't know better, I'd say you were actually having fun with this. Did you mean it when you said you're starting to believe in Beauregard?"

Sam shivered. "I'm so serious it's sending chills up and down my spine. I never wanted to believe in ghosts, but how else can you explain Kim being so accurate with all those little details?"

"I can't," Indie agreed. "It really is pretty spooky, isn't it? It's just that we've always gone on the assumption that Beauregard wasn't real, up till now. It's kind of hard to change my way of thinking so quickly."

"Well," Sam said, "let's just go and do this. If we find Henry Beauregard's grandkids and they really do need some kind of assistance, that will pretty much nail it down."

Indie nodded and they began packing in earnest. Kenzie was running through the house excitedly, her cat, Samson, tumbling along at her heels. Sam noticed, and quickly called Jim Peterson, his friend down the street, who agreed to let Samson come and visit with them for a while.

It took less than two hours to get everything ready. Since it was a Sunday, Sam left a note in the mailbox telling the postman to hold their mail until further notice, and then they climbed into their Honda Ridgeline and headed for Grace's house. Grace and Kim were packed and ready, so they loaded everything into the back of the little truck and got onto the highway.

From Denver, Colorado, to Murfreesboro, Tennessee, was about an eighteen-hour drive, when Sam factored in stopping to eat and other necessities. Since it was almost noon by the time they got on the road, he planned on stopping somewhere for the night, but first it was time for lunch.

"Anybody hungry?" That question got a chorus of affirmative answers, so he stopped at a burger shop just before they got onto I-70. Four deluxe combo meals and an Adventure Meal later, the Ridgeline made the sharp turn out of the parking lot and onto the ramp.

Kenzie, her car seat comfortably sandwiched between her grandmothers, was asleep before they made five miles. The grandmothers followed her less than ten miles later, leaving Sam and Indie as the only ones awake.

"Thank you for this," Indie said.

Sam glanced at her with his eyebrows high. "For what?"

"For taking us all along. We haven't gotten out of town to just relax for a long time, so this will be a nice break." She glanced into the back seat, then turned back to Sam with a smile. "And while she'd never admit it, I don't think Mom has been on any kind of vacation in at least five years, unless you count the times Harry has shipped us all off somewhere. We had some fun at Disney World, but just knowing we had all that security watching us kind of ruined some of it, you know?"

Sam nodded. "Yeah, I can imagine. Well, this isn't going to be all fun and games, but we should be able to find time for a little relaxation. I just want to work the case as much as I can, just in case Beauregard is right and there are people in trouble."

"Oh, let's face it, Sam," Indie said. "We know he's right—he's always right. I don't know who his descendants are, but I'm quite certain they need some kind of help or he wouldn't have known about it."

"That's pretty much how I feel about it," Sam said. "And I'll admit there's a little part of me that is curious, now, that wants to know just who Beauregard really was. I've read a lot of books and articles about so-called ghosts, and I've never heard of anyone actually being able to verify that one existed. The more he talked this morning, though, the more I began to believe. When you were able to find a record of him and his children, that just about clinched it for me."

"Yeah, I understand. Are you thinking about writing a book of your own, once we've proved he really did exist?"

Sam shook his head. "No way," he said. "Good grief, can you imagine what would happen? Your mother would never have another moment's peace. Between the scientists who would want to try to study Beauregard through her and the loonies who would want Beauregard to tell them where to find the missing family fortune, I'm afraid it would drive her crazy."

Indie shrugged. "You could always do it the way most of them do," she said, "saying you had to change the names to protect everybody. That way no one could actually track her down."

"If you can't publish the name of the person who

really is the proof of what you're saying, then why bother to write anything about it at all? That wouldn't be any different than writing a fictional story. Besides, I don't know that it would be good for people to believe in life after death, not this way. If everyone thought they would simply end up as a ghost, it might be too easy for them to stop paying attention to how they live. There aren't any ghosts in the Bible, you know."

"Yes, there are," Indie said. "I don't remember exactly where it is, but King Saul went to the medium and asked her to call up the ghost of the prophet Samuel, and she did. Samuel told Saul that he would die the next day, so that means that maybe ghosts really can see the future."

Sam glanced at her for a second before turning his eyes back to the road. "Okay, good point," he said. "Still, I don't think I'd want to try to tell the world about Beauregard. Somehow I don't think it would be fair to him or your mother."

The road droned on beneath them, and it wasn't long before Sam glanced over to find Indie sleeping, as well. That was okay with him, though; Sam felt that he always did some of his best thinking while he was behind the wheel.

Of course, that was when the irony of the entire situation struck him. He had spent the last couple of years trying to deny that Beauregard could possibly be real, and now he was on a quest to prove that the old soldier really had existed. He decided to fall back on one of his favorite maxims.

Life, he told himself, *is what happens while you're making other plans.*

Sam stopped for gas in the middle of Kansas, which woke everyone and precipitated a short break. It got longer when they decided to have dinner, and then they were back on the road. They made it to just short of Kansas City before stopping for gas again, then drove on for a couple hours more, finally stopping for the night at Columbia, Missouri.

The long drive, despite being comfortable in the Ridgeline, had taken its toll on everyone. Sam paid for two rooms and confessed to Indie that he was relieved when Kenzie decided she wanted to stay with her grandmothers.

Indie agreed. Being four and a half months pregnant, she was feeling the effects of carrying her second child and was looking forward to a good night's sleep. She took a quick shower and climbed into bed, and was sleeping peacefully by the time Sam got back from his own.

They took advantage of the continental breakfast at the hotel the following morning, then checked out and hit the road. Sam predicted that they would reach Murfreesboro by four p.m., but between Kenzie and Indie, the potty breaks added an extra hour to the trip. They rolled into town just after five, and Sam was delighted to see a selection of motels. He checked them in, and then they went out in search of a nice dinner.

Murfreesboro, Tennessee, was of major importance during the Civil War. Following a battle between the Union's General Rosecrans and Confederate General Bragg between December 31, 1862, and January 2, 1863, it became a Union base of operations that allowed the North to push further into the South. Rosecrans decided to use the city as a supply depot, and Fortress Rosecrans was ordered built. This was the largest military structure of the Civil War, covering two hundred and twenty-five acres and comprising sawmills, small factories, and other forms of industry within its borders. The fortress was never attacked, primarily because of the constant training of artillery at that location.

After the war, the city remained and slowly began to recover. It had become an educational center of the state of Tennessee, earning it the nickname "Athens of Tennessee." As time passed, it continued to grow as an educational center, culminating with the formation of the Middle Tennessee State Normal School, an institution for training teachers. In 1965, this became the Middle Tennessee State University, a major educational institution that is still growing today.

After dinner and some relaxing television time, the family once again split into two rooms and settled down for the night. The following morning, Sam decided to let them rest while he began his search for information regarding Martha Chase Wellington and her daughters,

Clara and Beatrice.

His first stop that morning was at the Rutherford County Courthouse. He knew that Henry Beauregard's daughter, Winnifred, and her husband, Arthur Chase, had moved to Murfreesboro sometime after they were married in 1871, so he asked the clerk about researching the records from that time.

The woman gave him a knowing smile and escorted him to a room in the basement that was lined with shelves holding massive books. "You can start here," she said, indicating a particular section of a particular shelf. "This would be the first book of records for 1871."

Sam's eyes got wide as he looked at the thick book and all the others that followed it. "You mean, none of this has been digitized?"

"I'm afraid not," the clerk said. "We've asked repeatedly for the budget to do so, but it's just never come through. If you find the names you're looking for, then there will be a catalog number on the far right of the page. Write it down and bring it to me, and I'll be able to show you where to find all of the actual records pertaining to those individuals."

She turned around and left Sam standing in the room, so he sighed heavily and took down the first book she had indicated. There was a table against one wall with an ancient desk lamp, so he sat down and began going through the book page by page.

Running his finger down the names on the third

column of each page, Sam found that he could search each book fairly quickly. Still, it took him almost forty minutes to scan through the first book alone, and he was halfway through the third book for the year before he spotted the name Chase, Arthur. He wrote down the catalog number on a slip of paper and started to put the book away and head back to the clerk, but then he had a thought.

He recalled that Martha Chase had married Charles Wellington in 1895, so he found the books for that year and began scanning through them. He only made it halfway through the first book when he came across Wellington, Charles, and copied down that number, as well.

He put the book away and made his way back up the stairs to the clerk's office. The same woman smiled when he handed her the slip of paper with the names and catalog numbers on them, and then escorted him to yet another room that held a number of microfilm viewers. She showed him how to use the catalog numbers to find the specific film that would have copies of documents relating to the names he had listed, and Sam shook his head in disbelief.

"Microfilm? Do they still make those machines?"

"Oh, no," the clerk said with a grin. "These are probably fifty years old, but they still work."

"That's good, I suppose," Sam said. "I'm just surprised those books weren't already converted over."

The clerk rolled her eyes and shook her head. "They did all this before my day," she said, "or those would have been converted first. Someday, we'll be able to scan all the microfilm and convert it to computer files. There are machines that do that now, and they only take a few seconds to convert an entire film. Unfortunately, that's another budget request that keeps getting turned down."

She turned and went back to her office, and Sam started looking through the drawers that held the film sheets. It only took him a few minutes to find the reference numbers he wanted, but each of them occupied the better part of three sheets.

He took them over to the viewer and sat down, inserting the first sheet into the machine. It took him a couple of minutes to figure out how to operate the device, but then he began gliding the pointer over the various images and reading through them on the screen in front of him. Halfway through the very first sheet, he found a document that confirmed that Arthur Chase had purchased a home at 532 East Main Street. His spouse was listed as Winnifred Chase. They still owned the home when Arthur died in 1889.

Excited, Sam jotted down the address on a sheet of paper and then began looking at the films for Charles Wellington. It took him only minutes to find the record of his marriage to Martha Chase, and then he found another record showing that they had also purchased a house, on Lytle Street, and two others recording the births of their daughters, Clara in 1897 and Beatrice in

1898. That house was their home until Charles died in 1901. Shortly after his death, Martha sold the house, which is when she and her children must have moved back to the house on East Main Street.

Interestingly, the same catalog number that had referenced documents relating to Charles Wellington also referenced those relating to Martha. Sam continued searching through them until he found a notation regarding a 1913 dowry transfer from Martha to a man named James Landon. There was no further reference to Landon, but in a document recorded a year later, a second dowry was transferred from Martha to Walter Ashley.

Sam checked through the rest of the films but found no further mention of either man's name. He copied them down onto his notes, put away the films, and made his way back down to the basement. Since he knew the dates of the two girls' marriages, it didn't take him long to find the relevant catalog numbers for Landon and Ashley, and then he limped back up the stairs to the microfilm room.

James and Clara Landon had lived in a home that belonged to him prior to the marriage, on East Vine Street, only a short distance from the Chases' home on East Main Street. They had one child, a boy named Jeremiah, in 1914. Another document recorded the death of Clara only two years later, with the cause of death listed as "atrophy of the brain." Sam noted down Jeremiah's name.

He then looked for Walter Ashley and quickly found a reference to his marriage to Beatrice Chase. Unfortunately, that was the final document under the catalog number he had found. They had apparently moved away, and there was nothing in the public records to indicate where they had gone.

Back down the stairs Sam went, and he began looking up Jeremiah Landon. It wasn't terribly difficult, since his record of birth contained the catalog number that would follow the rest of his life in local records. By the time he got back upstairs to the microfilm room again, his bad hip was issuing complaints that he could not ignore.

He found the single sheet of microfilm pertaining to Jeremiah and slid it into the machine. A quick scan of its contents brought him to Jeremiah's own marriage in 1932 to Mary Porter. The newlywed Porters had purchased a home a short time later but sold it only three years afterward. That was the last reference to them on the film.

Still, Sam felt that he had gained some useful information. He thanked the clerk for all her assistance and asked her if she might know of anyone who was intimately familiar with the history of Murfreesboro between 1900 and 1925. She thought for a few moments, then nodded.

"Abigail Morton," she said. "She's ninety-two years old and works at the Murfreesboro Historical Society. If anyone can tell you anything about the people you're researching, it would be her."

Sam thanked her and left the courthouse. As he got into the Ridgeline, he took out his phone and called Indie. His family had had breakfast there at the hotel, but since it was almost half past noon, they were definitely ready for lunch.

3

Because Sam had made so much headway but still had more to do, they decided to keep lunch simple and went to a restaurant just across the street from the motel. The food and the service were both good, and they were finished in fairly short order. They went back to Sam and Indie's motel room, and he went over what he had learned so far.

Indie pulled her computer close to her and entered the addresses he had found. "Well," she said, "the house on East Main is still standing. Not surprisingly, it's known as the Chase House, and it's on the national historic register. The others are apparently gone."

Kim grinned. "Beauregard says he would love to see the house his daughter lived in," she said.

"We'll take a drive by later this evening," Sam said. "Right now, I want to go and track down Abigail Morton. From what I've heard, she's sort of a walking encyclopedia about Murfreesboro and its history."

"Then get to it," Indie said playfully. She leaned over and kissed him, and he headed out once again.

The place Sam was looking for turned out to be the Murfreesboro Historical Association, but it came up when he tried to google the address. Luckily, it was only a short distance from the motel. He pulled into its parking lot only fifteen minutes after kissing his wife goodbye.

Three elderly women sat at the counter in its lobby, and Sam put on his best smile as he approached. "Hi, there," he said. "I'm looking for Abigail Morton. Would she happen to be in today?"

One of the ladies looked at the one in the middle. "Abby," she said, "how is it all the nice-looking young men come in asking for you?"

The lady in the middle giggled like a schoolgirl and smiled at Sam. "You found her," she said. "How can I help you?"

"My name is Sam Prichard," he said, handing her one of his business cards. "I'm a private investigator from Denver, Colorado, and I'm trying to find any information I can get on some people who used to live here, quite some time ago. The lady down at the county clerk's office told me that if anyone could help me, it would be you."

"And she's probably right," Abigail said. "I seem to have a lot of information stored under these gray curls, especially when it comes to names. Probably goes back to the fact that my father was one of the most popular doctors when I was a little girl. Who is it you're looking for, young man?"

"Well, I have a number of names, but the most important one would be Jeremiah Landon. He was born to James and Clara Landon in 1914 and was married to a Mary Porter in 1932. I managed to trace him that far, but I couldn't find anything after that."

Abigail, who didn't look anywhere near her reported age of ninety-two, stuck the tip of her tongue between her teeth and narrowed her eyes in thought. "Landon, Landon," she said. "Now, there was a Jeremiah Landon, and I believe he did marry a Porter. Give me just a minute." She turned and walked to a large bookcase behind her and reached out to take down a thick volume. She carried it back over and laid it on the counter, flipped it open, and began quickly riffling through its pages. "Here we go," she said. "Jeremiah and Mary Landon. Yes, they were married in 1932, and then they moved off to Evansville, Indiana. They lived there for about fifteen years and then moved to Smyrna, right down the road."

Sam's eyes grew wide as she spoke. "They moved to Smyrna? But isn't that here in Rutherford County?"

Abigail nodded. "Yes, it is," she said, "but if you're wondering why you didn't find any reference in the county records, it's because Jeremiah was incapacitated by that time. He had had a stroke, you see, and my daddy used to drive all the way out to Smyrna to see him. His oldest son was serving as the man of the family by then. His name was Alvin."

"Fifteen years," Sam muttered. "That would have been 1937. Ma'am, would you happen to know if Alvin might still be alive?"

"Oh, no," Abigail said. "Alvin went off to Europe during the second war and never came back. Actually, I tell a lie. Alvin left Smyrna in 1938, but we heard later that he was missing in action somewhere overseas."

"Oh," Sam said. "I don't suppose you'd know if he ever married or had any children?"

"No, I'm sure he didn't. Now, his sister, Roberta, she stayed and took care of their father until he died in 1943. I mean to say that she stayed, even after that. She married, let me see, she married John Wingo, back in '37. They had two daughters, and if I remember correctly, their names were Judith and Millicent. They were born in '38 and '39, respectively. Yes, here's a reference. Judith still lives down in Smyrna, in the same house her mother inherited when her grandfather died. She never married, but I do recall hearing that Millicent did." She looked through the pages of the book, which seemed to be filled with handwritten notes. "I'm afraid I don't know who Millicent married—that was after she left here. I remember that it was quite a scandal, though, because she was in a bit of a family way at the time."

Sam was grinning. "Ma'am, is there any chance you might have an address for Judith? I'm sure she'd be able to tell me about her sister and her children."

Abigail looked up at him, and the expression on her face caused Sam's grin to fade away. "I can give you an address, but I'm not sure Judith will tell you anything. You see, the reason she never married is that the man who got Millicent in her predicament was engaged to Judith at the time. From what I understand, the two sisters never spoke again, and Judith is known to be one of the most stuck-up and hateful old biddies in the whole county." She took a slip of paper from the counter and scribbled down an address, then passed it to Sam. "I wish I could give you something better to go on," she said. "Frankly, I'll be quite surprised if Judith agrees to speak with you at all."

Sam winked at her. "Just leave that to me," he said. He slipped the address into his pocket and blew her a kiss as he turned and walked out the door. Behind him, he could hear the other two ladies gasp, while Abigail simply chuckled.

Sam punched the address into the GPS app on his phone and began following the directions it gave him. According to the app, he should arrive at his destination in just a little over twenty minutes, but Sam had a tendency to push the speed limit. He got there in just over eighteen and parked the car at the curb in front of a beautiful antebellum home.

He walked up to the front steps and leaned heavily on his cane and the handrail as he made his way up. When he got to the front porch, he had to stop and rest for a moment because of the sharp pains in his hip, and the front door opened before he even got a chance to knock.

An elderly woman stood there glaring at him. "Whatever you're selling," she said angrily, "I'm not buying. You're wasting your time."

She started to slam the door, but Sam quickly held up a hand. "Ma'am," he said urgently, "I'm not selling anything. I'm actually a private investigator, and I'm trying to track down the heirs to a man named Henry Thomas Beauregard."

The door stopped swinging shut, and the old woman glared out at him. "Beauregard? Henry Thomas Beauregard was my great-great-great-grandfather. What's this about heirs?"

Sam had made it to the doorway by then and smiled as he leaned on his cane. He flashed his ID and let her look at it, then went on. "Ma'am, it seems that Mr. Beauregard owned some property that was willed to his children, but they were never found. Now, normally when that happens, the property ends up being claimed by the state, but Beauregard was extremely intelligent and apparently pretty wealthy. He had put the property into a trust whose sole purpose was to locate any legitimate heirs and see that they were granted ownership. He endowed that trust with a substantial amount of money so that its attorneys could continue looking for those heirs. Somewhere along the line, the case sort of fell through the cracks and was forgotten, but I was recently engaged to try once more to locate any living descendants of Mr. Beauregard, and that's what brought me to your door."

Judith Wingo seemed to have a miraculous change of attitude, swinging the door open and inviting Sam to come inside. "Oh, this is such a surprise," she said with a smile. "So, just what would be the value of this property?" She motioned for him to sit down on the big sofa.

"I'm afraid I'm not privy to that information, ma'am," Sam said, "but it must be pretty substantial. The trust is still in existence and has paid me considerably well to try to locate you and your sister. If you could tell me..."

"My sister? What the hell has she got to do with any of this?"

Sam tried to look innocent. "It's the terms of the will, ma'am," he said. "The estate must be divided equally among all surviving heirs. I've been able to establish that you, your sister, and any children she might have had would be in the line of inheritance. Before the trust will release any of the assets, however, it's necessary for all of the prospective heirs to certify that they were notified and signify their acceptance or rejection of their portion."

Judith's demeanor went back to being cranky. "Millie's dead, as far as I know. I haven't spoken to her in more than sixty years, but she used to send these stupid Christmas cards every year until about eight years ago. I figure she must've died, so there's no need for you to look any further."

Sam looked confused. "But did she never have any children? It was my understanding that she was pregnant at the time she was married. If she did have children, then they and even their children would also be in the line of inheritance."

The old woman looked around, as if trying to come up with a good answer, then grinned at Sam. "Nope! I'm all there is."

Sam simply looked at her for a couple of seconds, then lowered his eyebrows. "Ma'am, I should point out to you that withholding any information about other possible heirs could constitute fraud and would immediately disqualify you from receiving any share in the estate. It could also, if any other heirs were to see fit to file complaints, result in criminal charges being filed against you. Are you absolutely certain she never had any children?"

Judith narrowed her own eyes and glared at him. "Fine," he said after a moment. "She had a daughter and a son, but I've never met either of them. Far as I know, they might be dead, too."

Sam nodded. "And that's certainly possible," he said. "However, it's absolutely necessary that I find out for certain. Could you tell me where I might find them?"

"Hell, no," Judith said. "I don't even remember their names. All I know is she used to send me Christmas cards and put their pictures in them as they were growing up. God only knows whatever happened to them; they really might be dead for all I know."

Sam continued nodding. "And I'll be happy to find out for sure," he said. "You said your sister used to send you Christmas cards—would you happen to have an address, and perhaps her married name? It would give me a place to start, in looking for her children."

Judith glared at him for a couple more seconds, then turned and walked into another room. She came back a few minutes later with a box and set it on the coffee table. She sat down on the sofa and opened the box, then began digging through it. After almost five minutes, she held up a single envelope and squinted at it. "Millie's married name was Cameron, on account of she married Donald Cameron, the son of a bitch who knocked her up. Can't make out the address," she said, "but the postmark is from Thompsonville, Illinois. That's the most recent one, from eight years ago. Of course, Millie would've been about seventy or seventy-one by then, so her kids were long grown and gone, I'm sure."

"And you're sure you don't remember your niece's or nephew's names?" Sam asked, looking pointedly into the box. There appeared to be dozens of envelopes of roughly the same shape and size within it. "Didn't your sister ever include any notes or anything?"

Judith tossed the one she was holding into the box and slammed the lid shut. "No, she didn't," she said emphatically. "How long am I going to have to wait for you to try to track them down before you give me my property?"

Sam reflected that the old woman was not only angry and bitter, she was extremely selfish. "Well, to be honest, Ms. Wingo," Sam said, "there actually isn't any inheritance. The truth is that I'm just trying to track down the most recent generation of your family, and you've just been good enough to help me do that."

A moment later, Sam hurried out the front door as the old woman inside screamed a number of unpleasant insults at him. He had learned early on in the PI game that even the people who were most reluctant to answer questions would usually speak right up if they thought there was money in it for them. He had used the "unknown heirs" routine a couple of times in the past, and it had yet to fail him.

He got back into the Ridgeline and pointed it back toward Murfreesboro and the motel. The afternoon traffic was beginning to pick up, so the drive took him almost half an hour. Still, it wasn't even 3:30 yet, so Sam felt like he had actually accomplished quite a bit.

There was no one at either of the motel rooms, so

Sam took out his phone to call Indie and find out where they were, but then he heard the unmistakable sound of Kenzie's laughter coming from the direction of the swimming pool. He put the phone back in his pocket and turned in that direction.

The pool was in a fenced-off area in between the two buildings of the motel. It was surrounded by a privacy fence that was eight feet tall, and there was only one entrance. Sam opened the gate slightly and peeked inside, and saw his wife and their mothers in bathing suits, sunning themselves in chairs near the shallow end of the pool, while Kenzie was splashing in the water with other children. Their backs were to the gate, so he slipped in unnoticed and managed to make it all the way up to just behind Indie's chair without being seen. He quickly slipped his hands around and put them over her eyes, and he laughed when she squealed in surprise.

"Guess who," he said, and then he let out a yelp. Indie had reached up and grabbed both of his thumbs and twisted them backward.

"Guess who's going to get broken thumbs if he ever tries that again," Indie hissed at him. "Sam, you know I don't like to be startled like that."

Despite the mild pain in his thumbs, Sam was laughing. "Okay, okay," he said, "I'll make sure I never forget that again. I just wanted to surprise you all." He spotted an empty chair nearby and dragged it over beside his wife. "So, this is how you spend your time

41

while I'm out working?"

"Working vacation, remember?" Indie said. "That means you work, and we take a vacation."

"You did say that, Samuel," his mother said. "I heard you say it, so don't try to back out of it now."

"I'm not backing out of anything. Actually, I'm glad you guys are having fun." He saw Kenzie and two other little girls, all of them wearing what Indie called "floaties" as they played together in the shallow end. "Kenzie sure seems to be."

Indie nodded and smiled. "Those two little girls spotted her when we came out and came running over to ask her to play with them. She got so excited she almost forgot we were with her, but then she remembered. They've been having a blast, and we've been soaking up some sun."

"So I see. That's fine—I really am glad you're having fun. Meanwhile, I've been gathering up some information."

Kim leaned forward so that she could look closely at Sam. "Did you find out anything about Beauregard's family? About where they might be now, I mean?"

"Well, I got to speak with his great-great-great-granddaughter a bit ago," Sam said. "Let me tell you something—that is one bitter old lady. She's probably in her mid to late eighties, and she has hated her one and only sister for more than sixty years."

"Well, don't stop there, give us details," Grace said.

"We're women, Samuel, we need details."

"I'll give you what I've got," Sam said. "Apparently, Judith—that's the one I met today—was engaged to be married back around 1937, but her fiancé apparently seduced her sister, Millicent. Millie got pregnant, so when it all came out Judith called off the engagement, Millie married the former fiancé, and the two of them moved off somewhere else. I haven't been able to get any direct information about where they went, but it seems Millie never stopped trying to make peace with her sister. She sent a Christmas card every year until about eight years ago, when they stopped coming. The postmark on the last card was from a tiny little town called Thompsonville, Illinois. I googled it on the way back here—it's got like six hundred people. I figure somebody there ought to remember Millie, and hopefully we can get a lead on where her kids might have gone."

Kim's face brightened. "She had kids, then?"

"At least two," Sam said. "Judith knew of a boy and a girl, but she either couldn't or wouldn't tell me their names. I'll be honest, I've seen people filled with hate and anger before, but Judith pretty well took the prize. Can you imagine hating someone in your family for more than six decades?"

"It's not that uncommon," Kim said. "My mother hated her family so much that I don't even know who my grandparents were. Every time I asked about them, she said we don't have anything to do with them and she would tell me why when I was old enough to understand, but then she was diagnosed with early onset Alzheimer's disease when I was only nine. She was so far gone within a year that it was all I could do to take care of her, and she couldn't even remember her own family. I never did learn the truth about that."

"Didn't your father know?" Grace asked. "Seems to me he would probably have known who they were, anyway."

Kim gave her a sad grin. "He might have known," she said, "but he never told me, and I don't think I ever thought to ask him. He started drinking after Mom's mind went, and he had a bad wreck when I was eleven. He was drunk at the time, so he was charged with vehicular manslaughter and sentenced to prison. When that happened, somebody from the state put my mother in a nursing home, and I was shuffled from one foster home to another and lost track of my dad after my mom died a year later." She sighed and shook her head. "Of course, then I got pregnant at sixteen, so I was emancipated by the State of Kentucky, and that's how Indie and I ended up on our own. I tried to find out about my dad a few years later, but he'd already been released by then, and I never found him. He had some health issues, so I assume he passed away."

"We did okay, Mom," Indie said. "For a single mom, I think you did really well. I mean, I turned out pretty good, right?"

Kim smiled at her daughter. "Yes, you did. I'm just glad you were lucky enough to find a man like Sam so you didn't have to raise Kenzie all alone. I'll be honest and tell you there were times I didn't know how I was going to make it, and if it hadn't been for Beauregard... He kind of came along just when I needed him most."

Sam cocked his head to one side and looked at Kim. "You said the first time you ever heard him was after you moved into that old house in Hazard, Kentucky, right?"

"Yes, that's right," Kim said. "I heard this voice tell me to get Indie out of her playpen, and a couple minutes later a big piece of the ceiling fell down. If he hadn't warned me, she could have been killed. Of course, at the time I thought it was God talking to me, so it took him a few minutes to convince me of who he was. He told me he had died in that house, and that he been waiting there for a long, long time, hoping that someday, somebody would be able to hear him."

"Okay, but I'm just curious," Sam said, "why did he stay in that house all that time? Why didn't he go out into the world and try to find someone who could hear him?"

Kim shrugged, with a half smile on her face. "He always said it was because he couldn't leave the house," she said, "until he met me. I thought about that, too, wondering if maybe that makes more sense if we think about him as something I dreamed up."

Sam shook his head. "That's not what I'm trying to

say," he said. "I was just curious, that's all. I mean, I think everybody's read stories about ghosts that haunted certain places, as if they could never leave them, right? I just wonder why he's been able to stay with you ever since."

"I don't know. He said that as soon as he knew I could hear him, he was able to stay with me all the time. He doesn't follow me somewhere; he's just always with me."

"And you tell everyone about him," Grace said. "Now I understand why you never found a stepfather for Indie. It must be hard to keep a boyfriend when you got a ghost hanging over your shoulder all the time."

Kim scowled at her. "Boyfriends were easy to get, and they aren't that hard to keep," she said. "That is, assuming you want to keep one. I had several over the years, but you want to know who was the only guy who was always there for me? The only guy who was always keeping an eye on Indie, always helping me do my best to raise her properly? It was Beauregard. I'm not saying I'm in love with him, nothing like that, but he was more dependable than any other man I've ever known." She turned and looked at Sam. "Up until now, anyway."

"I could've done without a few of your boyfriends," Indie said. "Remember Mitch? Right after I came back from MIT? He made a pass at me, and you took his word over mine, kicked me and my daughter out. I'm over it, but I just wanted to get my little dig in there, you know?"

Kim gave her a sly grin. "Actually, do you remember that I kicked him out the same day? Beauregard told me you were telling the truth, Indie, but Mitch could be pretty violent. All I really wanted to do was get you out of the house safely before I lit into him, but you're the one who wouldn't talk to me for almost a year after that, remember? And even when I tried to explain, you wouldn't let me. All you would say was that you forgave me, and to let it go at that, so I did."

Indie looked at her for a moment, then bowed her head in acceptance. "You're right," she said. "I never gave you the chance to explain. I'm sorry, Mom." She raised her head and looked around in the air for a moment. "And, Beauregard, if you're listening—thanks for the times you helped Mom figure out what to do while I was growing up."

Kim chuckled. "He says you're welcome."

4

When they went out for dinner that evening, Sam took them on a drive past the Chase House on East Main Street and then drove down to Smyrna and showed them the big old house that Judith Wingo occupied. Kim had assured them that Beauregard could see anything she could see, which made Sam start wondering again if the old soldier was some kind of mental construct. A ghost hovering near you shouldn't be able to see through your eyes, should it? And yet that's how things seemed to work with Kim and Beauregard.

They got up the next morning and checked out of the motel, had some breakfast, and then headed for the highway. They passed through Nashville, where they picked up Interstate 24 and followed it up through Kentucky and into Illinois. The whole drive took about four and a half hours, and then they rolled into

Thompsonville at just about lunchtime.

Sam looked around and thought that he should really be able to hear a lonesome harmonica, and maybe see a couple of tumbleweeds blow by. The little town didn't seem to have much in the way of commerce, though it was rather picturesque. There was a single gas station, a small eatery called Jim's Fresh Stop, and a number of houses. They were all starting to get a little hungry, so Sam pulled into the Fresh Stop parking lot, and they all went inside.

"Welcome to Jim's," a waitress called out. "Sit wherever you want—be right with you."

They sat down at a table, and Sam snagged another chair for Kenzie. The waitress, a girl who looked to be in her late teens or very early twenties, was there a moment later with a tray full of glasses of water. She set one in front of each of them, then passed out menus.

"I'm Crystal, and I'll be your waitress today. The special today is a sloppy joe with fries and coleslaw for five ninety-nine," she said. "We are out of biscuits at the moment, so we can't do the biscuits and gravy. I think we got everything else, though."

All three of the ladies decided the sloppy joe sounded good, but Kenzie and Sam weren't the type to follow everybody else. Kenzie went for the chicken strips with mac and cheese, but Sam's choice was the Philly cheesesteak sandwich. He said that if it tasted half as good as it looked in the photo on the menu, it was bound to be the best thing he'd eaten in years.

"It'll surprise you," Crystal said. "It's Marcy's own special recipe, though, so I'll warn you it's a little spicy."

"Spicy is good," Sam said. "Bring it on. By the way, is Jim here today?"

"No, I'm afraid not," Crystal said with a frown. "Jim owns the place, but Marcy runs it. Did you need to talk to him about something? I mean, Marcy is back in the kitchen. She can probably help you with just about anything you might need."

"Well, it's not something I need to speak to Jim about directly," Sam said. "I was wondering if you might know of a family that lived here for a while, a family named Cameron? Would have been an older couple, Donald and Millie Cameron, but I heard they had a couple of kids who might have grown up here. Ring any bells?"

Crystal's eyes went completely blank, and she stared at Sam. "What do you want to know about them for?"

Sam was surprised at how dead her voice sounded, but he put on a reassuring smile. "Actually, I was hired to try to find them by a distant relative. Do they still live around here?"

Crystal shrugged. "I'm really not sure," she said, avoiding his eyes. "Let me see if Marcy knows."

She picked up their menus and walked stiffly toward the door that led into the kitchen, then went through it. They could hear some muffled voices coming through the door, and a moment later a short, stout woman walked out of the kitchen and came straight toward their table.

"Okay," she said sternly, "just who are you people? Ain't that family been through enough already?" The obvious surprise on all of their faces seemed to register with Marcy, and the look on her own face softened a bit. "Good Lord," she said, "you don't even have a clue, do you?"

"No, ma'am," Sam said. "We literally just arrived in town, and our interest in this family is purely beneficial, I assure you."

Marcy reached behind her and grabbed another chair, pulled it over close, and sat down. "Just about everybody around here knew Donald and Millie Cameron," she said, "and most of us knew their kids, those of us what's over thirty years old, anyway. Ross and Debbie, that's their names, if it matters. Donald died about ten years back, heart attack. You honestly don't know what happened to Millie?"

"Oh, my God," Indie said, looking at her phone. "Sam, we should have googled before we came. Millie Cameron was murdered eight years ago, beaten to death in her own home. Her son, Ross, was arrested and convicted of it, even though this particular story says the evidence was only circumstantial. He was sentenced to life in prison. His sister, Debbie, has been trying to prove his innocence ever since."

Marcy had been watching Indie, but now she turned her eyes back to Sam. "So, what's your deal? Are you another reporter, trying to make your name on this ugly story?"

Sam reached into his pocket and produced his business card and ID. "No, ma'am," he said. "My name is Sam Prichard, and I'm a licensed private investigator from Denver, Colorado. This is my wife, Indie, my mother, Grace Prichard, Indie's mother, Kim Perkins, and our daughter, Mackenzie. I was hired by a distant relative to try to locate the Camerons. My client only knew that he had some relations out there but didn't know who they were, so I've had to go back and dig into history a bit. I was hired to find all the descendants of a man named Henry Thomas Beauregard, a Confederate soldier, and that led me to Mrs. Cameron. If she's dead, then her children and theirs would be the relations he was looking for."

"Well, he'll probably not want anything to do with them after you tell him this," Marcy said. She had looked at each of them during the introductions, but Sam noticed that her eyes kept returning to his mother-in-law. "Or maybe he'd want to talk to Debbie and her kids. Nobody accused them of doing anything wrong."

Sam nodded. "Of course, of course. Would you happen to know where I can find them?"

Marcy looked at his ID once more, then passed it back to Sam. "I haven't talked to her in a couple of years," she said, "but Debbie and me used to be best friends. When this happened, it got so ugly around here for a while that she had to move away, just to protect her own kids. See, Debbie came along late in life for her mother, when Millie was already past forty. Ross, he was already grown by then, but with his problems, he never moved out on his own. When Debbie came along, he was just the big brother she idolized, and she absolutely does not believe he's guilty."

"You mentioned Ross's problems," Sam said. "Can I ask what kind of problems you're referring to?"

She looked at Sam for a long moment, then let out a sigh. "Ross Cameron is autistic," she said. "He wasn't quite like Rain Man—I mean, he could function fairly well around here. He worked for Gary Burgess at his auto shop, and Gary claims Ross was a pretty fair mechanic's helper, especially in the easy, routine jobs. He had a knack for being able to take something apart and then put it back together perfectly."

Sam looked at his wife and his mother-in-law, then turned back to Marcy. "The article my wife found said the evidence against Ross was circumstantial. Do you know much about the case? What kind of evidence they had?"

"Oh, yeah," Marcy said. "That's what made it all so ugly. See, somebody called the sheriff and said they heard Millie screaming, but when the deputies got there, they found Ross sitting in a chair right beside the one his mother's body was in. Somebody had beat her brains in, and there was blood pretty much everywhere. Well, Ross told the deputies that he had been out for a walk and found his mother that way when he came home, but there was blood on his hands, so they arrested him. I don't know what they did to him after that, but somewhere along the line they got him to confess. He tried to tell the judge the day he was sentenced that he didn't do it, but the judge said the confession would stand, and that was that." She shook her head. "They originally sentenced him to death, but then the governor signed a law that made the death penalty illegal, so it was changed to life in prison."

"Marcy, can you tell me how to find Debbie? It sounds to me like there may be more to this case, and maybe I can help."

Marcy looked at him from under lowered eyelids. "Debbie don't have any money," she said. "Why would you want to help?"

"I've been known to take on pro bono work from time to time," Sam said. "This sounds like it might be a case that would be worthwhile taking on that way."

Marcy continued to look at him that way for another moment. "Tell you what," she said at last. "Let me think about this while you eat your lunch. Just promise me that if I tell you how to find her, you're not going to make her life even worse than it already is. Can you promise me that?"

"To be perfectly honest," Sam said, "no, ma'am, I can't promise you that. All I can promise you is that my client only wants to try to help her. I'm curious, though—you said Debbie doesn't believe Ross is guilty, but what do you think?"

Marcy glanced around, as if to reassure herself that there was no one else in the establishment who might be listening. "Debbie doesn't believe he did it because—well, there's rumors that there was some kind of curse on that family, and Debbie is the one who always insisted it wasn't true. But since you asked me, I'll tell you the truth. No, I don't think he did it. I think he was set up to take the fall for it, but I don't believe he would ever really have hurt his mama, no matter what anyone says."

Sam nodded. "Something in your voice when you were telling me about it made me think you didn't believe he was guilty," Sam said. "I'll promise you this: if it's true that he was convicted on only circumstantial evidence, I'll do my best to find out the truth. If he's innocent, I'll prove it. Would that help?"

Marcy rose from her chair and pushed it back toward the table she had borrowed it from. "It sure couldn't hurt," she said. "That poor family has been through enough, and I know it would do Debbie and her kids a world of good. But let me tell you this," she said with a menacing glare. "Around these parts, we're a bunch of hillbillies. You ever had a couple hundred angry hillbillies on your tail?"

Sam's eyes went wide. "No," he said, "and I don't think it's something I ever want to experience."

"Then you just make sure you don't hurt that family any more than they've already been hurt. Wouldn't take me ten minutes to put together a posse to come after you." She turned without another word and walked back into the kitchen.

Crystal came out a few minutes later with their orders, and Sam realized that she must be as capable in the kitchen as she seemed to be in the dining room. Marcy must've said something positive to her, as well, because she had her smile back in place.

The food was good, but Marcy didn't wait until they were finished eating to make her decision. She came out while they were halfway through and slipped a piece of paper into Sam's shirt pocket. "Ross is doing his time in Stateville Prison, up by Joliet. Debbie moved up there to be close to him. That's her address and phone number," she said. "I also put my own phone number on there so you can get hold of me if you need any more information. My gut tells me you're a pretty good guy, Sam Prichard, but I don't always trust my gut. I went back there to the office and googled you. I had already thought your name sounded familiar, but when I saw that you were the guy who almost got killed stopping that wacko at Lake Mead, that's when I decided you're probably on the up-and-up. Let me know if I can help, okay?"

Sam nodded, his mouth too full to allow him to speak, and Marcy took that as good enough. She went over to a bulletin board next to the cash register and used a thumbtack to put Sam's business card up on it, then walked back into the kitchen and didn't come out again.

"They'll be pointing at that card and bragging about you having lunch here for years to come," Kim said. "They probably don't get a lot of genuine heroes through here."

Sam scowled. "I'm no hero," he said. "You don't become a hero by just doing what you have to do."

"No," Indie said. "You become a hero by doing the things you don't have to do. Sam, no one would have blamed you if you had gotten off that dam that day, and you know it. And yet you stayed there and waited for Jamal, and you almost died even though you saved millions of people. Sam, you might as well give up and accept it. You're a hero, whether you ever meant to be or not."

"Yeah, whatever," Sam growled. He got up and walked to the register where Crystal was waiting, paid their tab, and then told Crystal to tell Marcy goodbye for them. He followed his family out and got behind the wheel of the Ridgeline, then pulled the slip of paper out of his pocket.

Deborah Jenkins
114 South Garden Way

Joliet, Illinois

815-555-2110

Marcy Elimon 618-555-9895

He showed the paper to Indie, and she googled the address. "Looks like it's about five hours north of here. Straight up Interstate 57 for the most part."

Sam nodded and headed toward the interstate. It was about eleven miles away, through the town of Benton, and everyone was ready for a potty stop by the time they got there. Sam pulled into a gas station just a short distance short of the on-ramp to gas out, while the ladies all took Kenzie and headed inside.

Sam was leaning against the truck and watching the numbers climb on the gas pump, so he was startled when a voice behind him suddenly said, "Samuel." He jumped slightly, then spun around to find his mother-in-law standing there.

He corrected himself. He found Beauregard standing there, wearing his mother-in-law's face.

"Beauregard?" Sam asked.

"Of course," Kim said. "Samuel, I just wanted to say thank you. Just the fact that you have found my grandchildren has given me great hope."

Sam nodded. "And it appears you were right," he said. "Sounds like one of your descendants is definitely in need of help. Any chance you can do your little hocus-pocus thing and tell me whether Ross is really innocent on not?"

Kim shook her head. "I'm afraid it does not work that way. I have no control over the things that I see. However, it occurs to me that if he is in fact not guilty, then there is a killer running loose somewhere. My previous statement that there is no danger to yourself or your family may no longer be true."

Sam looked into Kim's eyes, then nodded once. "We'll be in a better position to judge after we meet Debbie. You're right, though—if Ross really is innocent, then that means the real killer is getting away with murder. Whoever it was might not be too happy about me poking my nose around in this. I may need to send the rest of you home."

Kim stood there and looked at him for a moment longer. "Samuel, I have no way to pay you for this..."

"Don't even bother," Sam said. "Beauregard, no matter what you are, you saved my life and my family's lives more than once. I think I can afford to repay those favors this way, and I wouldn't think much of myself if I wasn't willing to."

Kim smiled, and then a moment later her eyes closed and she wobbled on her feet. When she opened her eyes again and saw Sam standing in front of her, she sighed heavily. "I knew he wanted to talk to you again," she said, "but I wish he'd stop just taking control when he feels like it."

"I think it was something important, Kim," Sam said. "I think maybe he felt like he couldn't wait any longer."

Kim nodded, then turned and went back into the gas station. Sam finished topping off the gas tank and hung up the nozzle, then started toward the men's room. A few minutes later, fresh cup of coffee in hand, he climbed back behind the wheel of the Ridgeline.

"Everybody ready?"

"We're all ready," Indie said. "I checked, and there is a motel about a mile from Debbie's place. I went ahead and reserved us a couple of rooms."

Sam grinned at her. "That's my smart girl," he said. He put the truck in gear and made the turn from the parking lot, then immediately made another turn onto the northbound ramp. He set the cruise control as they passed the little airport on the left, then settled back into his long-distance driving mode.

Stateville Prison is a maximum-security facility located on twenty-two hundred acres. While it is often considered one of the Joliet prisons, it is actually situated in the community of Crest Hill, Illinois. Sixty-four of those acres are surrounded by a thirty-three-foot-tall concrete perimeter that is capped with concertina wire and ten wall-mounted guard towers. It routinely contains more than thirty-five hundred inmates. Housing them costs more than thirty-two thousand dollars per year for each inmate, giving the prison an operational budget of more than one hundred and twelve million dollars per year.

Stateville was also the site of many of the executions

that had taken place in Illinois and was the home of Illinois' Death Row from 1977 until 1998. Infamous serial killer John Wayne Gacy was executed there in 1994.

Sam had suggested they get their motel rooms before contacting Debbie, so Indie directed him to the one she had already discovered. It was one of the more common chain hotels, and Sam went inside to get their usual two rooms. It took only a few minutes, and then they carried their bags inside.

"It's only a quarter to five," Sam said. "Why don't we give Debbie a call and invite her and her family to dinner?"

Indie's eyes went wide. "Don't you think it might be better to approach her privately, first?"

"Why? I'd say we've located the particular descendants Beauregard's premonition referred to, wouldn't you? We know that Debbie doesn't believe her brother is guilty of murdering their mother, so our approach can be that a distant relative has hired me to look into the case." Sam raised his eyebrows at her. "I think that's pretty close to the truth, don't you?"

Indie stuck her tongue out at him. "Okay," she said, "but I still think taking her out to dinner is the wrong approach. Sam, you should meet with her privately, give her the whole story about the distant relative and all that, but without an audience. From what I've been able to find online, she spends most of her time writing letters to congressmen and senators and anybody else she thinks might listen, trying to convince them that Ross was railroaded and deserves a new trial. The problem is that there's no new evidence; without that, she's just wasting a lot of postage."

Sam smiled at her. "All right, if you feel that strongly about it. Should I give her a call this evening, do you think, or just show up at her door tomorrow morning?"

"Just show up there tomorrow," Indie said. "It's gonna be hard enough to believe that someone would suddenly appear out of nowhere to help. If you try to convince her of it over the phone, you may scare her off completely."

Sam nodded. "Okay, tomorrow morning it is. For tonight, however, I'm still hungry. I saw a place called the Route 66 Diner, and a bit of nostalgia might go down well this evening."

5

The skies were overcast in northern Illinois, and there were hints of thunder and lightning up in the clouds, so they spent the evening watching a movie in Kim and Grace's room. When it was over, Sam carried Kenzie back to their own room and tucked her into one of the queen-sized beds. He and Indie took turns in the shower, and then they both fell, moderately exhausted, into the other one.

It wasn't until they had finished the complimentary breakfast at the motel that Sam finally got on the way. The motel was only five minutes from Debbie Jenkins's house, and he pulled into the driveway of a slightly rundown ranch house. He climbed out of the Ridgeline and leaned on his cane—the weather had his hip screaming loudly—as he walked up to the door.

He rang the doorbell and waited, and a moment later a woman who looked a bit like Kim opened the door and looked out at him. "Yes? Can I help you?"

Sam had his ID ready and held it up for her to see. "Mrs. Jenkins? My name is Sam Prichard, and I'm a private investigator from Denver, Colorado. I've been employed by someone who wishes to remain anonymous to look into your brother's case, to see if I might be able to find any new or overlooked evidence that could conceivably prove his innocence."

Debbie was staring at the ID the whole time Sam was talking, but she looked up into his eyes as he finished. "Are you serious?"

Sam nodded, keeping a smile on his face. "Yes, ma'am, I am. As I said, I've been hired by a distant relative of yours, someone who wishes to remain anonymous, who believes as you do that your brother is not guilty. I'd like to sit down with you and talk about the case, because as it stands right at the moment, all I know is what I can read in the news articles about it."

Debbie swallowed hard, and a couple of tears began making their way slowly down her cheeks. "Do you have any idea what an answer to prayer you are? Come in, please come in," she said as she pushed the storm door open wide.

Sam walked into the house and noted instantly that it was in far better condition on the inside than the outside would lead one to believe. He waited until she had closed the door behind him and then followed her into the kitchen.

"Would you like some coffee? I've got some made, I just haven't had a chance to sit down and have a cup yet."

"Sure," Sam said, "coffee would be great." He took a seat at the kitchen table as she poured two cups and brought them over. She set one in front of him and then pushed the sugar and cream set toward him as she sat down at her own chair. Sam added sugar, which suddenly reminded Debbie that he didn't have a spoon. She jumped up and snatched one out of the dish strainer for him.

"So, somebody actually is paying you to do this?" Debbie asked. "Somebody hired you to prove he didn't do it?"

Sam held up one finger. "Actually, somebody hired me to find out for sure whether or not he did it. As I said, my employer believes that you are correct and he is innocent, but it's necessary for me to look at it as simply a case. I have to examine all the evidence I can find, and if it shows that he is not guilty, then we'll do all we can to get him a new trial. On the other hand, you need to prepare yourself for the possibility that I cannot find the proof you're hoping for. If that is the case, then there's probably nothing we can do."

"But at least someone wants you to try, right? Somebody believes there's a chance, right?"

Sam smiled at her. "Yes, ma'am," he said. "More than one person, to be honest. In the course of looking into this situation, I went to Thompsonville and spoke with an old friend of yours there. Marcy Elimon? She said the two of you used to be very good friends?"

"Yes, we're good friends," Debbie said. "I've just been so busy lately, I just haven't had time to really sit down and write to her, or even pick up the phone and call."

"Well, she's another one who believes your brother is innocent. Believe me, I got an earful about it while I was there, and from the way she talks, a lot of other people there believe he's innocent, as well."

"Some do," Debbie said, shrugging. "Others—not so much. It blows my mind how quickly people can turn on you when you've been accused of something terrible, even people who've known you all your life. Before this happened, no one would ever have believed that Ross could hurt anyone, let alone our mother. But once the deputies arrested him, most of the town decided he was no good and that was that."

Sam nodded. "I understand," he said. "I've seen it happen to a lot of people. Can you tell me anything about the evidence that was actually used against your brother in court?"

Before she could answer, they were interrupted by the arrival in the kitchen of a much younger woman—it was obviously Debbie's daughter. Debbie looked up at her and smiled, then indicated Sam. "Mindy," she said, "this is Mr. Prichard. He's a private investigator, and somebody has hired him to help prove Uncle Ross was innocent. Mr. Prichard, this is my oldest daughter, Mindy."

Sam rose stiffly to his feet and shook Mindy's hand, then sat back down as the girl gave her mother a questioning look. "Somebody hired him?" Mindy asked.

"Yes, somebody who's related to us but who doesn't want us to know who they are at the moment."

Mindy made a sour face. "You know, Mom, you've always told me if something sounds too good to be true, it probably is? Don't you think you ought to check this out a little bit before you invite strange men into the house?"

Sam couldn't stifle the grin that spread across his face. "You know, she's actually right. Mindy, could I suggest that you google me? I promise you I really am who I say I am, and you shouldn't have too much trouble finding proof of that online."

Mindy looked at him for a moment, then took out a smartphone. She spoke to it softly for a couple of seconds, and then her eyes grew wide. She skimmed through a couple of the links that came up, then looked back at her mother. "Okay, this is the guy who foiled the terror attack plot on Lake Mead a couple years ago. I guess we can give him the benefit of the doubt, right?"

Debbie's own eyes went wide, and she stared at Sam for a moment. "That was you? Wow, I never would've expected to have a real hero in my house."

Sam grimaced. "Please, I'm not a hero," he said. "I was just doing my job, just like dozens of federal agents who were on that dam with me. I don't deserve any more praise or pats on the back than they do."

"Hey, can I get a selfie with you?" Mindy asked. By the time Sam stopped sputtering, it was too late. She had already thrown an arm around his shoulders and held her phone out. Sam heard the shutter-click sound effect half a dozen times before she let go and stepped away. "Okay, anyway, Mom, I gotta run. Carly's picking me up so we can go job hunting together. I won't be out late—see you tonight." She blew her mother a kiss and hurried out the door.

"She's eighteen, just graduated last year. She started working at the bookstore while she was a junior, but they went out of business a couple weeks ago. She loves her uncle, but I'm afraid she's become disillusioned and doesn't believe we're ever going to get him out."

Sam was about to ask once more about the case when two more kids came in. Twin boys, about fourteen or fifteen in Sam's estimation, stepped into the room and started rummaging in the refrigerator.

"Hey," Debbie called out. "Boys, come meet Mr. Prichard. He's a private investigator, and he's going to help us try to find proof that Uncle Ross isn't guilty." The two boys turned their eyes toward Sam, and he instantly felt like he was being carefully examined under a microscope. "Mr. Prichard, these are my boys, Andy and Alex. They're missing school today because we're going to see Ross. They've been a terrific help to me these last few years, especially since my husband passed away."

Sam's eyebrows rose. "I'm sorry," he said, "I didn't know that you were a widow. To be honest, I don't know anything about your husband at all. Once I tracked you down, I just concentrated on getting here and getting in touch with you."

"It's okay," Debbie said. "Randy died five years ago—car accident. Just seemed like everything that could go wrong was going wrong, for a while there. I mean, Ross's problems, my sister's disappearance, my dad dying, and then Mom being murdered and Ross being accused of it, then Randy falling asleep behind the wheel... They used to say my family was cursed, and I'll confess that for a while there I began to believe it, myself."

One of the twins stepped close to Sam and looked hard at him. "What was your name?"

Sam took out a business card and handed it to him. "I'm Sam Prichard. Good to meet you boys."

The other boy was holding a cell phone and frantically pecking at its keys with his thumbs. "Yep," he said to his brother, "it's him." He looked up at Sam and grinned hugely. "We follow you on Twitter," he said. "Ever since that case when your bass player got arrested. That was slick, how you figured that one out, that it was the crime scene investigator who was actually the killer."

"What? You got all that out of Twitter?" Sam knew that Indie was running a Twitter account for him, but he avoided anything to do with it as much as he possibly could. He didn't even know for sure what his Twitter handle was.

"Not just off Twitter," the boy standing beside him said. "We follow you on Twitter so we know when the blogs get posted."

"Blogs? What blogs? What are you talking about?"

"Your wife, dude," the boy said, chuckling. "Indie. She writes up all your cases on her blog. That way we get to read all about them, and everything you have to do to solve each case." He looked at his brother, who gave him a thumbs-up sign, then turned back to Sam. "You're the reason we want to be private eyes when we grow up."

Debbie was shaking her head, just staring at the three of them. "My, what a small world it is," she said. "These boys have been telling me about their hero, the private eye who saves the world, for the last year or so, but I thought it was some fictional character in a book. And yet, here you are, sitting in my kitchen. There has to be something supernatural at work here, that's all I can say."

Sam looked at her, his face registering the latest shock to his system. "Ma'am," he said, "you have no idea."

The commotion, with the boys getting so loud in their exuberance, brought the last of Debbie's children into the room. A girl of about twelve, already showing hints of the beauty she would be when she was fully grown, walked into the room and leaned against the doorpost. She didn't even wait for Debbie to make introductions but looked Sam dead in the eye.

"Do you think he did it?"

"Mr. Prichard, this is my youngest daughter, Kaylee. Kaylee, this is..."

"I heard," Kaylee said. "So? Do you think he did it?"

"At this point," Sam said carefully, "I don't know enough to be entitled to an opinion. If I said I don't think so, that would only mean that I'm trying to say what I think you want to hear. If I said I think he did, then it would mean I am already prejudiced against him. Either way would be a mistake, since an investigator's job is to keep an open mind until there are enough provable facts to come to a conclusion. I don't have that many facts. As a matter of fact, I don't have any at the moment. All I know is that your uncle has been accused of murdering his mother, and that at least one reporter feels that there wasn't enough evidence to justify convicting him. I know that your mother believes he's innocent, and so do several other people, but that isn't a fact that can be used to substantiate either his guilt or his innocence. It'll be my job, now that I've taken the case, to find those facts. If I can find enough of them that indicate that he did not commit this crime, then it will be my job to work with an attorney to try to get the court to agree to a new trial."

"Then, you're saying that you don't know either way, right?"

"That's right. At this moment, I don't know either way."

Kaylee walked toward him and held out a hand, fingers together and palm facing upward. "Good. Everybody else who says they want to help tries to tell us how they 'just know' he's innocent, and they always end up wanting money. My mom doesn't have any money—she spends every penny she can get her hands on trying to get someone to listen to her."

Sam nodded. "I know about people like that," he said. "Here's a promise from me to you: I will never ask your mother for any money. I've already got a client on this case, so this isn't going to cost her anything. You have my word on that."

Sam reached out and slapped the girl's palm, then flipped his own hand over so she could return it. The power she put into the return slap suggested that he went too easy on her.

"Okay," Kaylee said. "So what do we do first?"

"And can we help?" Andy and Alex chorused together.

All three of the kids sat down at the table, and Debbie beamed at them, her pride in her children just about overwhelming her for a moment. Sam could see the tears threatening to brim over, but she kept them under control.

He shrugged. "Well, I need to know everything I possibly can about the case. I get the feeling all of you know it pretty well, so who wants to start telling me?"

Debbie started to speak, but Kaylee beat her to it. "Mom gets emotional, and my brothers just try to talk over each other all the time. You'll get it better if I tell it."

Sam, his eyes wide, glanced at Debbie for permission and then nodded toward Kaylee. "Please proceed."

"It was a little after three o'clock in the afternoon," Kaylee said, "June fourth, eight years ago. A lady named Geraldine Pyle said she heard my grandmother screaming, so she called the sheriff. She said it sounded like my grandma was begging someone to stop hurting her, but she couldn't make out the words for sure. 3:21 p.m., a sheriff's car pulled up in front of the house, and two deputies got out. They walked up and knocked on the door and heard someone yell for them to come in, so they opened it and walked inside. As soon as they opened the door and stepped in, they saw my grandmother with blood all over her head and face and clothes, and then they saw Uncle Ross sitting in the chair right beside the one she was in. He had blood on his hands, but the only blood on his clothes was from where he had touched himself. There were bloodstains on his pant legs from where he laid his hands on his thighs, and on his sleeves, because he has a tendency to hug himself a lot when he gets upset."

"Yeah," said one of the twins. "There was blood splattered all over the chairs and the wall behind them, but there was none on his shirt or his face. If he had been beating on her hard enough to make the blood fly around like that, then he would have got it all over him, right?"

Sam blinked. The boy was echoing his own thoughts. "That's how I would see it, yes. What about the murder weapon? Did they ever find one?"

"No, they didn't," the boy said. "Their theory was that Uncle Ross beat her with just his fists, but they never had him examined. They never had anyone look at his hands to see if they were bruised or had any kind of injuries on them. If he had managed to bash her skull in with just his fists, he would have had bruises on all his knuckles and fingers. There's no possible way to avoid it, and some doctors will even say it's impossible to break somebody's skull that way."

"What was the actual cause of death?" Sam asked.

"Penetrating depressed cranial fractures due to blunt force trauma," Kaylee said. "The medical examiner said it means that pieces of her skull were driven into her brain and that's what actually killed her."

Sam turned back to the girl. "Go on, please." He was amazed at how calmly and logically the girl was telling him the story.

"3:29 p.m., Deputy Johnny Moore came walking out with Uncle Ross in handcuffs and put him in the back of the car, and he told a bunch of people standing around that Uncle Ross had killed his mother. He called the sheriff's office on the radio and told them what they found and that he had already arrested Uncle Ross. The sheriff's detective, Ray Weimer, showed up about ten minutes later and took over. He looked everything over and said there was no doubt in his mind that Uncle Ross did it, so he took Uncle Ross back to the jail and locked him in the little room they use for interrogating criminals. That was about four thirty in the afternoon. At three o'clock the next morning, Weimer came out and said Uncle Ross confessed."

Sam stared into the girl's eyes. "And that was the extent of their investigation, right?" He turned toward Debbie. "Debbie, how soon did you find out what was going on?"

"Oh, right after they brought Ross out," Debbie replied. "I only lived a couple blocks over, and one of my mother's neighbors sent her little boy to get me. He didn't tell me what was going on, just that I needed to get over to my mother's house right away. I dropped everything and told Mindy to watch her brothers and sister and took off running. When I got there, some of the neighbors kept me from going inside, and then the other deputy, Bob Fry, he came out and told me that my mother had been beaten to death and that Ross did it. I told him then there was no way Ross could do such a thing, he was too gentle, but they said it was obvious and I would have to learn to accept it."

"Did you go with your brother to the jail?"

Debbie pulled her head back a bit and widened her eyes. "No, they wouldn't let me," he said. "Besides, I had kids at home. I had to go back and take care of them, and had to tell them that their grandmother was gone."

Sam nodded his understanding. "Okay, did your brother ever get to speak to an attorney?"

"Weimer said he refused one," Kaylee said. "He said Uncle Ross was advised of his rights but refused the services of an attorney and agreed to answer questions."

Sam snapped his attention back to her. "But I'm sure I've been told that your uncle has autism? I realize there are different types and levels of autism, but shouldn't that have some effect on whether he was mentally competent to understand what was happening, the questioning and everything?"

"Judge Hausman ruled," Kaylee said, "that the fact he held a job and was able to manage his own money meant that he was mentally competent. Since they claimed he had given his statement of his own free will, and had refused an attorney when it was offered to him, that meant his confession had to stand. The prosecutor didn't even bother to present any other evidence against him, resting his entire case on the statement he gave during interrogation. The public defender tried to argue that Uncle Ross didn't understand what they meant when they said he could have an attorney, and that the statement should be thrown out, but the judge overruled him."

Sam looked at the young girl for a moment, then nodded. "Something tells me you're thinking about a career in law?"

Kaylee smiled sweetly. "I'm buying used law school textbooks online and studying them on my own," she said. "I plan to be number one in my class when it comes time to graduate."

"There's not a doubt in my mind that you'll accomplish it," he said. He glanced at her twin brothers. "You know, a really good defense attorney will need her own investigators. You might want to keep these guys owing you favors."

"She's already good at that," Debbie said with a chuckle. "She does these videos on YouTube where she talks about issues that kids face nowadays, and what they can and can't do about them. She's actually had several lawyers contact her and tell her how good she's doing, and it makes her several hundred dollars every month. Needless to say, her brothers are constantly indebted to her for one thing or another."

"So where will you start?" asked one of the twins.

"Well, since I'm here," Sam replied, "I think I need to go and meet with your uncle. Debbie—may I call you Debbie? If possible, I'd like to go with you to visit him. You can probably help me to explain to him what's going on, and how I'm hoping to help."

Debbie smiled. "We're heading out there this morning," she said. "I go twice a week, and the school is good about letting the kids go with me, sometimes. We could go now, if you like."

Sam smiled back. "Now is fine," he said.

6

Since the three younger kids were going along and Debbie's car was pretty small, Sam suggested they all go in the Ridgeline. With the teenagers snugly belted into the back seat and Debbie Jenkins riding shotgun, Sam followed her directions out to the prison.

Sam wasn't carrying his gun, so he didn't have to worry about going through all the headaches of putting it into a locker and such. Instead, his professional ID was taken into a security office for several minutes and then was brought back to him by the lieutenant on duty.

"Mr. Prichard? I'm Lieutenant Willoughby. I understand you're here to see Ross Cameron?"

"I am," Sam said. "I've been hired to look into the possibility that there was other evidence that might have exonerated him, evidence that was overlooked or never discovered. I need to speak with Mr. Cameron and see if he can give me any insight into where I might look for such evidence."

Willoughby frowned. "I'm not trying to tell you your business, Mr. Prichard," he said, "but I'm not sure how far you're going to get in trying to interview this guy. I mean, don't get me wrong, Cameron is a model prisoner. He never gives anybody any problems, and the only time he's ever even been in a fight is when he happened to be in the way while somebody else was being attacked. You ask me, this guy doesn't have a violent bone in his body, but I can tell you from personal experience that he will not discuss what happened to his mother. He'll tell you he didn't do it, but if you try to ask him about who else might have done it or how you can prove he didn't do it, he clams up. Won't say another word after that."

Sam narrowed his eyes. "Really? That seems odd. You'd think he'd want any help he could get in proving his innocence."

"If it was anybody else, I'd agree in a heartbeat," Willoughby said. "Cameron, though, he's an entirely different kettle of fish. I don't know why, but he doesn't seem willing to open up at all about that day. Our counselors have tried to work with him since he first got here, and they've gotten nowhere." Willoughby shrugged. "Of course, it could be that he doesn't trust anyone connected to the prison; I considered that, as well. Unfortunately, the state won't allow any outside psychologists to come in and talk with him."

Sam nodded slowly. "That could be a problem, if he won't talk," he said. "Thank you, Lieutenant. I appreciate you giving me a heads-up."

Sam was escorted into a room with Debbie Jenkins and her kids, and a few moments later Ross Cameron was brought in. They all sat down around a stainless steel picnic table, and Ross was watching Sam the entire time as he took out a small pad and a pen.

Sam, in turn, was watching Ross. Ross was about sixty years old, but he seemed to be in pretty good physical condition. He didn't appear to have any problems moving around and seemed to be in good health. His hair was showing some gray, but it was still mostly dark.

"Ross," Debbie said, touching his hand, "you remember how I've been praying for some kind of a miracle? Well, this is Mr. Sam Prichard, and he is a private investigator from Colorado. He's come to meet you today because he's been hired to help prove you didn't do this."

Sam held out a hand to Ross, but he only glanced at it and looked away. Kaylee reached out and took hold of Sam's hand, pulling it down to the table and gently shaking her head. "He doesn't shake hands," she whispered.

Sam grinned at Ross. "Ross, I'm glad to finally meet you," he said. "I'm hoping to be able to find evidence that will back up your insistence that you did not commit the crime that put you here."

Ross turned his face toward Sam, but it was obvious that he was not looking directly at Sam's face. Instead, his eyes seemed to be focused on a point slightly off to the right. "I didn't kill my mom," Ross said, and Sam was surprised at the clarity in his voice. "I know they said I did, and I guess it looked like I did, but I didn't."

Sam nodded. "And a lot of people believe you're telling the truth," he said. "Ross, do you have any idea who might have actually done it?"

Beside him, Kaylee whispered, "Uh-oh," but Ross simply continued to look at the same point, not turning his head even slightly toward Sam. "I didn't do it," he said, "but somebody else did. I don't know who the somebody else was. I was out for a walk, and when I came home, Mom was all bloody."

Ross suddenly turned to his sister and, looking at the wall just to the left of her face, asked about the oldest girl, Mindy, so Sam took the opportunity to lean close to Kaylee. "Hey, quick question," he said softly. "Did anybody report seeing Ross out walking that day? Did anyone see him coming or going from the house?"

"No, but that's probably because he would have gone in and out through the back door. He liked to go walking in the woods, and where they lived was right on the edge of town. At the back of the yard was all woods and forest, so he could go straight from the back door out into the woods and come back the same way."

"And I'm assuming no one saw anybody else enter or

leave the house?" Sam asked.

Kaylee narrowed one eye. "There was one kid, Jason Garrity, who said he saw somebody running out the back door into the woods. The deputies said it must've been Uncle Ross, but Jason insisted that it wasn't. The trouble was that Jason was always into some kind of trouble, so nobody believed him."

Sam nodded and sat up straight again. When Ross turned to look his way again, Sam was ready. "Ross, did you see anybody else in the woods when you were walking that day?"

There is almost no such thing as a person sitting absolutely still. There are enough motions going on inside the human body to make perfect stillness nearly impossible, from breathing and heartbeat to the simple little unconscious twitches that take place in different muscles at different times. Because of those things, it's almost impossible for a human body to be completely still other than in death, but Ross almost achieved it. As soon as Sam asked the question, he froze, and there was an absolutely eerie stillness about him for several seconds.

It passed as quickly as it began. Ross looked at the same point off to Sam's right and shrugged. "I saw somebody," he said, "but I don't know who it was."

Sam nodded calmly, trying to keep his own excited sense of discovery from transmitting itself to Ross. "Did you tell the deputies that you saw someone?"

Ross froze again, and Sam realized that what he was seeing was a manifestation of Ross's concentration on remembering specific details, the way another person might study a picture or read through a note on the subject. Ross was literally reviewing the actual moments he was thinking about inside his mind, and was distancing himself from the outside world and all its distractions while he did so. Once again, it lasted only a few seconds and was gone, and Ross focused on the wall again. "I told the deputy Bob Fry," Ross said, "but he told me there was no one else out there. He told me not to say it again, so I didn't."

Ross turned back to his sister and began talking to her about the past few days since he had seen her last. He had reached some level of accomplishment in his ceramics class and seemed excited when he told her that he was making a set of canisters for her. Debbie responded by telling him about the new recipe she had tried the day before and about a new television show she had started watching.

Kaylee tugged on Sam's sleeve, so he leaned down close to her. "Sometimes it doesn't matter," she whispered, "what we talk to him about. For him, it's just important to have some kind of interaction. He can be serious and answer your questions for a few seconds at a time, but then he has to have a break and just be himself for a few minutes. If you can be patient with him, I'm pretty sure it'll pay off. You've already gotten more out of him than anyone else's been able to in all this time."

Sam raised an eyebrow and looked at her. "How so?"

"I studied the case from one end to the other," the girl said, "but that's the first time I've ever heard that he told a deputy about seeing someone else in the woods, or that he was told not to mention it again. If we could prove it, that would be enough to overturn his conviction, wouldn't it?"

"I think it might," Sam said. "The problem is going to be getting that deputy to admit it." He winked at the girl. "But you can bet your latest copy of the *Law Review Journal* that I'm going to try."

It was several minutes later when Ross finally turned his attention back to Sam. "And then," he said without preamble, "the detective Ray Weimer told me I would not have to go to jail if I admitted it. He said I would be able to go back home, but I had to say I did it." Ross put his arms across his chest and gripped his upper arms, hugging himself and rocking gently back and forth. "I told him I didn't want to say that, because I didn't do it, but he said it was the only way I could go home."

Sam sat there and stared at Ross for a moment, then shook his head. If he had anything to say about it, Ray Weimer would no longer be a detective by the time Sam Prichard was finished with him.

"Ross, the person you saw in the woods," he said, "was it a man or a woman?"

Still hugging himself and rocking, Ross started

shaking his head from side to side. "I don't know," he said. "I don't know if it was a man or a woman. They were too far away and off through the trees, so I couldn't tell."

"I understand," Sam said. "It's okay, it's no problem. Do you remember that day very well?"

Ross began nodding vigorously, and Debbie leaned toward Sam. "He remembers everything," she said softly. "Roughly one in ten autistics display exceptional memory, and one in a hundred have an actual eidetic memory. Ross is one of those. Ten years from now, he could tell you every word of this entire conversation. If you give him a scripture and verse reference from the Bible, he can tell you exactly what it says. Ask for an entire chapter, and he'll quote it word for word. It's the same with any other book he's read. If you can give him a page number, or the first few words on a page, he can start from there and quote everything after it."

Sam looked at her for a moment, then turned back to Ross. "Ross, what time did you go out to walk in the woods that day?"

"It was 9:42," Ross said. "I looked at the clock as I went out the door—I always look at the clock when I go out the door. It was 9:42."

Sam nodded. "And what time did you see the person in the woods?"

"The first time I saw them was 1:18," Ross said. "I was down by the creek, and I saw them through the trees. I looked at my watch, and it said 1:18. The next time I saw them was 2:51, I looked at my watch again because I always look at my watch when something happens that I don't expect. They were too far away, but I could see they were moving out toward the creek, back the way I came from, moving really fast."

"Moving fast? Was the person running?"

"Not running, just walking fast. No, not running. Just walking fast."

"Ross, what color was this person's clothing? Could you tell?" Sam asked.

"Yellow shirt and brown pants," Ross said. "They had a hat, but they threw it down. I went and looked at it, and it was all dirty, with stuff stuck to it."

Sam's eyebrows lowered. "Why was it dirty, Ross?"

"It was all dirty because stuff was stuck to it, like dirt and grass, and stuff was stuck to it because it had blood on it, and blood is sticky."

Ross turned suddenly to Debbie and started jabbering about some of the other inmates. From what Sam could gather, there were a few of them who watched over him, who tried to make sure Ross was safe in that terribly dangerous environment.

Sam was amazed at the information he was learning, and even more amazed that none of it had come out before. The trick, he figured, was to ask the right questions. The problem was knowing which questions were the right ones to ask. He carefully planned his next few questions while Ross and Debbie and the kids talked about simple, everyday things.

Ross suddenly turned back to him and simply looked at him, expectantly. Sam realized that was his cue and took advantage of it.

"Ross, did you tell anyone else about the hat and the blood?"

"No. Nobody asked about it."

Sam nodded; it was the answer he had expected. "Do you know what kind of hat it was?"

Ross froze for a moment, then shook his head. "It wasn't a cowboy hat." He froze again, then shook his head once more. "It wasn't a cowboy hat. It was a black hat, and it had a feather in it."

A number of images flashed through Sam's mind, ranging from fedora hats that might have been worn by private eyes in the forties to the outrageous designs often worn by Gothic girls in recent years. He doubted that any of these would actually match the hat in question, but he wished there was some way to get a glimpse of the hat. It might give him some minor clue as to the identity of its wearer.

"Ross, can you tell me exactly what happened from the moment you stepped back into the house that afternoon?"

"I went in the back door, and I yelled to tell Mom I was home. She always wanted me to tell her when I got home. I went in the front room, 'cause that's where

Mom liked to watch TV, and I saw her in her chair with blood all over her. I went over and asked if she was all right, but she didn't answer, so I shook her a little bit and her head fell over on her shoulder. I knew she was dead, but I didn't know what to do, so I sat down and watched TV. Mom always told me if I didn't know what to do to just sit down and wait, and her or Daddy would come and tell me what to do. Then the deputy Johnny Moore came in and he threw up on the floor, then he kept asking me if I killed my mom and why I killed my mom, and I said I didn't do it. He said he had to put me in the car so I wouldn't be in the way, and I had to let him put handcuffs on so I wouldn't hurt anybody."

Sam scribbled furiously on his pad, making sure to get every detail as accurately as he could. Each and every bit of this information, if he could substantiate it, would increase the likelihood of getting Ross's conviction overturned. That didn't necessarily mean he wouldn't be charged and tried again, but that was another problem.

If only someone had found that hat and turned it over to police at the time. The blood undoubtedly would have been from Millie, so the hat's very existence would have cast at least some doubt on Ross's guilt. Surely even an idiot like Weimer would have felt the need to determine who owned the hat, at the very least.

Ross didn't seem interested in talking to Sam anymore, so he sat quietly while the family visited. When the time was up, they all said goodbye and Ross thanked Sam for coming. They were escorted out of the visiting room and allowed to pick up their things, then headed back to Debbie's house.

"That was so awesome," said one of the twins. "You got him to tell you things that nobody else even knows."

"I think it was just about asking the right questions," Sam said. "I'd love to say I was smart enough to think of that, but the truth is that I think I just got lucky."

"I don't know," Debbie said. "I've never seen Ross react to anybody like that. It's like he wanted to tell you, but he didn't know how to do it until you asked a specific question. Maybe he sensed something about you that gives him hope."

Kaylee shook her head. "I'm gonna stick with Mr. Prichard on this," she said. "It was a case of asking the right questions. It never occurred to any of us to ask about what the person in the woods might have been wearing. If somebody had asked him that way back then, then maybe that hat would have been found and he wouldn't be sitting in prison."

Sam nodded. "That's exactly my thought," he said. "Eight years ago, though. I'm afraid there is very little hope that we can track the hat down now. Either it was never found and has probably rotted away, or more likely it was carted off by an animal." He turned to Debbie. "I don't suppose you remember anyone who wore a black hat with a feather?"

She made a rueful face and shook her head. "I'm afraid not," she said. "And believe me, I wish I could come up with the name of somebody who did. I've never believed my brother could have done this, but it would be nice to have another potential suspect to vent my anger on."

Sam shook his head. "That wouldn't help, not unless we can be certain it's the right potential suspect. Look what happened to your brother when people automatically assumed he was guilty. Would you really want it on your conscience if some other innocent person were to be charged with this crime?"

Debbie stuck her tongue out at him, and Sam couldn't help laughing. "Look," she said, "I've been dealing with this for eight years. You can at least allow me a few minutes' fantasy about having someone else to blame, right? Don't spoil my day so quickly."

Kaylee, who was sitting in the back seat between her brothers, leaned forward. "You have to forgive Mom, Mr. Prichard," she said. "She doesn't have the logical mind of an investigator or an attorney."

Sam grinned. "Good thing she's got you three, then," he said. "Between all you kids, she's got a pretty good team of her own working on this."

"So what's next?" asked the other twin. Sam had given up trying to tell them apart, but he vaguely remembered Debbie telling Andy to sit behind Sam while Alex sat behind her. If he was correct, then it was Alex who had spoken.

"Well, Alex," he said, and then he mentally

congratulated himself when no one objected, "now I suppose I'm going back to Thompsonville. I need to see the crime scene and try to get some sense of what actually happened that day, and I want to track down the witnesses, speak with them."

"Witnesses?" Andy asked. "What witnesses?"

"Well, there is the guy your uncle used to work for," Sam said. "I'd like to get his take on this whole thing. Then there's the kid who said he saw someone in your grandmother's backyard, Jason Garrity. I want to talk with him and see if I can connect his statement to what Ross just told us. If Garrity can remember a yellow shirt, for example, then suddenly we've got corroborating statements." He suddenly set his jaw and looked at Kaylee in the rearview mirror. "And I want to get my hands on a certain detective named Weimer. That guy bullied Ross into a confession; he made promises to him he knew to be false to get him to admit to something he hadn't done. I could be giving myself more credit than I deserve, but I don't believe I would have jumped to the conclusion that Ross was the killer, and I can guarantee you I wouldn't have tried to manipulate him into a confession. As far as I'm concerned, this guy was just too lazy to actually conduct an investigation."

"Cool," the boys said together. "Can we go with you?" Alex asked.

"Oh, no," their mother said. "You guys have school—you're not going anywhere."

"But you let us skip school other times," Andy said, "when it's for Uncle Ross. Like today, when we go to visit him. You let us cut school on visiting days."

"Not all the time," Debbie said, "and only for half a day. As soon as we get home, your butts are on the way to class."

It was only a few minutes later when they pulled up to Debbie's house, and Sam let them out. He promised to keep them all up to date on what was happening and shook hands with the three kids, but then he had to put up with a hug from a crying Debbie.

"I don't know how to thank you," she said, "and I don't know who else to thank. Please, tell whoever hired you how much I appreciate this. And if it's a distant relative, then tell them not to be so distant. I don't have a lot of family left, so I'd sure be glad to get to know them."

Sam smiled and promised to relay the message, and then he put the truck in gear and drove away. He took out his phone and started to call Indie, but then he remembered that he was only a few minutes away and put it back. Sure enough, he pulled into the motel parking lot less than five minutes later.

The air in northern Illinois was too cool for splashing in the pool, so Sam found the entire family gathered in his and Indie's room. The three adults were sprawled across one of the beds, while Kenzie bounced in the midst of them. When she saw Sam come through the door, she squealed, "Daddy!" She flew off the bed and leapt into his arms.

A pair of hugs and two kisses later, Sam began telling them all about his morning. The more he talked about the things Ross had told him, the more irritated he was becoming, and it was obvious to the others.

"Sam," Kim said, "Beauregard says you need to calm down."

Sam jerked his head upright and back, and stared at her for a moment. "Calm down? I think he'd be just as ticked off as I am. His great-great-great-great-great-great-whatever-grandson is sitting in prison doing life for a crime he probably didn't commit."

Kim was nodding. "Yes, he understands that," she said, "but he says Ross may not be the one he was having the premonitions about. He says it changed all of a sudden this morning, and now he knows that someone among his descendants is going to be in very serious danger sometime in the next few days."

Sam stopped talking for a few seconds and stared at her. "But he still doesn't know who? What kind of danger, any idea?"

"He says all he knows is that it's somehow connected to Ross's situation, but Ross isn't the one in danger. He's pretty sure it's a woman, but the danger isn't here; it's back in that little town we stopped in yesterday."

Sam chewed the inside of his cheek for a moment. "Well, in that case," he said, "I'm going to rent a car and drive down there alone. You guys can stay here until I get back."

"Stay here?" Indie asked. "I thought we were making this a family trip?"

"Not if Beauregard is sensing danger, we're not. The only reason I agreed to let you come along is because he didn't think there was going to be any kind of danger, remember? If he's changing that story now, then I want all of you to stay well out of the line of fire."

"Yeah, I get that," Indie replied, "but did you listen? He's saying that the danger is for one of his descendants, not for us. Come on, Sam, I don't want to hang out here, and I don't want to go home yet. Let us go with you, please?"

Sam looked over at Kim. "Any danger for you guys?"

Kim close her eyes for a moment, then opened them and looked at Sam. "He says the only danger is for one of his great-great-greats. He just doesn't know which one, but he did say he thinks it might not be one of the ones you already tracked down."

Sam furrowed his brow. "As far as I know, Judith, Ross, and Debbie and her kids are all that are left. I don't think there are any other living descendants."

"Or there's some you haven't discovered yet," Indie said. "Apparently you will, if the danger comes to them because of what you do in Thompsonville. Maybe whoever it is lives around there."

Sam looked into his wife's eyes and let out a sigh.

She had the look, the one that told him there was no way he was going to win this particular debate and he might as well just give up and enjoy the inevitable. "Fine," he said after a few moments. "It's too late to check out today, so we'll leave in the morning. Who's ready for lunch?"

7

Marcy's cell phone rang as the lunch rush was beginning, and she couldn't help smiling when she checked to see who was calling. It was Debbie Jenkins, and she was expecting the call. "Hello," she said.

"Marcy, you darling, you," Debbie said. "Sam Prichard just left here a little bit ago, and he's going to try to help me prove that Ross didn't kill our mother. He said you're the one who told him how to find me, so I just wanted to call and say thank you."

"Well, you're welcome," Marcy said with a chuckle. "So, does he actually think there's any hope?"

"He really does, yeah. I took him along today to go visit Ross, and Ross told him some things that we never heard about before. It turns out Ross saw somebody in the woods behind the house that day, but he doesn't know who it was. The only thing he knows is that the person was wearing brown pants and a yellow shirt, and that they threw down a black hat with a feather in it, but the hat was covered in blood."

"Covered in blood?" Marcy repeated. "A hat? How come we never heard about that before?"

"Well, probably because Ross didn't realize it might be important. But Mr. Prichard also found out that that detective, Weimer, he did some pretty underhanded things to get Ross to give his confession. Of course, we sort of knew that, but now we know more of the details."

Marcy was shaking her head. "Deb, honey, this is great, I think. So, what does the famous private eye plan to do now?"

"Oh, he's headed back to Thompsonville," Debbie said. "He wants to talk to some of the people who knew Ross back then, and he wants to talk to Jason Garrity. Is he still around there?"

"Garrity?" Marcy snorted. "Of course. You can't get rid of a bad penny, remember? He gets in minor trouble now and then, but he never seems to do anything serious enough to get locked up for. He's in here every morning for breakfast, him and those Hammond boys. Said they're working the corn harvest up at the grain mill, so that ought to keep them from getting into too much mischief."

"Well, good," Debbie said. "At least he shouldn't be too hard to find. What about Weimer, is he still with the sheriff's office?"

"Nope. He's the police chief over at Benton. That

just happened last year, but I'm sure he's still there."

"Well, if Mr. Prichard has his way, he may not keep the job much longer. As far as he's concerned, Weimer didn't do his job properly back then, or he would have known that Ross didn't do it."

Marcy agreed, and the two women chitchatted for a bit while Marcy kept the phone clamped between her shoulder and her ear and continued cooking for the lunch rush. If there was one thing Marcy Elimon could do, it was multitask, but Debbie finally realized what time it was and let her go. Marcy put the phone away with a sigh of relief and kept hustling all the way through lunch.

* * * * *

Sam and his family rose early and were finished with the waffles available in the breakfast room before six thirty. By seven o'clock, they were checked out and on the highway once again, headed back to southern Illinois and the answers to a mystery that might have begun almost a century and a half earlier.

"*Along the southbound Odyssey,*" Sam sang as they passed the city of Kankakee, "*the train pulls out of Kankakee...*"

"*Good morning, America,*" Grace, Kim, and Indie joined in, "*how are you? Say...*" The four of them sang along through the chorus, with Sam chuckling when Kim got a few words wrong.

"Samuel, I can't believe you know that song," Grace

said. "My goodness, that's from back in my day. Arlo Guthrie did that when I was just a kid in the seventies."

"Willie Nelson recorded it in the eighties," Sam said. "That's where I know it from. Who is Arlo whatever?"

"Arlo Guthrie?" Kim interjected. "Didn't you ever see *Alice's Restaurant?*"

"Um, wasn't that a TV show?" Sam asked innocently.

"Samuel, I am never speaking to you again," Grace said. "You're mocking me, I can tell."

"Don't mock Grandma," Kenzie said, her voice stern. "That's not nice, Daddy."

The four adults burst out laughing, and Grace decided to mellow out. They found other songs to sing, including a number of children's songs that little Kenzie could join in on, and singing helped the time pass along with the scenery.

As they passed Effingham on the journey south, Indie googled for hotels around Thompsonville and found that there simply weren't any until you went at least twelve miles or more. She found one in Benton that looked nice and was reasonably priced, and Sam told her to go ahead and book a couple of rooms.

They rolled into Benton at about one o'clock, and it was only that late because of a couple of potty stops and lunch at the big truck stop on the Mount Vernon exit. Sam had made a mental note to himself to avoid stopping at big truck stops for lunch. Big truck stops always had big gift shops, and it was a toss-up whether it was harder to drag Kenzie out or her grandmothers.

Once they were checked in, Indie set up her computer and put Herman to work. Herman was a program, one she had written herself that could almost qualify as artificial intelligence. Herman was capable of running searches and deciding which items that came up seemed important, and even had the ability to learn as it went along. She fed him the data she wanted him to search—Millie Cameron's murder, Ross Cameron, Ray Weimer, Jason Garrity, and others—and turned him loose.

It was only a matter of seconds before the computer began to chime, and each time meant another page of links that Indie needed to look at. She and Sam huddled at the table while the grandmothers took Kenzie out to a playground they spotted near the hotel.

"Oh, look at that," Indie said. "Your boy Weimer is the police chief here in Benton, now. He probably built his career off of the Billy Cameron case."

Sam shrugged. "That'll just make him easier to find," he said. "What else has Herman got?"

"Did you know there have been three different books written about Millie's murder? According to this, all three of them support the notion that Ross was innocent and was bullied into a confession, but none of them have any idea who might have actually done it."

"Writers always try to attach their names to a big

story," Sam said. "Incidentally, what's this about you writing a blog about my cases?"

Indie leaned closer to her computer and pretended not to have heard him. "Jason Garrity seems to be quite a character around here," she said. "He's been arrested several times but always on minor offenses that seem to get dismissed."

"That means one of two things," Sam said. "Either he knows things he can tell the cops to buy his way out of trouble, or he knows things about the cops they don't want brought to light. In a Podunk burg like this, I'd almost bet on the latter. Now, about that blog..."

Indie let out a sigh and turned to face him. "You're not upset, are you? I just wanted something to do to help bring a little money in, and when the Twitter feed took off the way it did, I got the idea of starting a blog. You're up to about two hundred thousand regular followers, and it's bringing in about eight hundred dollars a month now."

Sam's eyes went wide. "Eight hundred dollars a month? Where is it going?"

Indie made a face that was halfway between a smile and a grimace. "Um—I've been putting it in a college fund account, for Kenzie and the baby. I didn't think you'd mind."

Sam burst out laughing and pulled her into a hug. "Mind? I think you're a genius," he said. "When were you going to get around to telling me about this?"

Indie shrugged, and Sam laughed again. "Okay, so let's get back to Herman. Anything else going on there?"

He let her go and she turned back to the computer. "Oh, hello," she said suddenly. "This is interesting. A year after Millie was killed, a man named Ralph Pinkham told a reporter for the Benton newspaper that he had proof that Ross was innocent. He claimed that Millie was killed over some kind of dispute, and that he had overheard the altercation that took place in her house that day, and even saw the killer."

"Seriously?" Sam asked. "Find me this guy."

Indie was shaking her head. "Sorry, babe, but the interesting part is that the day after he made that call to the reporter, Ralph Pinkham's car was found upside down in the Big Muddy River north of Benton, and he was still belted in behind the wheel at the time."

"Then I want the reporter's name." Sam's face suddenly became grave. "I'd have to say it sounds like Beauregard might be right," he said. "Sounds like it might be dangerous to dig into this story too deeply."

"Sam, he said it was going to be dangerous for someone descended from him. You don't have any Beauregards in your family history, do you?"

Sam shook his head. "Not that I know of," he said, "and Mom would probably know. Think you can figure out who it might be?"

Indie shrugged. "Well, I guess I can try having Herman run a scan through all the national databases on birth records, see if maybe one of the other descendants had a child or two that we don't know about yet. I mean, it's possible there's another whole branch of the family tree out there, but what are the odds that it would put another of his descendants here in this area? In order for one of them to be in danger because of this investigation, they'd almost certainly have to be close by, right?"

"Yeah, I guess that makes sense," Sam said. "Still, it's worth a try. How long will that take?"

Indie was entering data on her keyboard. "I'm giving him all the names we've collected, going all the way back to Beauregard's own children. Now, according to ancestry.com, most of them didn't have kids of their own, but you never know what might turn up in a government database, right? Birth records should be one of the first things to be converted to data, I would think, so hopefully some of these long-dead people had children and the birth certificates got recorded in a computer someplace." She hit the Enter key and looked up at Sam. "Don't get your hopes up too high," she said. "Even if it finds something, it'll be hours at least."

Sam looked at her and smiled. "And our mothers won't be back with Kenzie for at least another hour."

She looked up at him, and suddenly she broke into a smile. Sam locked the door while Indie turned down the covers.

* * * * *

Sam decided not to do anything until the following day, choosing instead to spend some time with his family. After googling for local tourist attractions, they took a drive out around Rend Lake, apparently one of the biggest lakes in all of Illinois. It was built in the 1960s by the US Army Corps of Engineers and covers nearly forty square miles to an average depth of about ten feet.

The scenery around it was beautiful, especially with the red and gold of the autumn leaves. They enjoyed the drive immensely and then decided to explore some of the smaller communities in the area. That took them to the neighboring community of Christopher, where they stumbled across an interesting little diner with a sign that read simply "Maid-Rite." Since it had been more than six hours since lunch and they were all a little hungry, Sam pulled the Ridgeline into the little parking lot and they wandered inside.

The nostalgic little place featured old soda-fountain-type stools around a horseshoe counter and offered sandwiches made of loose ground beef. After listening to a couple of customers tell them how good the sandwiches were, they all ordered one and some fries, and moments later they were all moaning with delight.

The lady behind the counter told him how that particular diner had been standing in the same spot for more than eighty years and planned to be there for at least eighty more. Sam assured her that he had no trouble believing they would achieve it, as long as they could keep those sandwiches tasting that good. He ordered four more to take with them, and they headed back to the hotel to relax and watch some TV.

The next day was a Saturday, but Sam had learned that the weekend was no deterrent to a private investigator. Indie had googled the addresses of the people he wanted to see, but Herman wasn't finished looking for Beauregard's missing descendants. Sam copied the addresses into his phone and kissed his wife while she lay sleeping in. He slipped out the door quietly and snagged himself a cup of coffee on the way out to the truck.

The first person he wanted to see was the potential star witness, Jason Garrity. From what Indie had read in excerpts of the books written about the murder, Garrity had never wavered in his story. He was only fourteen years old at the time the murder took place, which meant he would be twenty-two years old by now. Like a lot of young men, Jason was still listed as living at home with his mother. Sam started up the truck and headed for Thompsonville, but he had one stop to make first.

Millie Cameron had lived on Fifth Street, in the very last house on the north end of the street. Sam had been told that the backyard opened on to the woods, but when he went to look at the house, he realized that it was actually surrounded. The wooded area extended away from the street in both directions, though it was especially dense and thick to the west. Sam pulled up and parked on the street just in front of the old house, which had been sitting empty since the day Millie had died. Debbie had told him that she and her late husband had gone to the place and gathered up what they could of her mother's things, but that much of the furniture and such still remained inside.

Sam got out and just stood there for a moment, looking at the house and getting a sense of the area. Down the street, the nearest neighbor was about two hundred yards away. Sam could hear the neighbor's dog barking, probably reacting to the presence of the stranger in the area he considered his own domain.

Barking dogs, Sam knew from sad experience, weren't regarded with the same respect they once had been. There was a time when a barking dog would cause the homeowner to get up and look out the windows, just to make sure no one was prowling around the yard. Nowadays, though, most people simply wished the dog would shut up.

He walked up to the front door, putting his hands around his face to look through the window. It was dark inside, but he could actually make out the silhouettes of a couple of chairs, and a shiver went down his spine as he realized that he was probably looking at the precise spot where Millie had died.

He backed away from the door and began walking around the house, headed toward the backyard. It took him only a moment to get there, and he spotted the back door. He walked up to it and then turned to look at the woods behind the house.

Okay, I'm Ross, and I want to go for a walk among the trees. I come out the back door; now where do I actually enter the woods at?

Sam started walking toward the trees and suddenly realized that there was a natural break in the trees that bordered the back of the yard. He cut slightly to the right to reach it and could tell that there had once been a well-trodden path under his feet.

He had to duck slightly to get under an overhanging branch, but then he was inside the same woods Ross had visited on that fateful day. Even after eight years, the path that he must have walked was clearly visible, a line of stunted growth and bare spots where even grass had never managed to take root after the ground had been trampled. He followed it for about fifty feet, then turned and looked back toward the house.

It was like he was on a different planet. Despite the fact that many of the trees were bare and the rest were losing their leaves, the house couldn't be seen from where he stood. There was a peaceful sense about that spot, and Sam suspected that he might've found one of the places where Ross liked to stand and simply commune with nature.

He followed the path back to the house and made his way around it once more. When he got to the front of the house, though, he suddenly realized he wasn't alone. Standing beside the Ridgeline was a short, chubby woman dressed in dark slacks and a black hooded sweatshirt. Sam could see that the hood was sagging a bit as she looked through the window of his truck, but then she turned when she heard his feet crunching through the tall, dry grass. Dark glasses hit her eyes, but he could see gray curls inside the cavernous darkness of the hood.

"You got a reason to be snooping around here?" she asked pointedly, her voice a little shrill and cracking.

Sam withdrew his ID from his pocket and held it out as he approached her. "Yes, ma'am," he said. "My name is Sam Prichard. I'm a private investigator, and I'm working for the family of the lady who was murdered here. From everything I've been able to determine, the police didn't bother looking for any evidence that might have cleared this lady's son, but I'm convinced he's innocent. I just wanted to get a look at the place and get a feel for where the crime actually happened."

The woman looked at his ID for a long moment, then switched her gaze up to his eyes. "You working for Debbie, then?"

"Actually, I was hired by a distant relative of theirs to simply find his relations," Sam said, "but when I told him what was going on with Ross and Debbie, he asked me to try to find evidence that would get Ross out of prison. I'm working for him, and he wants to remain anonymous, but I'm also reporting everything I find back to Debbie Jenkins."

The woman looked him in the eye for another few seconds, then nodded and smiled, showing Sam a set of pretty rotten teeth. "I'm Marie," she said simply. "I keep an eye on the place for Debbie, so that's why I came over when I saw you walking around over here. Do you want to look inside? I have the key with me."

Sam glanced over his shoulder at the house and slowly nodded. "Yes, ma'am," he said as he turned back to Marie. "I think I'd like that."

Marie nodded and reached into a pocket of the sweatshirt she was wearing. She pulled out a key ring with two keys on it and handed them to him. "The gold one is for the front door," she said. "The silver one opens the back door."

Sam looked at her, his eyebrows crawling up his forehead. "You're not coming in with me?"

Marie's eyebrows rose over her sunglasses this time. "Who, me? No, sir, not me. I stepped into that house one time, about a week after Millie died, and that was enough for me. I will never go in there again."

"Was it that big a mess in there?" Sam asked.

"Mess? Yeah, it was a little messy, but that's not why I won't go back in there. It's on account of the things that happen in there. You go inside, you'll see what I mean. Things move around all by themselves, doors open and close—that place is haunted. I don't know if it's Millie or some other ghost, but I know I don't want no truck with it."

Sam felt a shiver run down his spine, but after having dealt with Beauregard for a couple of years, he wasn't about to let the thought of another ghost scare him off. He turned and walked toward the front door, slid the key into the keyhole in the middle of the doorknob, and turned it to the left. It opened smoothly, and Sam stepped inside.

The sun outside had been bright, so his eyes would take a moment to adjust. He took out his phone and turned on its flashlight feature, shining it around inside the living room.

Sure enough, there were the two chairs. The one on the left still bore the obvious darkenings of bloodstains. There were blotches across the top of the back of the chair, and it was obvious that blood had run down inside the wings on either side. The back corners of the seat cushion were also dark.

Sam glanced at the chair beside it and saw that there were only a few dark spots there. When he looked a little more closely, he could tell that there were spots from blood splattering. They were all over the back of the chair and the side of it that was closest to its mate, but there was also one bloodied handprint on the right arm of the chair. Sam was sure that it was probably from Ross, after he had touched his mother and determined that she was dead. He must have leaned on the arm of the chair as he sat down, leaving the handprint.

A sudden clunk to his right made Sam jump, and he spun and shined his light in that direction. A large metal can, the kind that coffee comes in, was rolling across the floor toward him. Sam raised the light and aimed it toward where the can was coming from but saw nothing. The only thing in that direction was a blank wall.

8

The hairs on the back of his neck were not only standing up, they were dancing a jig. Sam swallowed hard and forced himself to take a couple of steps toward that wall, and then he swallowed again when the can suddenly came to a stop a foot in front of him. He was honestly debating with himself about whether he should just leave the house immediately when a mouse suddenly ran out of the can and disappeared under a tall old bookcase.

The sigh of relief that came out of him sounded almost like laughter, but Sam wasn't in a humorous mood. He glanced around and saw Marie still standing by his truck and glared at her. She had primed him by telling him that the house was haunted, and even his determination not to believe it wasn't enough to keep him from feeling near panic when something unexplained happened. If he had run out the door before seeing the mouse, he probably would have gone to his grave thinking that he had honestly been in a haunted house.

"Sam Prichard ain't afraid of no ghost," he mumbled to himself. He shined the light ahead again and spotted a doorway that looked like it led into a bedroom. He walked over and looked inside, half-afraid he was going to see something wearing a bedsheet come flying at him.

Nothing happened. There was a bed in the room, but it had no sheets, blankets, or pillows. The mattress was also gone, and Sam suspected that it had ended up on Debbie's bed. He stepped into the room and shined the light around, but other than an empty wardrobe there was nothing else to see. He left the room and stepped into a short hallway.

To his right was a bathroom, and it took only a few seconds for his light to show him that there was nothing inside but the sink, toilet, and tub. To his left was a closet, and he opened the door cautiously, but nothing leapt out at him. That only left straight ahead, where another hall intersected this one on the left, but a door on the right led into what must have been Ross's room.

Sam opened the door and shined the light in, and then his heart almost stopped. Leaning against the wall on the far side of the room was a man, and Sam took an instinctive step backward when the light hit his face.

With his back against the opposite wall, Sam stared at the figure in the bedroom. It took him several seconds to realize that he was not looking at a living person, but at what appeared to be a manikin wearing bib overalls, a T-shirt, and a straw hat.

A minute later, when he had regained some semblance of his composure, Sam walked into Ross's room and examined the manikin more carefully. Nothing he knew about Ross gave him any inkling into the manikin's purpose, but the more he looked at it, the less sinister it appeared. It was leaning against the wall as if it had been posed that way, as if whoever it was supposed to be was simply relaxing there. Its face was turned toward the bed, and Sam imagined Ross lying there, looking up at the manikin and...

And what? No matter how he tried, Sam could not come up with a valid reason for the manikin to be there. Still, he really did feel that there was nothing sinister about it, so he decided to give Debbie a call later and ask her for an explanation.

Looking around the room a bit more thoroughly, he noticed several model cars and airplanes and a number of intricate little buildings made of Lego bricks. He had read somewhere that many autistic children were quite adept at assembling puzzles and models, and wondered if his parents bought them for him as some kind of therapy. Maybe they were just intended as something to keep him busy, something to occupy his mind at times.

Sam left that bedroom and walked along the intersecting hallway. A moment later, he found himself in the kitchen. A brief look around told him that this was one of the rooms where most of the contents had been left as they were. There were dishes in the dish strainer beside the sink and a couple of pans sitting on the stove, and a pair of coffee cups were still on the table. He imagined Ross and Millie sitting there that last fateful morning, perhaps even talking and laughing as they drank their morning brew.

That's when it happened, as he was standing there just staring at those coffee cups. The door of the cabinet over one end of the counter swung slowly open, and Sam's eyes were drawn up to it as those hairs on his neck switched from a jig to the Charleston. He kept waiting for the mouse to jump out of the cabinet, but it didn't, and the door slowly swung wider and wider.

He shined his light into the cabinet, and then he gasped. For a brief second, he would have sworn he was looking directly into an old man's face, complete with a handlebar mustache and goatee, but then that image vanished. Behind it, now clearly illuminated by the LED light from his phone, was what looked like a leather bag, and Sam might have simply dismissed it as just a bag if he had not seen the feather attached to it.

Slowly, Sam forced his feet to move toward the cabinets, but he kept looking around the room as he did so. It'd been a long time since Sam had felt anything close to terror, but he was quite sure he was on the verge of it at that moment. When he reached the cabinets, he steeled himself and shined the light in on the item that had caught his attention.

It was a hat, all right. It looked like a black leather version of a military garrison cap, and it definitely had a feather on it. Sam debated on whether to simply reach out and pick it up, but his training in handling evidence forced him not to do so. Instead, he used his phone to take a couple of photographs of it, then glanced around the room and spotted what looked like a stack of once-clean dish towels. He reached out to them, flipped the top one off because it would naturally be the dustiest of them all, then picked up the second and shook it out. A small amount of dust flew out from it, and then he used it to reach into the cabinet and pick up the hat.

There was mud on the hat, mud that had dried much darker than he would expect. He took a couple more photos of it with his phone, turning it over to be sure he got every angle. While Sam could not imagine how the hat had gotten into that cabinet, there was no doubt in his mind that he was looking at the same one Ross had seen the day his mother was killed. Was it possible he had actually picked up the hat and brought it home with him? No, that wouldn't make sense. He would have remembered, and surely, Sam told himself, he would have shown the hat to the deputies, wouldn't he?

Then again, would he have gotten the chance? From the stories Sam had heard, Ross had been arrested and hustled out to the squad car within minutes after the deputies arrived.

Sam looked around again, trying to find something to put the hat in. He opened a few other cabinets, then thought to look under the kitchen sink. Sure enough, there was a box of trash bags there. There was only a couple left, but Sam only needed one. He pulled it out and shook it open, slipped the hat and the dishrag inside, then carefully closed it up. He looked up at the cabinet he had taken it from, instinctively planning to shut the door, and suddenly realized that it was already closed.

"Okay," Sam said to himself, "that's enough." Another door led directly back to the living room, and he wasted no time in getting to the front door and out into the sunlight again. He pulled the door shut behind him and locked it, then turned to go back to Marie.

There was no one standing beside the truck. He looked around, but there was no sign of the short, chubby lady who had given him the keys. Sam swallowed hard, dropped the keys into his pocket, and slipped quickly behind the wheel of the Ridgeline. He slid the trash bag with the hat inside up under his seat and then started up the truck.

Jason Garrity lived with his mother, only a block away on Fourth Street, but there was no cross street that connected the two anywhere near the north end. Sam had to go all the way back to Division Street, turn left, and then left again to get to the house.

A glance at his phone told him that it was just hitting eight thirty in the morning, and he hoped that would be a good time to catch Jason at home on a Saturday. He went to the front door of the house and knocked, and it was open a moment later by a pleasant-looking woman.

"Good morning," Sam said. "Would Jason happen to be here?"

The woman smiled and chuckled. "He's here," she said. "Now, whether we can get him out of bed or not, that's another whole question. Won't you come inside?" She held the door open, and Sam thanked her as he followed her into her living room. "You just have a seat, I'll go wake him up."

Sam looked around the living room, taking in the décor that he could only describe as "rustic contemporary." There were two different styles of sofa in the room, four different end tables that didn't match at all, and a coffee table that didn't look like it was even remotely related to anything else in the room. Still, none of it looked like junk; each piece was in rather good condition, especially when he considered that some of them were undoubtedly antiques. Considering that the house was probably eighty or a hundred years old, many of these pieces could easily have been originals when it was built.

Mrs. Garrity came back a moment later and told him that Jason would be right out, and then Sam heard a toilet flushing somewhere toward the back of the house. A minute later, a short, stocky young man with hair that looked like a badger had tried to nest in it came stumbling down the hall.

Sam stood. "Jason?" He produced his ID when the young man nodded. "My name is Sam Prichard. I'm a private investigator. I've been hired by the family of Ross Cameron to try to find out what really happened the day his mother was killed, and I'm told that you might actually have been a witness."

Jason had stopped rubbing his eyes when Sam mentioned Ross, and they got very wide in his round face when Sam used the word "witness." He shook his head a couple of times as if to clear it, then looked Sam in the eye.

"Are you for real? I talked to a bunch of people over the years, and some of them even wrote books about that poor lady, but nobody ever took me seriously. I know good and well Ross didn't do it, because I saw the person who did. I tried to tell the cops and they didn't believe me, and nobody else has taken me seriously since then. I've just about got to the point I don't even want to talk about it anymore."

Sam waited until his little tirade was finished and then shook his ID. "Like I said, I'm a private investigator. That means I'm out to find the truth, not just try to make a buck off the story. I want to know what you saw that day, because it just might help me find out what really happened. Are you willing to talk to me about this? You might actually be saving Ross's life. I went to see him in prison day before yesterday, and that's not a very safe place for a guy like him to be."

Jason frowned, but then he sat down on the couch beside Sam. "I'll tell you the same thing I told everybody else," he said. "I was cutting through the trees between here and there, headed over to ask Ms. Cameron if she wanted me to mow her grass that week. It hadn't rained a lot, so it wasn't growing very fast; sometimes when it was dry like that she let it go an extra week between mowings. She gave me a few dollars each week to mow because—well, because when Ross tried to mow, he always ended up missing a bunch of spots. He could take the mower apart and put it back together perfectly, but he couldn't tell the difference between grass that was already mowed and grass that wasn't. It was kind of a joke around here."

Sam nodded. "Okay, I'm with you. Go on."

"Yeah, so anyway, it was about two thirty when I went over there, and like I told you, I took a shortcut through the woods between here and there. To do that, you have to go kind of north a little bit, so you actually come out a little below her house, know what I mean? Well, anyway, when I come out on her street, I seen somebody in her backyard. Now, at first, I thought it was Ross, but then I saw that they were too short and a little bit fatter than he was, y'know? So I stopped and I kind of leaned over so I could see a little bit better, and that's when I knew for sure it wasn't him. See, there's two things that told me that, okay? First off, Ross don't ever wear a hat, and this person had a hat on. And second..."

Sam cut him off. "Could you see the hat? Could you

describe it?"

Jason looked confused for a second, then shrugged and shook his head. "It looked black—that's all I could really tell from that far away. Is it important?"

"It might be," Sam said. "Anyway, go on. What was the second thing?"

Jason grinned. "Simple. I knew it wasn't Ross because the person who was running across the backyard was a woman."

Sam's eyebrows shot upward. "A woman? Are you certain?"

"If I'm lyin', I'm dyin'," Jason said. "See, I was in drama club in high school, right? That year, just not long before Ms. Cameron got killed, we did this play called *The Sneaky Old Lady*, about this burglar who never got caught. Well, the reason he never got caught is because he was always disguised as an old lady, and I got the title role. My drama teacher, Ms. Berkowitz, she told me that if I really wanted to play it right, I had to study the difference between how men and women walk, right? So I did. See, in the play, I had to do two parts. I had to be James, who everybody thought was a great guy, and I had to be old Ms. Lydia, who nobody would ever suspect of being able to climb the side of the building and slip the lock on the window, right?" He grinned and rubbed his hands together. "I studied makeup and all kinds of stuff, and I did such a good job that a lot of people refused to believe it was me dressed up as the old lady. And the reason I did it so well was because of what Ms. Berkowitz said—I studied how women walk. Men walk mostly with their legs and arms, but women put their whole body into it. I saw that, and then I walked that way when I was in that costume. That's how I know the person I saw was a woman. Because men and women walk differently, and that person walked the way a woman walks."

Sam sat there and looked at the young man for a moment, then cocked his head to one side. "Now, wait a minute," he said. "I've read some bits and pieces out of the books that were written about the murder, and the authors mentioned that they talked to you. Nowhere in any of that stuff did it ever say that you thought the person you saw was a woman."

Jason looked smug. "That's right," he said, "and you wanna know why? Because everybody else who's asked me about this didn't give a rat's ass about Ross, but you do. I can tell because of what you said. You said that place isn't a good place for Ross to be, and you wouldn't have said that if you didn't care about him."

Sam looked at Jason and grinned. "You seem a lot sharper than your reputation would lead one to believe," he said. "I'm gonna play a hunch, here. Jason, tell me what else you think you figured out about this case."

Jason glanced at his mother, who was smiling proudly at him, then turned back to Sam. "Well, there's a couple of things," he said. "I drove myself kind of nuts for a while, trying to figure out why anybody would want to kill that sweet old lady, but I couldn't even come up with a guess. Nobody around here ever had anything bad to say about her, I can tell you that. So I started thinking about the reasons people usually commit murder, you know, like over money or jealousy or that kind of thing? None of that seemed like it could fit, either, because she didn't have any money to speak of and I couldn't imagine anyone being jealous over her, so none of that added up. So what does that leave? You're the private investigator, you tell me."

Sam chewed the inside of his cheek gently. "Well," he said, "while there are many different things that are considered motives for murder, such as domestic violence, self-defense, vengeance, to collect life insurance, that whole endless list, when you investigate murders as often as I've had to do, you realize there are actually only three motives for anything. Those are greed, survival, or revenge. A greed motive would be if you wanted to collect life insurance or an inheritance; a survival motive would be like the abused woman who kills her husband because she can't escape him, or somebody who kills a person who knows something that would hurt them; and the revenge motive would be like the person who kills the one their spouse left them for. Am I warm?"

Jason shrugged. "Could be. Want to try one more time before you give up?"

"Well, as you said, she didn't have any money and I

already know that her life insurance was barely enough to pay for her funeral, so that rules out greed. Nobody stood to gain anything financially or materialistically from her death."

"Right," Jason said. "She didn't even own her house at the time; her son-in-law did. He bought it and fixed it up for her after he married Debbie, but they never wanted to rent it out or sell it or anything after she died. No, I don't think there was any kind of greed involved."

Sam nodded. "All right, let's look at survival. From what little I know of her, and part of that is based on what you've told me today, it's highly doubtful that she was any kind of threat to anyone. I don't think anybody was suffering under her control, so there was no reason to kill her to get free of her."

"Bingo, right again."

Sam looked into the young man's eyes and was surprised to see that Jason really wanted him to get the answer right. He wasn't sure why, but it definitely mattered to the boy.

"That only leaves revenge," Sam said. "We have to find someone that felt she had done them wrong, somewhere along the line. The problem with that is that, as you said yourself, nobody had a cross word to say about her."

Jason started to speak, but Sam was suddenly lost in his thoughts. *Actually, someone did have some pretty cross words to say about Millie. Her sister, Judith. Millie stole Judith's fiancé and had his children. Millie got the wedding and the marriage and the romance and the children and everything. If anyone had a vengeance motive, it had to be Judith Wingo.*

Something Jason said caught Sam's attention, but he couldn't quite catch it. "Sorry? Would you say that again?"

"I said, there was only one person in the world who might have any bitterness or anger toward Ms. Cameron," Jason said. "And that one person would have to be..." He looked expectantly at Sam.

Sam blinked. "You know about her sister, then?" he asked.

Jason yanked his head backward and narrowed his eyes. "Sister? She had a sister?"

"Yes," Sam said. "In fact, her husband was originally engaged to her sister, Judith. He left her after Millie ended up pregnant with his child, and he and Millie were married and moved away."

Jason's eyes were about as big around as a dinner plate, and he gave a low whistle. "Well, that really throws a monkey wrench into the machinery," he said. "Because I didn't know anything about a sister. I figured it had to be her daughter."

It was Sam's turn to look confused. "Debbie? As far as I know, no one has ever suspected Debbie..."

"No, not Debbie," Jason said. "I'm talking about her other daughter, Debbie's sister. The one that up and disappeared when she was only thirteen or so."

Another brief memory suddenly surfaced, a snippet of Debbie's voice: *"I mean, my sister's disappearance, then Mom being murdered and Ross being accused of it, then Randy falling asleep behind the wheel—they used to say my family was cursed..."*

Sam looked at Jason. "What else can you tell me about this other daughter?"

Jason looked at his mother, who leaned forward. "Her name was Lynette," Mrs. Garrity said. "She was a beautiful girl, but she was always—well, precocious. I think she was about thirteen when she disappeared, but she looked more like a sixteen-year-old if you take my meaning. The boys were constantly sniffing around her, and she was eating up the attention. Unfortunately, it wasn't just boys who were paying that attention to her, and she got caught with a local man. He was arrested and taken to jail, but she disappeared a couple of days later. Without her, the prosecutor said he couldn't make the charges stick, so the man was released and everything was dismissed. Nobody knows for sure whatever happened to Lynette, but there were rumors."

"What kind of rumors?" Sam asked.

Mrs. Garrity glanced at her son, then turned her eyes back to Sam. "Well, that she was sent away to have a child, that she'd gotten pregnant. But the worst rumor was that she had been killed, of course, though nobody really believed it around here. It just seemed kind of odd to everybody that, after she was gone, the man she got in trouble with suddenly seemed to be best friends with her mom and dad."

9

"Did anyone ever ask Millie what happened?" Sam asked, his eyes wide. "I'd think she would have wanted to quash any rumors."

Mrs. Garrity shrugged her shoulders with an expression that said she wasn't all that sure what Millie would want. "She always claimed she didn't know where the girl had gone," she said, "and it was no secret that both Ross and Debbie—she was only about six at the time—they both kept asking what happened to Lynette. Some people thought she ran away, some thought she got dropped down one of the old mine shafts around here, but most said she got shipped off somewhere because she was pregnant."

"You said Lynette was thirteen, but Debbie was only about six," Sam said. "So, we're talking about roughly thirty years ago?"

"Something like that," Mrs. Garrity said. "I'd say

probably thirty-two, maybe thirty-three years."

"Did the sheriff ever look into it? I would think he would have been pretty pissed off if his only witness against a child molester vanished on him."

Mrs. Garrity shook her head. "I think he might have asked Millie, but that would have been about all. And they didn't consider it any type of molestation; the guy was only charged with statutory rape. That's pretty much how they used to look at such things around here."

Sam rolled his eyes. "So, who was this guy? Is he still around here?"

Mrs. Garrity lowered her eyes to the floor for a moment, then looked back up at Sam. "He's not around anymore," she said flatly. "He got into his car one day about six months later and said he was running up to the store to get some cigarettes, and he never came back. Nobody has seen or heard from him since."

Something in her expression made Sam look closely at her. "Okay," he said, "but who was he? Do you know his name?"

"Oh, yeah," the woman said. "His name was Bill Parkinson. The son of a bitch was also my father."

That explains the animosity I'm sensing, Sam thought. "Do you have any kind of theory on where he disappeared to?"

"Nope," she said. "And absolutely no interest in finding out. Lynette and I were the same age, and we were pretty much inseparable most of the time. She was my best friend, and when it all blew open I found out that she and my dad had been sneaking around together for three months. It started one night when she was sleeping over at my place, and then they just kept finding chances to meet up. I don't know whether she was really pregnant or not, because I never got to talk to her after they got caught, but if I had to make a guess I'd say she probably was. I'm one of those who thinks she was sent away, maybe shipped off to some other relative to have the baby and then just never wanted to come home. As for my father, just about everybody believes he found out where she was and went to be with her. Wouldn't surprise me even a little bit if that's the case."

Sam glanced at Jason for a moment, but he could see that the boy had obviously heard all this before. "So, Jason," he said. "You were thinking that maybe it was Lynette who came and killed Millie?"

The younger man shrugged. "Well, that's what I thought until you told me about her sister. I can imagine she would have wanted some kind of revenge, too, don't you think? Gives us another whole suspect."

"Actually, I think we have three suspects now," Sam said. He held up one finger. "There's Judith, Millie's sister, who hated her for stealing her fiancé away." Another finger went up. "There's Lynette, who might have hated her mother for sending her away, that's possible." A third finger joined the other two. "And we've got Bill Parkinson, your grandfather. If he and Lynette are together out there somewhere, it's possible he's the one who killed Millie, in retaliation for whatever damage he thinks the exposure did to their lives."

Jason gave him a calculating look, but then he shook his head. "It wasn't him," he said. "I'm telling you, the killer was a woman. I couldn't get a good enough look to make any kind of guess on how old the woman might have been, but it was definitely a woman."

Sam chewed his cheek and thought for a moment. "Let's get back to the person you saw. Can you remember what kind of clothes she might've been wearing?"

"Yeah, sure. Looked like a yellow shirt, and the pants were either brown or a dark red, I'm not certain."

"That helps quite a bit," Sam said. "Ross saw the same person in the woods, not long before he came inside and found his mother dead. He specifically mentioned a yellow shirt and brown pants, and that the person was wearing a black hat. He said he saw whoever it was drop the hat, so he went and looked down at it and saw that it had a feather on it. Did you notice anything about a feather?"

Jason screwed up his face and thought for a moment, then shook his head. "Seems like I might have noticed something back then, but I really can't remember now. I don't know if I'm remembering that I saw a feather or if I'm imagining I saw one because you mentioned it, know what I mean?"

Sam grinned. "I understand, and that's good thinking

on your part. Have you ever thought of going into police work? You think like an investigator, I can tell you that."

Jason smiled and blushed. "Actually, I've applied to every police department within fifty miles but always get turned down. I've had some little scrapes with the law, and they probably ruined me."

"Don't give up," Sam said. "As long as you don't have any felonies on your record, you can still become a cop. Think about going to college, maybe study criminal justice. You might have to go farther away to find a job, but I'm sure you can." He rose to his feet. "You've given me a lot of information, and I really appreciate it. Now I'll give you a bit. I went over to Millie's house before I came here, just to look it over, and a lady came over and gave me the keys, so I went inside. I..."

"Oh, oh," Jason said, and his mother's face suddenly looked ashen. "Did you—did anything weird happen?"

Sam grimaced. "Well, she had warned me that, as she put it, the place is haunted. At first, it just felt kind of weird in there, but then all of a sudden this tin can, like a big coffee can, came rolling across the floor at me, and it just about scared me to death. But then it stopped, and a mouse came running out of it, so I managed to get my heartbeat back under control. I did see a couple of other weird things, though; in one of the bedrooms, the one that I think must have been Ross's room, there's a manikin all dressed up in bib overalls and a straw hat. Would you know anything about that?"

"Yeah," Jason said. "After old man Cameron died, Ross found that thing somewhere and dressed it up like his daddy. I guess it helped him cope with the old man being gone, or at least that's what everybody said."

Sam nodded. "That would make sense, I guess. I just wondered about it. The other thing, though, it was pretty spooky. I went into the kitchen and was just standing there, and all of a sudden one of the cabinet doors opened up, one of the upper cabinets. For a second I thought I saw a face looking out, but then it was gone and I saw something else inside." He took a deep breath. "I'm pretty sure it was the hat that the person you saw was wearing. It's a black leather hat, like one of those military-style hats that fold flat, and it had some kind of a feather attached to it. I was wondering if you might have any idea how it could have gotten into the cabinet?"

Jason's eyes were wide, and so were his mother's. Mrs. Garrity was the first one to speak.

"I don't think we have any idea at all," she said. "I can tell you this, though. It wasn't there the last time I was in that house, but that was back when Debbie and her husband were trying to gather up whatever they wanted to keep from it, maybe a couple weeks after the old woman died. I know it wasn't there because I was helping her, and I opened every cabinet in the kitchen to see if there was anything in it they might want." She shivered, and the look on her face reflected fear. "That's really, really strange. I can't imagine who would've put that there, or who might have known it even existed. I don't think I ever heard about a hat until today."

"It doesn't make any sense," Jason said. "You said Ross saw the hat after whoever it was tossed it away, but did he say anything about picking it up?"

"No," Sam said, shaking his head. "Quite the opposite. According to Ross, he left it laying right where it was. He had said that it had gotten dirty because dirt had stuck to blood that was on the hat, and the one I found has dark mud stains on it. I found a trash bag and tucked it inside, I'm going to take it to the sheriff to see if maybe there might be some hairs inside it from whoever was wearing it. If there is, a good lab can pull DNA from them."

"Man," Jason said, "that is really weird. The only other person who would even have known the hat existed would be the killer, and she surely wouldn't have gone back to put it inside the house. Maybe one of those cops? But that wouldn't make any sense, either, because they wouldn't have put it in a kitchen cabinet."

"I agree, that wouldn't make any sense. Listen, the lady who gave me the keys didn't wait around, and I didn't see where she went. She said her name was Marie. Would you..."

Mrs. Garrity had leapt to her feet. "Marie?" she asked, her eyes wide. "What did she look like?"

A chill went down Sam's spine. "About five feet tall, kind of chunky. Looks like she might be in her sixties?"

"And she gave you keys?"

Sam reached into his pocket and pulled the key ring out. "Yeah, these," he said.

The woman stared at the keys in his hand for a moment, then looked up at his eyes. "Mr. Prichard," she said slowly, "the only Marie I ever knew around here was Marie Logan, and you just described her pretty well. The only problem with that is that she died three years ago. Up until then, she looked after the house for Debbie and her husband, but when she died no one could ever find the keys."

Sam stared at her for a moment and then looked at the keys in his hand. "This is getting crazy," he said. "I don't know what to think, let alone what to believe. You're trying to tell me that a ghost gave me these keys?"

Mrs. Garrity shrugged, but the expression on her face did not change. "This is an old town," she said. "You ask around here, you'll find an awful lot of folks who believe in ghosts. Like Mrs. Jackson—she died back in '71 when the tornado came through town, but there are at least a couple dozen people around here who saw her walking around at her own funeral, and she's been seen many times since then. Marie Logan—there's only one other person who ever claimed to have seen her since she died, and that was her son, Lester. He claims he's seen her two or three times, and always just before somebody dies."

Sam shook his head and started to turn toward the door. "Okay, listen, thank you both for your time. I need to..." He stopped and turned back to Jason. "One more question," he said. "You said you were on the way to see Millie when you saw this woman running out the back door, right?"

Jason frowned. "I didn't actually see her come out the door," he said, "but I did see her hurry across the backyard and into the woods."

Sam nodded. "Okay, I got that. What did you do next? Did you go on up to the house?"

"Yeah, I went up and knocked on the door, but nobody answered. I yelled a couple times to see if she was home, then I turned around and left."

Sam looked at the boy for a moment. "You didn't look through the window on the door?"

Jason shook his head. "Well, no," he said. "Mom always told me it was rude to look in somebody's windows, so I guess it just didn't even occur to me."

Sam nodded and thanked him, then walked out the door toward his truck. As he opened the driver's door to get in, Jason suddenly appeared beside him.

"Mr. Prichard," he said, "I know this is going to sound crazy, but I've got to tell you. I think maybe there's something about the way Ms. Cameron died that —well, that nobody has figured out. You know the cops said Ross just beat her to death, right? With his hands, I mean?"

"Yeah," Sam said. "You have another theory?"

"I read something not long ago that made me think

about that again. See, the human skull can take an awful lot of pressure, like five hundred and twenty pounds on average, so those TV shows where somebody crushes somebody else's skull, that's bogus. Now, just to fracture a skull to the point that it penetrates into the brain takes about three hundred and twenty pounds applied to a particular spot. So I checked out how much force the average person can deliver with a fist, without any kind of martial arts training, and it's about a hundred pounds, give or take twenty percent. But then you have to take into account the fact that most of the damage to her skull was done on the sides, so you have to factor in the fact that it would be moving with every blow. That would take away some of the force of each blow, so it's really just about impossible to believe that he could've done that much damage just by swinging his fists at her."

Sam nodded. "You're not the first one to come to that conclusion, but that's the first time I've heard it explained so well. The problem is that once the police decided Ross was guilty, they didn't even look for a murder weapon. Now, eight years later, it's a pretty cold trail. I don't know that we can ever determine exactly what it might have been."

"A forensic pathologist could," Jason said. "Even after eight years of being in the grave, the damage to her skull won't have changed. If it could be arranged to have the body exhumed, and a good forensic pathologist examine it..."

"You're right, of course," Sam said, "but exhuming a

body is not necessarily an easy thing to do. Do you happen to know where Millie was buried?"

"Yeah. She was buried at the cemetery out south of town. Freeman Cemetery, that's what it's called."

Sam nodded thoughtfully. "Let me mull this over, and I'll probably talk to Debbie about it. If we can establish that it was physically impossible for Ross to have done this the way the police say, then it would cast some doubt on the whole investigation. The fact that they never came up with any kind of murder weapon might just show how incompetent the sheriff's office was in this case."

Jason grinned and shrugged. "Cool," he said. "And thanks for hearing me out. Nobody else would even listen to me."

Sam patted the boy on the shoulder and climbed into his truck. He started the engine and turned around, then headed back toward Benton. Despite the fact that it was a Saturday, Sam wanted to try to speak to the sheriff's deputies who had arrested Ross.

The sheriff's office was located in the Criminal Justice Center on East Main Street, and Sam pulled in and parked in front of the building. As he climbed out, he reached under the seat and retrieved the trash bag that contained the hat and tucked it under his arm. When he got inside, a receptionist greeted him and directed him to the actual sheriff's office, just off the lobby.

The dispatcher, a young woman, smiled as he entered. "Hi there," she said. "I'm Jill McCann. How can I help you today?"

Sam showed her his ID. "My name is Sam Prichard, and I'm a private investigator looking into a case that happened here in Franklin County about eight years ago. It was the murder of an elderly woman named Millie Cameron, and I'm wondering if any of the deputies who were involved might be available. Their names were Johnny Moore and Bob Fry."

"Oh, goodness," she said. "I remember that. They said her son did it, right?"

"Yes, ma'am," Sam said. "The trouble is that there are a number of people who don't believe he's guilty, and from what I've seen so far, there were avenues of the investigation that were never followed. From what I understand, there was only one witness, but his testimony was discounted, and I may have actually stumbled across some potential physical evidence that lends credibility to his statement at the time."

"Oh, my. Well, Johnny Moore is our chief detective, now, but Bob Fry passed away about a year ago. Johnny is off today, but let me see if I can get hold of him for you." She turned away and picked up a telephone, then dialed a number quickly from memory. Apparently it was answered on the first ring, because she smiled into the phone. "Hey, Johnny, this is Jill," she said. "I got a private investigator here who's got some questions about a case you worked on eight years ago. It was the murderer of that old lady in Thompsonville—Millie Cameron, do you remember that? Okay, yeah, but this man says he may have come across some evidence that he thinks might change the situation. Could you come in and talk with him? Okay, great, I'll tell him. Bye-bye." She hung up the phone and turned back to Sam. "If you'd like to have a seat, he'll be here in about five minutes. He just lives a couple blocks away, and he said he was already heading out the door, anyway."

"Thank you," Sam said. There was a row of chairs against the wall opposite the reception desk, and Sam took a seat.

Detective Moore showed up right on time and came directly to Sam. "You're the private eye?"

Sam showed his ID to the detective and rose to his feet. "Yes, sir, Sam Prichard. I've been asked to look into the case against Ross Cameron, and I wanted to discuss it with you a bit."

Moore nodded and motioned for Sam to follow him. "Come on back to my office," he said. "We can talk there."

"I appreciate it," Sam said. He followed the detective past the reception desk and into a hallway, where they turned into the second door on the left.

Moore motioned Sam into a chair in front of his desk, then sank into the one behind it. "I remember this case very well," he said. "I was actually the arresting officer. Jill said something about new evidence?" He looked pointedly at the trash bag that Sam had placed in his lap.

"Well, I'm not certain whether it's new evidence or not. I met with Ross the day before yesterday and asked him to tell me everything he could remember about what happened that day. He said that he was walking in the woods and came home to find his mother dead, in the condition you saw when you arrived. However, he also told me that he had seen someone else in the woods that day. He saw them in the morning, as he was walking around, and then again shortly before he got home. When he saw the person the second time, he said they seemed to be in a rush, and he observed them throwing a hat onto the ground as they hurried through the woods. He was curious and went to look at the hat, and described it as a black hat with a feather."

Moore frowned. "He never said anything like that to any of us," he said. "And as far as I know, no hat was ever found anywhere around there."

Sam nodded. "Well, today I spoke with Jason Garrity, who claimed he saw somebody leaving the house that afternoon. He also told me that the person he saw seemed to be wearing a black hat, but he couldn't remember a feather."

Detective Moore made a scoffing sound. "There you go again. I talked to Garrity that day, and Detective Weimer spoke to him a couple of times afterward. I remember him saying he saw somebody leaving the backyard of the house, but he never mentioned any hat."

"He told me that, but he said it was because he didn't really think about the hat until I mentioned Ross saying he had seen one. However, both of them told me that the person they saw was wearing a yellow shirt. Ross said the pants were brown, while Jason said they were either brown or a dark red. Now, I highly doubt the two of them ever had a chance to compare their stories, so that gives me a pair of closely matching descriptions of the same individual."

Detective Moore had been leaning back in his chair, but now he sat forward and put his elbows on his desk. "Okay, you got my attention," he said. "However, that doesn't really provide any kind of new evidence, now, does it?"

Sam held up a finger in the universal gesture that asks someone to wait. "On its own, I would agree with you, though it does at least lend some credibility to Ross's story. However, before I went to see Jason today, I decided to just go by and take a look at the house where Millie Cameron died. I parked and got out, and was looking through the windows when a woman suddenly started talking to me. She was a short, heavyset woman who called herself Marie, and she asked me if I wanted to go inside. When I said I'd love to see the inside of the house, she handed me a set of keys and told me that she had been asked by Millie's daughter to keep an eye on the place. I went inside, and..."

"Did you see the ghost?" Moore asked. "All the locals claim they've seen a ghost inside that house, looking out the windows and such."

"To be completely honest, I'm not sure," Sam said. "A couple of strange things did happen while I was in there; one of them was when a cabinet in the kitchen opened on its own, very slowly. I—well, for a moment I thought I saw what looked like a man's face looking out at me, but when I blinked it was gone. However, before I could go running out the door—and I'll confess that I almost did—something else inside the cabinet caught my eye." He picked up the trash bag and laid it on the desk. "This was inside the cabinet. I didn't want to touch it, so I used an old dish towel to pick it up and put it in that bag."

Moore's eyes narrowed as he gingerly opened the bag and let its contents spill out onto his desk. They widened again when he saw the hat, with what looked like the remains of a decorative feather affixed to it. He stared at it for several seconds, then looked up at Sam.

"This was inside one of the kitchen cabinets?" he asked.

Sam nodded. "Yes, and you're not half as surprised as I was. That was the last thing in the world I expected to find inside that house. Ross had told me that when he saw the hat, it was, as he put it, 'sticky with blood' and getting dirt on it. Considering how dark those little mud stains on it are, I have to believe that's the very hat he saw that day."

Moore was using a pencil to move the hat around. "But how in the hell could it have gotten inside the house? I mean, even though we were pretty sure we had the right guy, we still searched through the house as part of our investigation. I can guarantee you that hat wasn't there then."

"It wasn't there two weeks later, either. Jason Garrity's mother said she helped Debbie and her husband gather up what they wanted to keep from the house, and said she looked in every cabinet in the kitchen at that time. I have no idea how it could have gotten there, unless there was another witness that we don't know about who thought it might be needed at some point."

"Did you ask that woman who gave you the keys about it?"

Sam grimaced. "Yeah, about her," he said. "When I came back out of the house, she was gone. I didn't know where to find her, so I asked Jason and his mother about her, and they both told me that there was a woman named Marie who had been watching the house for Debbie, but that she had died and no one ever found the keys."

10

Moore looked up at Sam, and his own eyes got wide. "Are you telling me a ghost gave you the keys to the house?"

"No," Sam said, shaking his head. "I'm telling you that a woman who claimed to be Marie and fit her description gave me those keys. I have spent most of my life denying the existence of ghosts, even though I've seen some pretty strange things over the years. I'm not quite willing to start admitting I actually believe in them now." Mentally, Sam crossed his fingers, remembering that he had actually said that he was starting to wonder about Beauregard.

"I know what you mean," Moore said. "I don't believe in them, either, but there have been a few pretty strange things that have happened in my life, too." He looked back down at the hat. "As for this, I'm not sure what to make of it. If we had found it back then, if Ross had told us about it, it might have made a difference. I'm really not sure about that. Now, though, when we can't even be a hundred percent certain that it's the same hat..."

"I understand, but I think it should be processed, anyway. Most hats end up with hair from the wearer stuck inside them. There's at least a chance that DNA could be recovered on that hat. I have a short list of possible suspects, and if it would match any of them..."

"Suspects?" Moore asked, his eyes meeting Sam's again. "Then I take it you honestly believe Ross Cameron is innocent?"

"I do," Sam said. "Ross is autistic. I know a bit about autistic people from my days as a policeman, when I had to deal with them every now and then. One thing I learned is that they don't seem to have a lot of imagination. Generally speaking, they are just about incapable of lying. They react to the world precisely as they see it, and one of the most common traits of the autistic is an inability to either recognize or utilize deception. For example, Ross says Weimer told him that if he would admit to killing his mother, he could go home. While the thought of being dishonest by admitting to the crime displeased him, he accepted Weimer's statement as fact. Since saying he did it meant he could go home, and he wanted to go home, then he was willing to say he did it even though he did not. If Ross tells me he saw someone in the woods behind the house, and that that person was wearing and discarded a hat that matches this one, then I am essentially certain he's telling me the truth as he knows it."

Moore stared at him for a moment. "I'm gonna tell you something I've never said to anyone else," he said slowly. "There have been many times since that day when I have felt that everything just went too easy, if you know what I mean. I'll grant you, my first reaction when I saw Mrs. Cameron was to grab the person who was closest and say he did it, and it wasn't until months later that I began to really wonder if he did. I think it was my sister's kid who made me think about it. I mean, he knew Ross because he used to take his motorbike to the garage he worked at, and Ross would always figure out the problem and fix it pretty quickly. He told me one day that he and his friends didn't believe Ross was guilty, because even when they would tease him and taunt him when they were younger, Ross never got mad." He rubbed at his nose for a moment, as if it were itching. "The beating that killed Mrs. Cameron looked to me like something done in anger. It looked like somebody had let out an awful lot of rage on that poor old woman, and if a bunch of kids torturing a man they thought of as retarded wasn't enough to make him lose his temper, then I can't imagine what could be."

"But you never wanted to look deeper into it? You never took any action to try to find out what the truth might be?"

Moore licked his lips. "Yeah, I did," he said. "I actually tried to reopen the case about a year afterward, but I was told to let it go. Since I didn't have any kind of new evidence, nobody wanted to work with me on it." He pointed at the hat lying on his desk. "I don't know if this is going to be enough, to be honest with you, but I'm definitely going to give it a try."

"What about Weimer?" Sam asked. "Is he going to object?"

Moore made a grimace of his own. "I don't think he's going to be any problem. Ray Weimer is the chief of police here in Benton, now. He ran for sheriff a couple years ago, but he lost the election, so he took the job when it came open about a year back. I won't say he and I are close, but we get along okay."

"I'm glad to hear that," Sam said. "Frankly, I don't feel he did his job very well on this case, but I'd just as soon not have him offering any resistance. Ross's been sitting in a prison long enough, and I'm actually starting to have some hope that we might get him out of there one day soon."

"I'm not sure I'd go that far just yet," Moore said. "Now, tell me about this short list of suspects. Who are you thinking of?"

"Well, Jason Garrity said he thought the person he saw leaving the house was a woman, and he gave a pretty logical argument for why he thought so, based on the way the person walked. Millie Cameron had a sister named Judith, couple years older than herself, and it just so happens that Donald Cameron, Millie's husband, had originally been engaged to the sister. He left her and married Millie after they had a little affair, and Millie ended up pregnant. Ross was born sometime after they left Tennessee together."

Moore cocked his head to the left and looked at Sam with a slight grin. "So you're thinking the sister might have had motive? Sixty years or so seemed like a long time to wait for revenge, don't you think?"

"Well, I can't disagree, but I've met the woman. There's an awful lot of hate there, and she actually seemed to know that Millie was dead even though she claimed to have no contact with her."

Moore nodded. "Okay, that's one. Who else?"

"I've learned that Millie and her husband had a third child, another girl," Sam said. "According to Mrs. Garrity, Lynette was caught in an affair with her father, Bill Parkinson. Parkinson was a much older man and was apparently arrested for statutory rape, but not long after that, Lynette disappeared. Charges against Parkinson were dropped, and it was speculated that Lynette was sent away because she was pregnant. She never came back, though, and a few months later, Parkinson also disappeared. Jason has speculated that Lynette may have held a grudge against her mother, especially if she was forced to have an abortion or give up a child she wanted to keep, and I can say that there could be some validity to that. Lynette would probably be in her mid to late fifties now, so that would put her in late forties or very early fifties at the time of the murder."

"I found out about Lynette back when Mrs. Cameron was killed," Moore said, "but Dan Anderson—he was sheriff at the time—said that Lynette died around thirty years ago. I don't know how he knew that, but he seemed pretty sure."

Sam's eyes widened slightly in surprise, but he went on. "Then that could leave Parkinson himself, but he would probably have been pretty elderly by then. He's also a man, and I tend to believe Jason is probably right in his belief that the person he saw leaving the scene was a woman. We still haven't got any kind of evidence that says that person was the killer, of course, other than the circumstantial evidence of being in the woods behind the house both before and after the crime."

"You're assuming that Parkinson, when he took off, went to be with Lynette? Have you got anything concrete that makes you believe that, or is it a wild guess?"

"Again, just circumstantial evidence. I was told that after Lynette disappeared and Parkinson's charges were dropped, he and Lynette's parents became close. Now, the Camerons were from down in the South, where it wasn't uncommon for girls as young as thirteen or fourteen to get married back then. It's possible they were fully aware of the relationship, whether they approved or not, and if Lynette really was pregnant, then they might have been working out some sort of arrangement for him to eventually go to be with her and his child. That's the only reason I can think of for the parents of the girl to befriend the man who was sexually abusing their daughter."

"Well, you do have a point," Moore said, "and I have no idea whatever happened to Parkinson. I'll run him through the computers, see if I can track him down. Who else is on your list?"

"Well, this is sort of off-the-wall," Sam said, "but Mrs. Garrity. When she told me that her father was the one who was caught with Lynette, there was an awful lot of anger showing through her eyes. If she blamed Lynette for taking her daddy away, it's possible that anger boiled over at some point and she lashed out at the only connection she had to the object of her rage."

"Despite the fact that we weren't the most competent investigators back then," Moore said with a slight grin, "I actually did canvass the area and check the alibis of just about everyone in that little town. Royce Garrity was in the hospital here in Benton the day Mrs. Cameron was killed, having a hysterectomy. I don't think she would've been in any shape to beat someone to death that afternoon after having major surgery in the morning."

Sam nodded and grinned sheepishly. "I'm kind of relieved to hear that, because I actually like Jason. That kid has a natural gift for detection. He says he's applied at every law enforcement agency around here and been rejected, but I think he would be an asset. You really ought to sit down and talk with him about this case, get him to open up to you. You'll be surprised at just how intelligent he really is."

Moore burst out laughing. "Surprised? I wouldn't be a bit surprised," he said. "That little cracker used to run us all ragged. I personally picked him up on half a dozen different burglaries, and I'm dead certain he did some of them, but he always managed to wangle his way out of it. There was always an alibi, or some bit of evidence that he could cast enough doubt on to keep the prosecutor from pursuing the charges. I don't know about you, but I think the best criminals know how to think like the best investigators. Got to, in order to make sure your butt doesn't end up in a sling. In Garrity's case, I think he didn't want it to end up as some big guy's cuddle toy in prison."

Sam shrugged. "I can turn that around on you," he said. "I know half a dozen cops who had to get special waivers to join a police force because of their own juvenile criminal records, but the experience has made them valuable officers. They seem to have a natural talent for spotting a lie, or maybe they can just sense when someone they pick up is guilty because they recognize the signs from their own criminal days. I suspect Jason would be one of those."

"I'll talk to him," Moore said after a moment, "but I'm not going to make any promises. I have a pretty hard time getting past the fact that he's outsmarted me in the past." He reached into a drawer, took out a pair of nitrile gloves, and slipped them on before turning the hat over and looking inside.

"Hmph," he said. "Did you look in here?"

Sam shook his head. "No, I didn't want to take a chance on contaminating any evidence that might be inside it. You see something?"

Moore nodded and turned the hat so Sam could look inside, as well. "Those look like hairs to me," he said. "Don't you think so?"

Sure enough, there were two long thin strands of what looked like gray hair stuck to the satiny lining of the hat. "Sure does. And if this is the hat Ross saw, that means we have a DNA sample."

Moore nodded and then carefully put the hat into a large Ziploc bag. "I'm sending this to the lab down in Marion. Give me a number and I'll let you know what I find out, and I'm sure you know I want to hear anything you run across. I'll call Sheriff McCollum today and let him know I want to reopen this case."

Sam passed over his business card and accepted one of Moore's cards in return. "My cell number is on there," he said. "And yes, I'll call you if I learn anything new."

He got to his feet and walked out of the office, waved at the receptionist, and made his way back to the Ridgeline. He climbed behind the wheel and started the truck, backed out of the parking space, and then eased out onto the street. The motel was on the other end of town, so he had to make his way around the town square to get there. The old Italianate courthouse that stood in its center caught his eye, and he realized he was looking at the place where Ross had been quickly convicted and sentenced.

His phone rang as he was just about to turn into the motel parking lot, and he saw that it was Indie calling. "Hey, babe," he said. "I'm just pulling in at the motel. You guys ready for lunch?"

"I'm starving," Indie said, "but lunch may have to wait. Hurry up and get in here. Beauregard needs to speak with you, and he says it's urgent."

"Urgent?" He let out a sigh. "Let me park, I'll be right in."

It only took him a couple of minutes to get the truck parked and ride the elevator up to their floor, and then he was inside his room. Both of the others were there, but Grace was keeping Kenzie occupied with a coloring book at the table. Sam sat down beside his wife on one of the beds and looked at his mother-in-law.

"Okay," he said, "what's so urgent?"

Kim looked at Sam nervously. "Beauregard says Ross isn't the only one that's in trouble. He said there is another of his descendants who is actually going to be in danger."

Sam squinted at her. "Is he talking about Debbie? One of her kids? Or maybe Judith herself?"

Kim was shaking her head. "He doesn't know who," she said. "The only thing he knows is that it's a woman.

Something is going to happen pretty soon, like in the next day or so, that is going to put her in serious danger."

Sam put his elbows on his knees and held his head in his hands. "If it's a woman," he said, "then it must be either Judith or Debbie. Right now I'd bet on Debbie. If there's going to be any kind of new danger, it's probably because somebody isn't going to like the fact I'm digging into this case."

"The real killer, you mean," Indie said. "Right?"

"I'd assume so." He brought them all up to date on the things he had learned that morning, and even told them about getting the keys to Millie's house from what might have been a ghost. "Is it only me, or does anyone else think it's ironic all this spooky stuff is happening with Halloween only a few days away?"

"It's definitely strange," Indie said. "Sam, let's turn Herman loose on Lynette and Bill Parkinson. I understand Detective Moore is going to try, but Herman has a tendency to find things the police would overlook." She got up and grabbed her computer off the dresser, then sat down and opened it up. "I'm giving him Lynette's name, and Parkinson's as well. I'm going to instruct him to look for any correlation between the two. With any luck, if they did get together after he left, he'll be able to track them down." She finished typing and hit the Enter key with a flourish.

"That was my mother's name," Kim said. "Lynette, I mean, but her maiden name was Smith."

Sam looked at her. "You never talk about your parents much," he said. "I know you have some unhappy memories, there. What was your father's name?"

"Bill. William, I mean, but everybody called him Bill."

Sam's eyebrows shot up. "Wow, that's a weird coincidence."

"They both died before I was born," Indie said. "I never got to meet either of them."

Kim smiled at her daughter. "They would have adored you," she said. "I know that."

Herman chimed, and Indie turned the computer so Sam could see a list of links. Most of them were unrelated, but then she stumbled across one that seemed to have promise.

"Here's a news article," she said, "about a girl named Lynette Cameron who was staying at the Virginia Home for Unwed Mothers in Bluefield. She gave birth to a baby girl, but the day after they were released from the hospital she disappeared. The police said it wasn't uncommon for girls to run away from the home after giving birth, but they usually left the babies behind. Lynette took her child with her, but they never found any trace of her after that."

Sam chewed his cheek for a moment. "That could lend credibility to the thought that Parkinson went to be with her. If he made contact with her before the baby was born, he might have been waiting to take them away once they got out of the hospital."

"I'll bet on it," Indie said. "It just makes sense, a lot more sense than thinking this young girl would try to make it on her own with the baby."

"And there's nothing about her after that?"

Indie shrugged. "There's a couple of references that might be her, but there's no way to verify them. Nothing that could positively identify her, anyway." She scrolled down the page a bit further and clicked on another link. "There are thousands of links to men named William or Bill Parkinson, but unless you can give me something more to go on, there's no way I would know if any of these are the right man."

Sam thought for a moment. "What about a marriage license? If he and Lynette were together, they probably got married at some point."

Indie tapped on the keys for a moment and then hit Enter. A moment later, she shook her head. "Herman says there are no references to Parkinson and Cameron getting married that match the first names."

Sam shrugged. "Well, it was a thought," he said. "Moore says the sheriff at the time told him that Lynette died years ago. Nobody knows whatever happened to Parkinson."

Sam felt a tug on his arm and turned to see Kenzie smiling up at him. "Daddy, can we go get lunch now?"

Sam smiled. "Of course we can, sweetheart," he said.

"What would you like to have for lunch?"

"Pizza!" Kenzie said, and everyone agreed that pizza sounded pretty good. There was a pizza place only a couple of blocks away, and the weather wasn't too cool, so they decided to walk.

"What really bothers me," Grace said, "is that ghost woman giving you the keys to that house. That's just really, really weird."

Sam made a grimace. "I don't believe she was a ghost," he said. "She was as solid and real as you are. I'd stake my reputation on it."

Grace rolled her eyes. "Then how do you explain it? How did she happen to show up at just the right moment, when there was a private investigator there who needed to look inside the house?"

"I didn't say I had an explanation," Sam said. "I just said she's not a ghost. The only thing I can figure is that, whoever she was, she probably got the keys from the real Marie and happened to see me pull up there. She might've only stopped out of curiosity, and it's possible she panicked after she realized who I was and decided to just dump the keys on me and split."

"Samuel," Kim said in the now-familiar Southern drawl, "do you still have the keys?"

Sam stared at his mother-in-law for a moment, then slowly nodded. "I do."

"Then, after you have eaten, would you take me to see the place? It's possible I might see something new, if

I go to the place where it actually happened."

Sam continued staring for a moment, then nodded again. "Okay. When we finish, I'll take everybody else back to the motel, and you and I will go take a look. If there's anybody getting nervous over my poking around over there, I don't want them getting a good look at Indie or Kenzie."

Kim blinked, then smiled at Sam. "Me again," she said. "Beauregard says he understands."

It wasn't long before they were done eating, and they all walked back to the motel together. Sam kissed Indie in the parking lot, then he and Kim got into the Ridgeline and headed back to Thompsonville.

"It's really pretty around here," Kim said as they drove along. Sam nodded but didn't reply. The rest of the ride was silent until they pulled up in front of Millie Cameron's house.

They got out and walked toward the front door, and Sam was looking around to see if anyone might be watching them. He didn't see anyone, but hairs on the back of his neck were standing up. He had the very strong feeling that someone was paying attention, but he couldn't spot anybody.

He used the key to open the door, then forced himself to step inside. The eerie feeling that someone was watching got even stronger, and he glanced at Kim to see if she was feeling it as well.

It took him only a second to realize that Beauregard

had once again taken control.

"That's the chair they found her in," Sam said, pointing at one of the pair of chairs. He knew which one it was because of the deep brown stains that were still visible.

"How interesting," Beauregard said. "Samuel, do you notice anything strange about that chair? Compare it to the one beside it, and I think you'll see what I mean."

Sam looked from one chair to the other and suddenly realized that they were quite different. The chair with the majority of the bloodstains was otherwise pristine; the other chair, the one Ross had been sitting in, had rips and tears that appeared to be the work of mice or rats over the years.

"The mice have been at that chair," he said. "But not the one Millie died in. I suppose that could be because of the bloodstains, don't you think? Maybe there is an odor or something that the mice avoid?"

Kim shook her head. "I wouldn't think so. Despite the fact that they normally tend toward the vegetarian, mice and rats will eat meat if they can. They certainly wouldn't shy away from blood that was so old and dried. There may be a perfectly reasonable explanation, but I find it interesting nonetheless."

Kim looked around the room and then started walking. She went through the door that led into the kitchen, and Sam followed. "In which cabinet did you find the hat?" Beauregard asked.

Sam looked up at the cabinet that had opened when he was there earlier in the day and slowly reached up toward it. He half expected it to open again, but it hadn't moved by the time his fingers reached the knob. He gave it a tug and realized that it moved far more easily than he expected. The hinges were so free that he suspected they had been recently oiled.

While Kim peeked into that one, Sam reached up and opened another. Unlike the first, this one was stiff. He took out his phone and turned on its flashlight, then shined it up on the hinges of the first cabinet door.

"Sure enough," he said. "It opened so easily I figured it must've been oiled, and I can see signs of fresh oil on the hinges." He shined the light upward and suddenly let out a gasp. "Son of a bitch," he said. "Somebody was yanking my chain."

Kim raised her eyes to follow the light and saw what had caught Sam's attention. Attached to the cabinet door in the top outer corner was a thin thread, and it ran over to the wall and through a screw eye. From there it ran along the wall and then disappeared between the cabinet and the wall itself.

Sam turned and walked out the back door, then stepped around the corner so that he was standing outside the wall the cabinet was mounted on. The string hung down from a hole in the wall, a small metal button secured to it as a weight.

Kim had followed. "Look at that," Sam said. "It had

to be that woman, the one who gave me the keys. Once she saw me leave the living room, she must've come around here and waited until I entered the kitchen." He pointed at a window. "She could have seen me through that window, even though I missed her completely. Once I was there, all she had to do was pull that string and it was almost certain that I would find the hat."

Kim was nodding slowly. "Then whoever she was," Beauregard's voice intoned, "she somehow knew the importance of the hat. I would surmise that she would be the one who placed it there. She undoubtedly found it sometime after the murder and must have considered it to be a valuable clue. I wonder how long it laid in that cabinet, waiting for someone to discover it."

"I don't know," Sam said, using his phone to take pictures of the string. He went back inside and got photos of the string attached to the cabinet door, as well. "I want to show these to Detective Moore. Somebody around here knows something, and we need to find out who it is."

Kim walked around Sam and went back into the living room, then stood there and stared at the chair. When Sam joined her, she looked up at him.

"What?" Sam asked, and Beauregard's reply left him staring with his eyebrows trying to climb over his forehead. A second later Kim wavered, and then she was blinking at Sam.

"Sam? Oh..."

Sam nodded. "Yeah, Beauregard just left, and if I could get my hands on him, I'd strangle him."

Kim's eyes went wide. "Why? What did he do?"

Sam shook his head, muttering under his breath, but then he looked at his mother-in-law again. "He just told me I need to find the witch."

11

Sam locked the house back up and drove straight over to the Garrity place. He left Kim sitting in the truck as he limped up to the door and knocked again. Mrs. Garrity opened a moment later, her face friendly but cautious.

"Mr. Prichard? Jason's not here, said he was going to see his girlfriend over at Benton. Is there something I can help you with?"

"I'm going to ask you a really strange question," Sam said. "Do you know anything about someone around here who might be considered a witch?"

Mrs. Garrity's eyes grew round. "A witch? Oh, there's only one person you can be speaking of. That would be Daisy Willis—she lives in a trailer off by itself, on the north edge of the woods. There's a little trailer park there just off the highway, but hers is an old silver trailer that sits way back from all the others."

Sam nodded. "By any chance, would Daisy Willis fit the same general description as Marie, the one I asked you about earlier?"

A sudden smile came across the woman's face. "Oh, I never would've thought about it until now, but yes," she said. "She'd be about the same size and shape as Marie was when she died. She got the reputation of being a witch because of these ointments and potions she makes out of stuff she finds in the woods. To be honest, some of them work better than the medicines you get from the doctor, but everybody's just a little bit afraid of her."

"I can imagine," Sam said. "All right, thank you very much." He turned and hurried at his best pace back to the Ridgeline and got behind the wheel again.

It took him only a couple of minutes to drive around onto the main highway that led back toward Benton, and he spotted the trailer park immediately. He pulled in and wound his way through its driveway, then spotted the old Airstream travel trailer sitting just at the edge of the woods. There was no driveway leading to it, but he saw tire tracks in the tall grass and followed them.

He climbed out of the truck and walked to the door, then knocked. When there was no answer after a few seconds, he knocked again, calling out, "Daisy? Daisy Willis? I need to speak with you."

"She ain't there," a voice called, and Sam turned to see someone standing on the back porch of another trailer. He turned and walked toward the person and saw that it was another elderly woman.

"Do you know when she might be back?" Sam asked.

"No idea," the old woman said. "I saw some car pull up there a couple hours ago, and some woman went up to the door. Then a few minutes later Daisy came out and got in the car with her. Don't know who it was, or where they might have been going, but she didn't look a bit happy about it. Daisy don't hold with cars—she says they're all from the devil."

Sam had gotten close by this time and squinted at the woman. "Then why do you think she would've gotten into it?"

"Well, there's them around here think I'm just another crazy old lady," the woman said, "but it sure looked to me like whoever it was with her had her scared to death. Held on to her arm all the way to the car and opened the door and kinda pushed her inside, then hurried around and got in and took off."

"Did it look to you like she was being threatened?"

"Well, son, ain't that what I just said?" The old woman huffed at him, then turned and stepped back inside the door and slammed it behind her.

Sam turned and looked at the Airstream again, then got back into the Ridgeline. Kim, who had had her window down, looked at him nervously.

"You think something happened to the witch?" she asked.

Sam shrugged and shook his head. "I don't know," he said, "but it strikes me as odd that this old woman thinks she was forced into that car, just a few hours after meeting me."

"But why? Who would know she talked to you?"

"I'm not sure," Sam said as he started the truck and put it in gear. "I do know that it felt like someone was watching me when we were at the house a few minutes ago. Did you feel anything?"

Kim's eyes went wide. "I don't even remember being there," she said. "That was Beauregard, remember? And before you ask, he says he didn't feel anyone watching."

Sam shook his head in frustration. "The only people I even mentioned getting the keys to were the Garritys and Detective Moore. That old woman said she was hustled into a car by another woman, though. I don't believe Mrs. Garrity would have any motive to bother her, since she had an ironclad alibi for the original murder. This case just gets stranger and stranger." He took out his phone and then got out the business card Detective Moore had given him. He used his thumb to dial the number and then put the phone to his ear. It was answered a moment later.

"Johnny Moore," the detective said.

"Detective, this is Sam Prichard. I came back over to look at the house once again, and I discovered a couple of strange things. First off, I found a string, a dark thread, that was rigged so someone standing outside the house could cause that cabinet door to open. The only possible person that could have done it would be the woman who gave me the keys, and I think I know who she was. There's a woman named Daisy Willis who lives in a trailer park in Thompsonville, and she fits the description of the woman I saw. I found out where she lived and went to her trailer, but a neighbor said another woman came by some time ago and appeared to have forced Daisy into a car."

"I know Daisy," Moore said. "She's been around here just about forever—people think she's a witch. You said she got into a car?"

"There's a blue trailer just across from hers in that park, a little distance away, and the woman there said it looked like whoever showed up forced Daisy to get into the car and go with her. It strikes me pretty odd that something like that might happen just a few hours after she talked to me."

"I agree," Moore said, "it does sound strange. Daisy's got a son who lives down in Carbondale. Let me call him and see if he knows anything. I'll call you back in five minutes."

Sam ended the call and set the phone in his lap. He made it about halfway back to Benton by the time it rang again.

"Prichard," he said.

"I talked to her son, and he doesn't know anything about it. He said his mother won't even get into his car, so her being forced does make sense. You said the witness was in the blue trailer?"

"Yes. The back door of the blue trailer faces directly toward the silver one that Daisy lives in."

"That would be Rosie Parks. I'll send a deputy out to talk to her, see if he can get any more information. I'll let you know what I find out. Meanwhile, tell me this: how many people knew that you got the keys from her?"

"Nobody, not specifically," Sam said. "Only you and Jason and his mother knew that I had gotten the keys at all. I just spoke to Mrs. Garrity, and she told me that Daisy might fit the same description as the woman I got them from, which is why I went looking for her." Sam neglected to mention that a reputed ghost had put him on Daisy's trail in the first place.

"I can't see Royce dragging Daisy into a car. All right, I'll call you again whenever I know something."

The two men said goodbye, and Sam put the phone back in his pocket. A moment later he pulled it back out and dialed Debbie Jenkins's number.

"Debbie," he said when she answered, "this is Sam Prichard. I'm down in the Thompsonville area, and there are some strange things going on."

"Strange things? What you mean?"

"Well, for starters, I went by your mother's house, and a woman showed up and offered me the keys so I could look inside. While I was looking around, I found what appears to be the hat that Ross saw in the woods that day. It fits his description, and there are some old, muddy bloodstains on it."

"You found it? Oh, that's wonderful."

"Yeah, but there's more. I was told by Royce Garrity that you had given the keys to a woman named Marie who died a few years ago, and that the keys had never been found. Is that correct?"

"Yes, it is," Debbie said. "Oh, my gosh, I had forgotten about that. Marie was the only one down there that had keys. Oh, my goodness, you don't think..."

"No, I don't," Sam said. "I think I've ascertained that the woman I met was a local character named Daisy Willis. I gather the locals think she's a witch."

"Crazy Daisy," Debbie said. "You know, she and Marie were good friends. I wonder if Marie gave her the keys before she died. That might make sense, right?"

"It could. My problem now is that I went to talk to Daisy and found that somebody may have abducted her. A neighbor said she saw someone apparently force Daisy into a car and drive away with her."

Debbie gasped. "Abducted? But why?"

"At the moment, I've no idea. The only thing I can suspect is that Daisy might know something about what actually happened that day, but I'm very surprised that anyone would wait this long to do anything about her. It's also odd that this happens only hours after she and I spoke. Can you think of anyone who might be concerned about me digging into the case down here?"

"Oh, my goodness, no," Debbie replied. "Of course, since we know Ross didn't do it, then somebody out there probably doesn't want the truth to be found out."

"Okay. Now, something else I never thought to ask you. Did you have anyone in mind as a suspect? Someone you thought might have actually been the killer?"

Sam could sense the slight hesitation before she answered. "Well, not really. Mom didn't really have any enemies, but there was one person she just couldn't get along with down there. I wondered for a little while if she might have done it, but..."

"Who was it, Debbie?" Sam asked.

"Well—it was Royce Garrity, but it couldn't have been her because she was in the hospital when it happened."

Sam nodded into the phone. "Okay. I actually considered her a suspect myself today, until I found out she'd had a hysterectomy that very morning. They didn't get along?"

"No, not at all. Mom thought Royce was a terrible mother, and there was some other kind of bad blood between them. You know I had an older sister, right? I probably forgot to tell you about her, but she was gone before I was born. She'd gotten pregnant, and the father was Royce's dad. Mom and Dad sent my sister away to have her baby, but then she ran away from wherever she was at, and then Royce's dad disappeared and everyone figured they ran off together. I think that was the thing that started all the trouble between them, between Mom and Royce."

"Yes, I'd heard about that. Do you know anything about what happened to your sister? I heard that she had died sometime back, but nobody seems to know anything for sure."

"Well," she said, "Mom told me she'd lost her mind and ended up in the loony bin, and died back when I was still a little girl. That's pretty much all I know about it."

"What about Bill Parkinson? The man she was supposed to have run off with? Did your mother ever mention him?"

"Not directly, no, but she did tell me once that he spent some time in prison. I never heard any of the details about it. I think the last time Mom ever mentioned him was maybe a year or so before she died. She said she got a letter from him but that she didn't want to bother with replying."

"Really? Any idea why?"

Debbie hesitated again. "She said—she said, 'dead things need to stay dead.' I remember asking her what she meant by that, but she just shook her head and wouldn't tell me anything else."

"If he's still alive, then he could conceivably be a suspect. Debbie, I need you to think hard. Did your mother ever tell you where he was?"

"No, she wouldn't talk about him at all after that. After she died, when we cleaned out the house, I found boxes and boxes full of letters, but I never took the time to look through them. It's possible that letter is still in one of them. I have them in the garage. I'll dig them out and take a look through them."

Sam chuckled. "Sounds like a good job for your twin detectives," he said. "Tell them I'll pay a fifty-dollar reward if they find it."

"You don't have to do that, Mr. Prichard," Debbie said. "If it will help solve this mystery, or help get Ross out of prison, then we're happy to do it."

"Tell them, anyway," Sam said. "Their goal is to become private eyes. Trust me, nothing motivates a private eye like the prospect of money. Now, one more thing. There are others who have come to the conclusion that your mother's injuries could not have been caused by Ross's fists, but it appears that the medical examiner at the time simply went with what the sheriff's office was telling him. Debbie, would you consent to having your mother's body exhumed and reexamined? A proper autopsy, even this long after the fact, could determine exactly what type of weapon was used on her. That could very well be enough to overturn Ross's conviction, though it wouldn't guarantee he would not be tried again."

Sam thought he heard a sob, but Debbie apparently pulled herself together quickly. "Mr. Prichard, if it will help my brother, I'll do whatever it takes. How would we go about it?"

"I'll check that out on Monday and get back to you. I'm already talking Johnny Moore. He's a detective now, and he admitted to me that he has also had doubts about whether Ross was guilty. He's trying to get the case reopened, and if he succeeds, then we might be able to get the state to agree to the exhumation. If not, we'll have to go after it privately and get a forensic pathologist to do it."

"But—Mr. Prichard, wouldn't that cost a lot of money?"

"You don't need to worry about that," Sam said. "My client on this case wants to see justice done, and that means doing whatever it takes to accomplish that goal. I happen to know that he isn't going to mind paying for it."

He said goodbye and cut the call off, then put the phone back into his pocket. Out of the corner of his eye, he saw Kim looking at him strangely.

"What?"

"Nothing," Kim said. "I just realized what you're doing. From what you said, Debbie doesn't have a lot of money. If you get Millie's body exhumed, you're going to be paying for that yourself, aren't you?"

Sam's lips twitched upward. "Well, look at it this way. Beauregard—no matter what he is or isn't—has helped me out a number of times, and even saved my life more than once. We'll just chalk it up to me repaying some favors, okay?"

"Uh-huh," Kim said. "It was also pretty nice of you to offer to pay those boys to help out. They probably don't get much of an allowance, so fifty dollars might be like winning the lottery to them."

Sam puffed up his cheeks and blew air out. "I kinda like those boys," he said. "And that Kaylee, she's got a mind like a steel trap. If she becomes a defense attorney, I pity the prosecutor who ever has to go up against her."

Kim smiled. "Beauregard says to tell you you're not nearly as mean as you pretend to be."

Despite himself, Sam smiled.

They got back to the motel about fifteen minutes later and found Indie, Grace, and Kenzie all piled up on one of the beds watching a movie. Kenzie jumped up to give her daddy a hug, but her attention returned to the television a moment later.

"Anything new?" Indie asked.

"You could say that," Sam said as the two of them sat down at the table in the room. He told her what had happened, with Beauregard telling him to "find the witch," and the strange apparent abduction of Daisy Willis. Indie's eyes got wider and wider as he told the tale, and she was shaking her head in wonder when he finished.

"Sam, this is really getting out-there. What are you going to do next?"

"Probably isn't much I can do over the weekend," he said. "Monday morning, I'm going to see the police chief here. He was the detective on the case when it happened, and I'd really like to know why he never discovered some of the things I've found out in the last couple of days. This should be a cold case, but it's looking pretty hot at the moment."

"And what if he won't cooperate?"

"Well, that brings up the second thing I'm going to do." He told her about asking Debbie to allow exhumation and a new autopsy. "We'll have to foot the bill for this ourselves," he said, "but it shouldn't cost more than a few thousand. We'll take it out of the reward money Harry gave us, and I can always write it off come tax time." He looked at her questioningly. "You don't mind, do you, babe?"

Indie smiled at him. "Mind? I'm not even surprised. I know the kind of man you are, Sam Prichard. Harry dropped an awful lot of reward money on us, not that you didn't deserve it. I think this is an appropriate way to use some of it."

"Yeah. I told your mom I'm just thinking of it as repaying some of the favors Beauregard has done me."

She kissed him on the cheek. "That sounds like a good enough reason to me." She was about to say something else, but there was a knock on the door. They both looked at it, and Sam got up to answer.

There was a tall, dark-haired man standing there, and

he was holding out a badge and police ID. "Sam Prichard?" he asked.

"Yes, that's me."

"I'm Ray Weimer, chief of police here in Benton. Could we step out and talk for a few minutes? I'll buy you a cup of coffee."

Sam's eyebrows went up a bit, but he simply turned around and waved at Indie before stepping out and shutting the door behind him. "There's a coffee shop right next door," he said, and Weimer nodded. They went down the elevator and out the front door, then walked across the parking lot to the restaurant.

A hostess seated them and took their orders for coffee. As soon as she had brought it to them, Weimer looked Sam in the eye.

"I understand you're looking into the Cameron murder," he said. "That was my case, back when it happened. I was with the sheriff's office then."

"I'm aware of that," Sam said. "In fact, I was planning to come see you Monday morning. There are a lot of things about this case that don't add up. I'm curious why you thought it was so open-and-shut at the time."

Weimer shrugged. "When the deputies arrived, they found Ross Cameron sitting next to his dead mother with blood all over his hands. Looked pretty obvious to them, and I agreed. The Cameron boy is retarded, and people like him have an awful lot of strength. Let his temper get out of hand, and God only knows what he might be capable of doing. Besides, he confessed."

"Chief, are you aware that there's a big difference between retardation and autism? Autistics display a number of common characteristics, and one of them that almost all of them share is an inability to understand deception. What that means is that they can't lie. To them, the world is simply as it is and there can't be any other truth, so they can't even formulate the possibility of a different version of events than what actually happened. On top of that, Ross Cameron is one of a percentage of autistics who remember absolutely everything. I spoke with him a couple of days ago, and he explained it to me that he didn't want to confess because it wasn't true, but you told him that if he did, he'd get to go home. He wanted to go home. Ergo, he had to say what you wanted him to say, whether it was really true or not."

Weimer grinned and shook his head. "I never said that," he said. "The only thing I told him was that he could never go home until he admitted he did. I never said he'd get to go home once he confessed."

Sam felt anger rising within him but shoved it back down. "To him, it amounted to the same thing. If he could not go home until he said what you wanted him to say, then logically he could go home if he did. That's how it works with people like Ross."

Weimer shrugged again, the grin never leaving his

DAVID ARCHER

face. "You believe whatever you want to," he said. "I put a killer away that day."

"No, you didn't," Sam said. "The fact is, Weimer, that it's physically impossible for anyone who hasn't had excessive strength training to do the kind of damage that Millie Cameron's skull suffered. A professional boxer might be able to crack somebody's skull, but they couldn't drive pieces of it into her brain, and that was the cause of death. There was a murder weapon, and you didn't even bother to look for it."

The grin faded away quickly. "Are you accusing me of not doing my job properly?"

Sam shrugged and grinned, just as Weimer had done a few minutes earlier. "Believe what you want," he said. "All I know is that I've uncovered evidence you didn't even bother to look for. Remember Ross telling you about a hat with a feather on it?"

Weimer's eyes narrowed. "He was talking a lot of crap," he said. "We looked around the house and the yard—there was no hat."

"But you didn't look in the woods behind the house. That's where Ross said he saw it, remember that? He does. He described it to me in great detail. Now, imagine my surprise when I went to look at the crime scene today and found that very hat inside one of the kitchen cabinets. It still has dried blood and mud on it, just as he described seeing it that day eight years ago."

"There wasn't any hat in any cabinet," Weimer

FACT OR FICTION

sputtered. "We looked through that house from top to bottom, just to be sure we didn't miss any possible murder weapon." He punctuated the last two words with finger quotes. "I don't know where this hat of yours came from, but I'll guarantee you this: if it turns out you're trying to manufacture evidence, I'll hang you out to dry."

"The sheriff's office has the hat, right now, but it's on its way to a lab to be tested. What I'm hoping is that there will be residual DNA, maybe a couple of hairs that got stuck inside, something that might help lead us to the real killer. But you might as well know now, I'm also going to start Monday working on getting Millie Cameron exhumed. I want a true forensic pathologist to examine her injuries. I can just about guarantee you that his findings will turn your original investigation on its head." Sam leaned forward across the table. "Weimer, I don't know how you managed to become a detective in the first place, and I sure can't believe you earned a shot at being chief of police. By the time this case comes to a conclusion, I expect Ross Cameron to be out of prison, and there's a good possibility you will be without a badge."

"Are you threatening me?" Weimer asked, raising his voice so that other people in the restaurant looked their way.

"Absolutely not," Sam said, still maintaining his calm. "I'm simply stating a fact. You bullied a man who was not able to resist into confessing to a crime he did not

181

commit, and then you wore that confession like a feather in your own cap. No matter how you look at it, you went for an easy conviction and didn't even bother to do a proper investigation at all. If you had, you might have learned some of the things that I learned today."

"Like what?" Weimer demanded. "Oh, yeah, you found some kind of a hat. That still sounds pretty fishy to me."

"How about the fact that Jason Garrity was probably a pretty reliable witness? If you had actually talked to the boy back then, he would've told you that he's pretty certain the person he saw hurry across the backyard that day was a woman, and his reasoning for thinking so is sound. That boy hasn't stopped thinking about this case since the day it happened, and he's actually done a better job of putting clues together than you ever did. Or you might have learned about Daisy Willis, the old woman everyone in Thompsonville thinks is a witch. She saw me looking at Millie's house this morning and offered me the keys, but she tried to pass herself off as the ghost of a woman named Marie." Sam grinned at him. "I figured out who she was, though, and went to her house trailer. Unfortunately, I got there a little late. A couple of hours earlier, somebody—apparently another woman—showed up there and forced Daisy into a car. They drove away, and nobody knows where she is now. Doesn't that strike you as kind of odd? My own thought is that if she had the keys to the house, then she might know something about how that hat ended up inside the cabinet. And if she knows that, then she just might know something about who had originally worn that hat, and that makes me wonder if the person who pushed her into a car and drove away with her might be the killer."

Weimer was leaning back in his chair, and his eyes had gone wide. "Daisy Willis? You do know they call her Crazy Daisy, right? What makes you think she could know anything about the case at all?"

"I think so because it would be almost impossible to come up with another reason for her sudden disappearance than the fact that someone saw her talking to me this morning. Now, if somebody doesn't want me to find out what she knows, then I damn well want to know it."

Weimer stared at him for a long moment, and it was interrupted when Sam's cell phone rang. He glanced at it and saw that it was Detective Moore calling, then held up a finger to tell Weimer to wait.

"Prichard," he said.

"Thought I better call you quick," Moore said. "We just found Daisy Willis."

Sam narrowed his eyes. "There is something in your voice that tells me I'm not gonna like what you say next."

"Probably not. She's dead."

12

"Dead? How..."

"Same way Millie Cameron died," Moore said. "Her head was bashed in. All the way around, just like Millie Cameron. I need you to come down to my office and give me an official statement about her dealings with you today."

"I'll be right there," Sam said, and then they ended the call. He put the phone back in his pocket and looked at Weimer.

"Crazy Daisy is dead," he said coldly. "Someone just found her body, and she died the same exact way Millie Cameron did. You know what that tells me, Weimer? It tells me that if you had done your job, then maybe you would have caught the killer back then, and maybe Daisy Willis would still be alive." Sam got up and threw a ten-dollar bill on the table. "The coffee is on me."

He stomped out the door and called Indie while he

headed directly to the Ridgeline. It took him only a couple of seconds to tell her what was going on, and then he was in the truck and headed east across town.

The woman at the front desk recognized Sam when he walked in and simply pointed down the hall toward Moore's office. Sam gave her a wave of thanks and leaned on his cane as he limped toward it. The door was open, and Moore was on the phone. He looked up at Sam and beckoned him in with his fingers.

"What I'm telling you is that I need that crime scene gone over by professionals," Moore said into the phone, "not by Barney Fife and Deputy Gomer. This woman may have been a witness in a cold case that I'm trying to reopen, and she was murdered in exactly the same way as the original victim eight years ago. That's a little bit too much of a coincidence for me, and I don't want our one lonely forensics tech to go out there and miss something that might be important." He listened for a couple of moments, then nodded. "That'll be great, and thank you." He hung up the phone and looked at Sam.

"That was the crime lab up at Mt. Vernon," he said. "They got some of the best CSI people around, and I just talked them into working this scene. Give me a minute to get set up, and I'll take your statement. Then you can ride out with me if you want, and they should be getting close by then."

"What about the hat? Are you turning that over to them?"

"No," Moore replied. "There's a private lab down in Carbondale that we send all that stuff to. Trust me, if there is anything there, they'll find it. Ready to do your statement now?"

Sam nodded, and Moore set up a microphone on his desk and pointed it at Sam. He turned to his computer and tapped a couple of keys, then looked at Sam. "Statement of private investigator Samuel Prichard," he said, adding the date and time. "Mr. Prichard appeared voluntarily to give his statement regarding interactions with murder victim Daisy Joanne Willis." He touched the Space bar on his computer and then turned to Sam again. "When I let go of this, just tell me in your own words what happened, how you met her and all that."

Sam nodded and Moore released the bar.

"At approximately eight thirty a.m. this morning, I drove to the former home of Millie Cameron, at 502 West Fifth Street in Thompsonville, Illinois. I have been engaged to investigate the possibility that Mrs. Cameron's son, Ross, who was arrested and convicted for the murder, might be wrongfully incarcerated, and I wanted to get a look at the crime scene. When I arrived, I walked up to the house and looked through the windows on the front door, which allowed me to see the chair that Mrs. Cameron's body had been found in. While I was looking through the window, I heard a voice ask me if I wanted to go inside and turned to find a short, heavyset woman standing near my vehicle. I approached her and said that I would like to see inside, and she handed me a set of keys. She identified herself only as Marie, saying that she was entrusted by Mrs. Cameron's daughter Debbie to hold them. I went into the house and found what may be a piece of evidence from the original crime, then came back outside to find the woman gone.

"At just after one this afternoon, I returned to the house to get another look at it, and that's when I discovered that the cabinet in which I have found the possible evidence had been rigged so that it could be opened in a haunting manner from outside the house. I concluded that the woman I had spoken to had waited until I was in the kitchen of the house and hurried around at the side to pull the string that opened the door and exposed the evidence. Upon asking a neighbor, Royce Garrity, about a woman who might fit that description, I had been told that Marie had died some years previously, but the description fit another woman named Daisy Willis. Mrs. Garrity told me where to find Ms. Willis's house trailer, and I drove there immediately. I knocked on her door but got no response, and a neighbor, later identified to me as Rosie Parks, called out to tell me that she was gone. She went on to elaborate that she had seen a car pull up at Daisy's trailer sometime earlier, and that she had observed what appeared to be a woman forcefully putting Daisy into the car and driving away with her. I reported all of this to Detective Moore."

Moore nodded at him and hit the Space bar again.

"That's very good," he said. "Clear and concise. The computer will transcribe it and print it out, and then I need you to sign it. Now, I have to ask, but where were you for the last three hours?"

"Well, three hours ago I was having lunch with my family. At one, my mother-in-law rode with me back over to Millie's house, so she can vouch for my whereabouts at that time. When we got back to my hotel, I was there for about five minutes, and then the police chief, Weimer, knocked on my door. I was having coffee with him and telling him—well, frankly I was telling him he's an idiot—when you called."

Moore's eyebrows shot upward. "Ray came to see you? How did that go?"

Sam shrugged. "He basically wanted to try to convince me he had closed the case eight years ago. I told him about finding the hat and that Daisy had apparently been snatched, and that I didn't believe he did a very good job. We were just getting good and warmed up into a friendly session of trading insults when you called. I walked out on him and came straight here."

Moore leaned back in his chair and looked up at the ceiling for a few seconds, then turned his eyes back down to Sam. "I can't help but jump to the conclusion this is the same killer," he said, "but that's not gonna be easy to prove. I checked you out, Sam. I know you were a detective in Denver, and I know you worked homicide for a few years. I've dealt with a total of four murders, including Cameron, over the last ten years. This will be my first as a detective, so don't you even hesitate on giving advice. Okay?"

Sam nodded. "I'll do what I can."

The printer made noises, and a moment later a single sheet of paper slid out. Moore picked it up and glanced at it, and then passed it to Sam. "Read through that if you would, and if it all sounds correct, then I need you to sign it. Just sign it anywhere under the printing and add the date, if you would."

Sam read through the statement and saw that it was exactly as he had given it, so he signed and dated it, then slid it back across the desk. Moore made a couple of copies of it, then put both the original and the copies into a folder and stuffed that into a drawer. He looked up at Sam while he got out of his chair.

"I'm headed out to the scene, now," he said. "You want to ride with me?"

"No," Sam said, "but I can't offer any advice if I don't know what's going on. Lead the way."

He followed Detective Moore out of the building and got into the passenger-side front seat of an unmarked car. He barely got his seat belt buckled before Moore drove out of the parking lot and turned east.

"Was she found near Thompsonville?" Sam asked.

Moore nodded. "Couple of boys out riding dirt bikes found her," Moore said. "Couple miles north of town off Amos Road. There's a pond just off the road, and a bunch of the local kids have made themselves some dirt trails out there. These boys actually stumbled across her accidentally, because one of them lost control of his bike and ran into some thick brush. She was laying right beside it, covered up with branches and leaves and stuff, but the bike hit some of it and they saw her hand sticking out. They pulled the rest of the crap off and realized who it was, then one of them called his dad. Daddy told him to check for a pulse, but when they didn't find one he told the boys not to touch anything else and to just wait for him and the police. He called in and one of our deputies was close enough to get there within twenty minutes."

Sam glanced at the speedometer and saw that the car was moving at about ninety miles per hour, but he didn't say anything. Moore obviously knew how to handle the machine, and it only took them about ten minutes to get to where Daisy's body lay. A sheriff's patrol car and an ambulance were already there. Sam got out and leaned on his cane as he followed Detective Moore through the tall grass.

Two boys, not more than fourteen by Sam's estimation, were sitting on their dirt bikes not far away. A couple of men were standing beside them, and it was apparent that these were their fathers. Moore walked up to the two men and shook hands with both of them.

"Bob Harris, Jim Ellman, this is Sam Prichard. He's a private investigator who's been looking into the old Millie Cameron murder case. He's also a former police detective from the big city, so I asked him to come out and give me his opinion on this."

Sam shook hands with both men and then followed Moore deeper into the brush. A moment later, they came to where the body was still partly covered, and Sam leaned hard on his cane as he knelt down to get a better look.

Even with the damage done to her head and face, Sam could see enough that his heart sank in his chest. "Yeah, that's her," he said. "The one who gave me the keys, I mean. The clothes are the same, and I recognize that purplish mark on the back of her hand."

Moore nodded as he glanced at his watch. "I don't want to bother anything," Moore said, "until the CSI team gets here. Shouldn't be more than another ten or fifteen minutes."

Sam nodded. "You said the boys found her," he said. "Were the two of them out here alone?"

Moore looked up at him, then turned and walked back to where the boys waited with their fathers. "Boys," he began, "was it just you two out here today? Was anybody else out here with you?"

The two boys looked at each other, then one of them shrugged. "We didn't see nobody else," he said. "Pete Talley was supposed to come out with us, but he got himself grounded yesterday. Just us, I guess."

Sam leaned on his cane and looked at the boy who was speaking. "When you got here, did you see anything unusual? Any cars around, maybe?"

Both boys glanced at Detective Moore, and he grinned. "Don't worry," he said. "Today you get a free pass for riding motorcycles on the road without a license. You think we don't know how you get out here?"

The boys grinned sheepishly, and the second boy looked at Sam. "There was a car," he said. "It was parked out on Amos Road when we come around the corner, but then it took off right after we hit the trails. Took off fast, too."

"Could you tell what kind of car it was?" Moore asked. "Or did you see who might have been driving it?"

"Didn't really pay no attention," the first boy said. "We was just out for a ride, you know?"

The second boy scrunched up one side of his face in thought. "It was white," he said. "I think it was a Chevy, maybe, an older Chevy. Like maybe ten years old, something like that."

Moore turned to the deputy who was first on the scene, and who was still standing close by. "Ned," he said, "let the boys show you where the car was parked. Don't tramp around through the grass, though, just kinda mark the spot. We'll need to figure out how the killer got from where the body is back to the car, especially if the boys didn't see them."

Both the boys walked off with the deputy, and their fathers chatted with Moore and Sam until they came back. They all agreed that while Daisy was a strange old bird, she didn't deserve to die like this.

A large van arrived while they were talking, and four crime scene technicians climbed out of it. One of them spotted Moore and walked up to him.

"Detective Moore? I'm Ron Caldwell, state police crime lab." The two men shook hands.

"I'm Moore," Moore said, "and this is Sam Prichard. He's consulting on this case for me. We haven't touched the body at all, and I kept everyone back away from it. When Sam and I got here, we only walked in spots that were already trampled down, so we didn't actually get up to the body itself. The boys who found her said there was a car out on the road when they first rode up here, and it took off shortly after the got on the trails. I had them show my deputy where it was parked; he can show your people."

"Sounds like good work," Caldwell said. He turned to one of his techs and told him to go with the deputy, then turned back to Moore. "Which way is the body?"

Moore led the way, and then he and Sam stood off to the side and watched as the CSI team did its job. Photographs were taken for several minutes, including photos of the body, all of the brush that had been piled on it, the tracks made through the tall, mostly dry grass, and even the black marks left by the car when it departed so suddenly.

Surprisingly, it only took them about thirty minutes to decide they were finished. Caldwell told the EMTs to go ahead and retrieve the body, then walked back over to Detective Moore.

"This lady was bludgeoned to death with something heavy," he said. "Coroner will make the final determination, of course, but it looks to me like cause of death will be extreme head trauma with penetrating cranial fractures."

Moore nodded. "Yeah, that's what we thought. You find anything that might help us identify the killer?"

Caldwell frowned. "Not a lot," he said. "There are some footprints that might belong to the killer, in which case you're looking for somebody wearing sneakers who weighs around one sixty-five."

"There's a witness," Sam said, "who thought it was a woman who took this lady away from her home. Find anything to indicate the killer might have been female?"

"The footprints aren't huge, but they are not so small. I'd be comfortable saying it's definitely a woman. From the extent of the damage done to the victim, I'd think the perpetrator was pretty strong, but the weapon could have been anything from a rock to a baseball bat, so its length and weight could compensate for lower strength." He shook his head. "I don't think I can seriously speculate as to the gender of the perpetrator, not at this point."

Another car pulled up on the road near where the ambulance attendants were loading the body inside, and Moore made a face. "That's Rob Girardi," he said.

"Reporter for the Benton paper." He motioned for Sam to follow and walked toward the man who got out of the car.

"Hey, Johnny," the reporter said. "Took me a little while to find the place. Is it really Crazy Daisy?"

"Yeah, it's her. Somebody beat her around the head."

Girardi clucked in sympathy. "Man, Thompsonville won't be the same without her. Any idea who did it?"

"Not just yet," Moore said. "However, it appears to be exactly like the way Millie Cameron was murdered eight years ago. The ironic thing about that is that Daisy may have known something about that case. Earlier today, she gave keys to the old Cameron house to this man. He's Sam Prichard, a private investigator who was looking into whether Mrs. Cameron's son was really guilty or not. Seems pretty strange that she'd be killed the same way just a few hours later, doesn't it?"

Girardi made a low whistle. "Damn right," he said. "So, do you think it was the same killer?"

"At this point, all I can say officially is that there are similarities. When you add in the pretty extreme coincidence that we were looking to talk to Daisy about the Cameron case just at the time when she was murdered, then I have to say it sure does look like a possibility."

"Are you reopening the Cameron case, then?"

"We are. Mr. Prichard stumbled across what might

be new evidence in that case today, but I'm not going to go into detail about what it is yet. If I get anything more, I'll give you a statement then."

Girardi nodded. "Okay, cool," he said. "I'll go get some background on Daisy and just hint in the story that there might be a connection. That okay?"

Moore nodded his head. "That's fine. You might mention that anyone who knows anything should give me a call."

Girardi agreed and got back into his car. As he drove away, Sam looked at Moore and grinned. "Your local reporters are easily satisfied," he said. "I've never had one give up that easily."

"He's got a murder in an extremely small town. Guy like him can spin that into a front-page story. Details will only get in the way." He looked around and saw that the CSI team was climbing back into their van. "I think we're done here. Got any advice on what I should do next?"

"I think the first thing I'd do is start looking for other killings around the region that have a similar MO. We've got two murders using identical methodology, eight years apart. If this is a person who already killed once, I'd be very surprised if they waited this long to kill again." He looked Moore in the eye. "I think we may be looking at a serial killer."

They got into the car and headed back toward Moore's office. "I can't recall ever hearing about a murder around southern Illinois that was really close to what happened to Mrs. Cameron," Moore said, "but I'll check. It's always possible one of the local jurisdictions had a case like it that never got compared to others. If local news didn't run the story properly, it might not have enough details to jog my memory, you know?"

"I know exactly what you mean. I had a case once where a serial killer had been getting away with it for years because nobody connected what appeared to be a bunch of random shootings. My wife is a whiz with computers, and when she started digging into old news stories and case files, a pattern turned up. In fact," he said, "she has her computer with her." He took out his phone and dialed Indie, setting it to speaker so Moore could hear.

"Hey, babe," she said. "Was it the lady you thought it was?"

"Yeah, it was her. Definitely the one who gave me the keys. Listen, she was killed exactly the way Debbie's mother was. Can you fire up Herman and see if he can find other killings that happen the same way? Bludgeoning deaths, all with massive head trauma."

"I'm sitting here with him right now. Give me a sec."

Sam could hear her fingers tapping on the keyboard for several seconds, but then he heard the first chime as Herman found results. Over the next minute, he heard the chime several more times.

"I'm just scanning news stories from the last fifteen

years at the moment," Indie said, "but I've got nine similar murders, most of them older women, including Millie Cameron. Her death is the oldest one, and then there's one in Golconda about a year later, then another in New Harmony, Indiana, almost a year after that one. The victim in New Harmony was a sixty-four-year-old man. There's one in Madisonville, Kentucky, a year and a half after that, another in Jonesboro, Illinois, six months after that one. One in Scott City, Missouri, a year later. Next one was Paducah, Kentucky, um, eight months later, but that's the odd one. The victim was a woman, but she was only twenty-nine. Then we got Hayti, Arkansas, ten months after that. Last one was nine months ago in Olney, Illinois."

Moore glanced at the phone and then at Sam. "How in the hell have I never heard about all these cases?"

"Probably because you're too busy dealing with your own," Sam said. "That's the way it was on the case I told you about. Every police department involved had enough of a caseload that kept them busy, so they never paid attention to other cases outside their own jurisdictions."

"And I was only scanning news stories within a hundred miles," Indie said through the phone. "You could probably check the FBI database and find more, or go out further. It looks to me like you got a serial killer on your hands."

"Yeah, I see that," Moore said. "And if you took a

map and marked all those places off, you'd find my county right smack in the middle of it all."

"If you add that to the fact that only Thompsonville has seen two of these murders, then it's quite possible our killer actually lives in this area. Somehow, he knew that Daisy had given me those keys, and something about her talking to me worried him. What are the chances that he just happened to be in the area on the day I go poking around inside that house?"

"Pretty slim, I agree," Moore replied. "I need to get all the information on those cases I can find."

"If you'll give me your email address," Indie said, "I can send all these links to you."

"Thank you, that would be a big help. It's j-m-o-o-r-e at franklinsherrif.il.gov."

"Okay, sent."

"Thanks, babe," Sam said. "I'll be back there in just a bit." He ended the call and put the phone back in his pocket. "So, Millie may have been his first, but she certainly wasn't his last. The victims are mostly similar, as well, mostly older women. That might actually lend credibility to the idea that it's a woman. Older women and men might be easier to subdue and beat to death."

"Yeah, but one of them was a younger woman. What about that one?"

Sam shrugged. "We don't have enough information to really make a reasonable guess. It's possible the woman was disabled in some way, might have been some kind of thrill for the killer to attack someone younger. Or, it could be just some kind of opportunity that struck and the killer couldn't resist, or maybe the victim knew something and the killer was forced to act to silence her. There could be any number of reasons why that particular victim ended up on the list."

Moore shook his head. "At least we have an idea why Daisy is on it. For whatever reason, she either knew something about the killer, or the killer thinks she did. Even without an autopsy report, I'm already convinced in my gut that we're dealing with the same killer. Now all we have to do is prove it and clear Ross's name."

"I'm with you," Sam said. "So I'll need you to back me when I start pushing for Millie's body to be exhumed and reexamined. I'll cover the costs, but we need the report of a genuine forensic pathologist, not your local coroner."

"Just meet me at the courthouse at eight o'clock Monday morning. I'll get us in to see Judge Middleton. Once I lay out the similarities in the cases, he won't be able to decline. Can you get permission from Debbie? Have her fax it down or something?"

"I'll take care of that, no problem. Once we get the order, who do we need to actually do it?"

"Well, Frank Hoover will dig her up for us, but the best forensic pathologist in the area is Dr. Havelock. He's down in Carbondale; he teaches pathology at the Southern Illinois University medical school and does forensics on the side. I know he's consulted on a lot of cases around the country, even up into Canada a couple of times."

"Sounds like the right guy, then. We'll want to get him on it as soon as we have the body."

"Middleton will give us whatever we need," Moore said. "I'll call Havelock as soon as we get Hoover scheduled. I've heard that he loves working on old cases, so this ought to be right down his alley."

13

Sam called Debbie as he was driving back across town. "Debbie, it's Sam Prichard," he said when she answered. "Can you do me a favor? I need you to write a letter granting your permission to exhume your mother's body, then fax it to me. I have a number you can fax to that will send it to my email, so I can print it out."

"Of course," Debbie said. She copied down the number and then asked, "Mr. Prichard? My friend Marcy called me last night and said there's been another murder, just like Mom's. Do you think there's any connection?"

Sam sighed. "I'm afraid there is," he said, "and I was going to tell you, anyway. The victim was Crazy Daisy. It's just a little too much to believe that this is just a coincidence, after she apparently talked to me just that morning. Johnny Moore, who was a deputy back then, is now the detective for the sheriff's office. I thought you'd like to know that he has also come to the conclusion that Ross is innocent, and he's trying to get the case reopened. He agrees with me that the fact Daisy was killed the same way your mother was is just too much of a coincidence. It's starting to look like we're dealing with a serial killer, and probably somebody local. As far as we can tell, your mom was the first victim, but there have been several others over the years since then."

"Oh, my goodness," Debbie said. "I'll get this letter done and out to you right away, but if this is the same killer, then that should be plenty of proof that Ross is innocent, right?"

"If we can come up with enough evidence that the killings are similar enough, then I'm sure of it. In order to do that, though, we've got to have your mother's body examined by a professional forensic pathologist. Detective Moore already has one in mind, somebody who's been a consulting pathologist on a lot of murder cases. He sounds like exactly the guy we need."

"That's good. I'd really like to be able to tell Ross some good news sometime soon. Oh, and I was going to call you in a little while, anyway. Alex and Andy found that letter from Bill Parkinson. They brought it to me a little while ago, and I read through it, but it's kind of strange."

"Strange, how?" Sam asked.

"Well, it's really just a short note. All it says is that he hoped she was doing well, but he just didn't feel like he could face her. He said it was too painful, anything to do with Lynette, but he just wanted her to know that he wished her the best."

Sam frowned into the phone. "That's not much, is it? What about the envelope, where did it come from?"

"That's the other strange part," Debbie said. "The envelope doesn't have a postmark, or even a stamp. It just has my mother's name written on the front, nothing else."

"Sounds like it might've been hand-delivered," Sam speculated. "Maybe he had been passing through the area and dropped it off. I saw the mailbox out near the street; he could have shoved it in there and driven away without being seen. Oh, well. Tell the boys I'll mail out a check to them."

Debbie thanked him again, and Sam ended the call. He got back to the motel just in time to hear Kenzie announce that she was getting hungry, so they all loaded up into the Ridgeline. Moore had suggested they try Mike's Drive-In in West Frankfort, only a few miles away, so Sam pointed the truck south. The place was appealing, and the food turned out to be very good, but it was the frosty mugs of root beer they all raved about.

Afterward, because it was simply too early to call it a day, they googled for theaters and drove a bit farther south to the town of Marion, where the latest Disney feature was showing. They did a little shopping before the movie, then finally got back to the motel at nearly eleven that night.

Kenzie was sound asleep, so Sam carried her into the room, but she woke up when he tried to lay her on the bed. There followed a few moments of Sam and Kenzie putting their hands on Indie's belly to feel the baby move around, which resulted in Kenzie insisting on sleeping with her mommy while Sam took the other bed.

Indie smiled at him, so he gave her a kiss and watched the two of them cuddled up for a few moments, then stripped out of his clothes and got into bed. The events of the day swirled around his head for a few minutes, but then he drifted off to sleep.

The next morning, since it was Sunday, Sam decided they needed to do something recreational. A few minutes googling led them to a few not so distant tourist attractions, so they spent the day on hiking trails and visiting a petting zoo. It was a nice day, and something Sam particularly needed after a week of digging through history and stumbling across murders.

It also left little Kenzie completely worn-out, so Sam got to spend that night with his wife again. Kenzie slept with her grandmothers, so the happy couple ended the day on an even happier note.

When the sun rose high enough for its light to penetrate the heavy curtains on Monday morning, Sam got up and dressed quietly. He kissed Indie and slipped out the door, and managed to eat two waffles in the continental breakfast room before heading for the courthouse.

He spotted Johnny Moore as soon as he stepped inside. He was waiting for Sam in the hallway and looked up with a smile when Sam came limping into view, then stepped up and held out a hand. Sam shook, and Moore said, "I got hold of the judge Saturday and let him know we'd be here this morning. He's waiting for us in his chambers." He turned without another word and led the way, and Sam followed along.

They passed through a clerk's office, and then Moore tapped on a large oak door. A voice inside called out for them to enter, and they stepped into the judge's chambers.

"Judge Middleton," Moore began, "this is Sam Prichard. Sam, Judge Harvey Middleton."

"Pleased to meet you, Your Honor," Sam said, shaking his hand.

"I think the pleasure is mine, young man," the judge said. "When Johnny called me the other day and told me about you, I thought your name sounded a little bit familiar, so I looked you up on the internet. Johnny, are you aware that this is the man who stopped the terrorists from dropping a nuclear bomb into Lake Mead?"

Moore's eyes bugged out, and he looked at Sam. "Damn it," he said with a grin. "No, I didn't realize that, but now I recognize your name, too. You could've told me, Sam."

Sam felt his face flushing a bit. "Oh, sure, that's the

way I start most conversations. Come on, Detective, what would you really think of me if I went around bragging about something like that? Besides, I wasn't the only one on that bridge that day. Some good people lost their lives that day, trying to stop that disaster. I just got lucky, is all."

"Lucky you lived through it, anyway," the judge said. "Anyway, all that aside, Johnny says you need an order to exhume a body?"

"Yes," Sam said. "I have a letter of consent from the next of kin, Mrs. Cameron's daughter Debbie." He produced the letter from a pocket and passed it over to the judge.

Judge Middleton read through it and then looked up at Sam. "All right," he said, "everything is in order. You don't actually need an order from the court to do this, but it might come in handy. There are a few people around here who don't really want this case reopened, but I'm sold. Give me fifteen minutes to dictate it, and the clerk will have it for you out front."

"Thank you, Your Honor," Sam said, and Moore echoed him. The two of them stepped out, and it was less than ten minutes later when the clerk printed out the order and handed it to them.

They walked out of the courthouse together. "I got Frank Hoover to clear his schedule today," Moore said. "If you're ready, we can head right out to see him now."

"Let's go," Sam said. "The sooner we get the

pathology report, the sooner I can start working on getting Ross out of prison. That's the goal, but I'm not going to run out on you with this current murder, either. Whatever reason Daisy may have had for giving me those keys, she definitely helped me get to where I can see daylight at the end of the tunnel for Ross. I don't think I could sleep at night letting her murder go unsolved."

"I couldn't agree more," Moore said. "Just leave your truck here; you can ride out with me."

The got into the unmarked car again, and Moore started it up and drove away from the courthouse, swinging around the square and heading out on North Main Street. Once they were rolling, Moore looked over at Sam.

"I got the judge to do something else for me on Saturday, when I called him," he said. "I got the okay to send Daisy Willis's body down to Havelock, as well. I figured it would be better to have the same pathologist do both autopsies, the current one and the old one. That way, we can get a definitive answer on whether the killings seem to have been perpetrated by the same person."

"That's fantastic," Sam said. "If he can say that there is a significant likelihood that the same killer struck again, then I'll get an attorney to approach the prosecutor on overturning Ross's conviction."

Moore nodded. "I figured you'd like that. Just so you

know, though, we've still got the same prosecutor that was here when Ross was convicted. He's probably not going to be too keen on flipping one of his own cases."

"In that case, I'll go to your friendly reporter, first. Let's see how he reacts to having a bungled case spread all over the news. By the time I give that reporter everything I know, that prosecutor's chance of reelection will be pretty slim."

Moore looked over at him with a sideways grin. "Man," he said, "you're not a bit afraid of making enemies, are you? Larry Zigler has been prosecutor here for fifteen years, and he's not going to take kindly to that kind of opposition."

"Then he should have make sure his investigators weren't bullying people of reduced capacity into confessions. Just about any decent defense attorney could have made a strong case that Ross was coerced, but he obviously didn't have one."

"Nope. Public defender, a guy named Paul Lambert. Lambert is all about plea bargains; I don't think he's ever actually defended a client."

Sam shook his head. "Unfortunately, that's the way most of them are," he said. "At least, that's been my experience with them."

"Ain't that the truth," Moore said. "By the way, I sent some deputies out Saturday to ask around that trailer park where Daisy lived. Rosie Parks wasn't the only one who saw Daisy getting shoved into a car, but nobody thought enough of it to get a license plate. One woman thought the car looked like her son's car, which is a late-model Nissan, but all we really know is that it was a white sedan. The trouble is that this could easily be called the land of white sedans. Probably a third of the cars in this area are white four-doors."

Sam frowned. "Too bad," he said. "In a town this small, you'd think that most people probably know what everyone's car looks like. Would have been nice if someone had recognized it."

"If it had been young men who saw it, somebody probably would have. Those trailers are mostly just old folks, though, and most of the ones I know can't recognize any car after about 1980."

They arrived at Hoover Excavation a few minutes later, and Sam followed the detective into the old brick building.

"Frank, this is Sam Prichard. He's a private investigator, but he's helping me out on a couple of murder cases. Do you remember the one I mentioned to you?"

Frank shook hands with Sam and then nodded. "I do," he said. "Mrs. Cameron, the lady who was murdered in Thompsonville a few years back, right?"

"Right. We got everything settled with the judge, so we're ready to go dig her up. I've already got Doctor Havelock arranged, and he's waiting for you to bring the coffin to him."

"Okay, then," Frank said. "Let's go do this. I already found out where she's buried, so I'll just meet you out at Freeman Cemetery."

Moore and Sam agreed and went back to the car, and Frank pulled out ahead of them a moment later in a truck towing a backhoe. Moore fell in behind him and followed as he headed south, then took a right onto Mcleansboro Street and followed it back over Highway 34 and then east toward Thompsonville.

It took almost twenty minutes to get to the old cemetery, mostly because the truck seemed to have a little trouble climbing a few of the hills with the big backhoe on the trailer behind it. Once they got there, however, it only took Frank a few minutes to unload the machine and drive it to where Millie's grave lay under a marble marker.

He set the safety legs of the backhoe once he had it in position and began digging. It was the work of only another fifteen minutes to expose the concrete vault that held the coffin, and then he put a chain on the bucket of the machine and used that to lift the lid away. Millie's coffin, protected by the vault from the elements and the earth, was still clean and relatively shiny.

Frank climbed down into the vault and passed a couple of straps under the coffin, then hooked them on to the bucket. He climbed back up onto the backhoe and pulled a lever, and Millie Cameron rose from her resting place. With the coffin swinging on the straps from the bucket, Frank raised the safety legs and drove the backhoe slowly toward his truck, where he set the coffin down gently on its flatbed.

Sam and the detective waited until he had the backhoe loaded onto the trailer again, then shook his hand and thanked him. "I'll stop by your office on the way back and pay the bill," Sam said.

Frank shook his head. "No charge," he said. "My wife used to babysit this woman's daughter Debbie. When I told her Johnny called about exhuming the body, and how it might finally come out that Ross didn't do it, she was pretty happy. I know the family don't have much money, so this is on me." He turned to Detective Moore. "I'll drop the backhoe at the shop, then head down to Carbondale. Ain't the first body I've taken down to Havelock. He'll have it in a couple of hours."

He climbed into the truck and started up, while Sam and Moore went back to the car and got inside.

"That was pretty decent of him," Sam said.

"I'd have to say," Moore said, "if anybody around here could be called a pillar of the community, it's Frank Hoover. He does an awful lot of good things for people around here."

Sam nodded. "It sounds like it. Well, all we can do now is wait for the pathology report. Anything come up on Daisy Willis's killing?"

"Not so much yet," Moore said. "I'll probably hear something from the CSI guys today or tomorrow, but

I'm not expecting much at this point. The footprints they saw at the scene might help if we come up with a suspect, but I kind of doubt they're going to find anything that points to somebody in particular." He let out a sigh. "Thing about Daisy is, she might have been a bit weird, but she never hurt anyone. There are some old folks around Thompsonville who swear by her potions. She made some kind of a tea drink out of some tree bark that apparently makes a pretty good painkiller for folks with arthritis and such. They're going to miss her."

"What about the other murders that fit the same pattern? Have you managed to get any further information on any of them?"

"Nothing yet, but I got calls out to police departments and sheriffs' offices in all those jurisdictions. Hopefully somebody will still remember the cases, and I might pick up something that could help."

"I can't help thinking we were on track about the killer being a local. If Millie was his first victim, then he probably did the next one trying to recapture the thrill he got from it. Same for the ones after that, he'd be looking for that adrenaline rush that serial killers talk about. With Daisy, though, the only thing that makes sense is that he somehow knew I'd be poking around this case. He might've been watching the house, waiting to see if I showed up there, and when he saw her talking to me it probably made him wonder what she knew, what she might've told me."

"I think the same thing. Whether she actually knew anything or not, I believe the killer thought she did. That's the only explanation I can come up with for why she's lying at the University morgue today."

He dropped Sam off at the courthouse and drove away, while Sam got into the Ridgeline and headed back to the motel. He didn't know what else to do at the moment, but it was not yet ten thirty, so he figured he would go back and hang out with his family until it was time for lunch.

Indie, however, had been busy. She looked up at Sam as he walked through the door and motioned for him to come to where she sat at the table with her computer.

"I thought I'd see how Herman was doing," she said, "because it's been a few days and he still hasn't turned up any new descendants we didn't know about—but you remember day before yesterday, I added in Lynette Cameron and Bill Parkinson? Well, I found out they definitely did get married; it was about two weeks after Lynette's baby was born, in a place called Pikeville, Kentucky. Unfortunately, that's the only thing he found. There is no record of Lynette's baby's birth, at least not in any database Herman can get into, and I can't find any reference to Bill or Lynette Parkinson that could possibly be them, not anywhere. It's like they fell off the planet right after they got married."

Sam frowned. "Did you try calling the county clerk in

Pikeville? Maybe they've got some old records that haven't been digitized, something they can look into for you."

"Tried that," Indie said. "A very nasty lady told me that a lot of their old records were destroyed in a flood back in 1977. The only reason I even found where they got married is because they had just started transferring records to microfilm at the time, and those had been moved to an upper floor of the courthouse. Marriage records were done by the time the flood struck, but a lot of other records were still on paper in the basement of the courthouse."

"Well, that sucks," Sam said. "Moore says Lynette is dead, but he doesn't know what ever happened to Parkinson. If we can track him down, it's possible he might be able to shed some kind of light on this, but I doubt it." He shrugged. "It was worth a try, though."

Indie looked at him, and her eyes were wide. "Worth a try? Sam, what I'm telling you is that there is absolutely no record of them after they were married in 1972. I mean nothing, not even any kind of Social Security records on either of them. Herman has a back door into the SSA database, so I told him to check. Parkinson had a Social Security account, just like every other adult American, and Herman was able to find him in the SSA database, but all activity on that account stopped within a month after they were married. Now, it's possible they went completely off grid and never paid taxes, but that would be pretty hard to believe. And as far as I can tell, Lynette never got a Social Security number at all."

Sam leaned back in his chair and cocked his head to one side. "Okay, I see what you're getting at. The chance that they could go completely unnoticed by the government after their marriage would be pretty slim. Even if Parkinson just did odd jobs, sooner or later he's bound to have run into something that would require him to use his Social Security number. Heck, even opening a bank account requires one."

"Yeah, and so does life insurance, getting a driver's license, and just about anything else you can do in our modern society requires that stupid number. Sam, I'm beginning to think he changed his name."

Her husband narrowed his eyes and frowned. "I know that it used to be possible to get a new identity by using the name and Social Security number of someone who died. All you had to do was get your hands on their birth certificate, because birth and death records weren't correlated at the Social Security Administration. With the birth certificate, you could get the Social Security card that was assigned to that person, and then you could get any other kind of identification. I think you're onto something, babe. Now, how do we find out what he changed it to?"

"I'm ahead of you, like always," she said with a grin. "I told Herman to search for death certificates of males who would have been around Parkinson's age within two hundred miles of Pikeville. Then, I told him to match them to Social Security numbers and check to see if any of those numbers became active again after the date of death. He's crunching on that now, and he's already found three SSNs that seem to have come back from the dead. I'm beginning to think it wasn't all that uncommon, back then, but it should hopefully give us a possible lead on Parkinson."

Sam smiled at her. "Did I ever tell you that I really just married you for your brains?"

"No, but I almost believe it."

He let his eyes roam up and down her body for a moment, then focused on her eyes again. "Good, because I didn't. You being brilliant is just a bonus—it's your body I'm really in love with."

She stuck her tongue out at him. "Lucky for you, I can take that as a compliment. And I need it right now, when I'm fat as a hippo."

"You, my love, are not fat," Sam said. "You are merely slightly fluffy. But don't worry, once the baby is born, that will go away."

"Yeah? They say baby fat is the hardest to get rid of."

Sam shot her a wicked grin. "Not with me around. I'll be chasing you all over the house—you'll get more exercise than you've ever had."

"Hey," his mother called from behind him, where she and Kim were watching TV with Kenzie. "Keep it PG, okay? There's a child present."

Sam and Indie snickered.

Sam called Detective Moore and told him what Indie had found out about Parkinson, then took his family to McDonald's for lunch. Kenzie particularly liked McDonald's, especially when she got the toy out of the Happy Meal. This one happened to be one of her favorite Disney characters, and she delightedly told all of them the story of the movie it came from.

"And then she fell in love with the Beast, 'cause he was really a nice guy, and she kissed him and he turned into a handsome prince."

"And was that all?" Sam asked. "Was that the end of the story?"

Kenzie shook her head. "No," she said emphatically. "They lived happily ever after."

"And do you know what that tells you?" Indie asked her daughter.

Kenzie looked up at her. "What?"

"It tells you you can't tell what a person is really like just by looking at the outside. Sometimes people aren't who they seem to be when you just look at them."

Kenzie screwed up her face and thought for a moment, then smiled and nodded. "Yeah," she said. "Like when they wear the skies."

Sam furrowed his brow. "The skies? Why would anyone wear the skies?"

The little girl looked at him as if he were stupid.

218

"'Cause they want to look like someone else."

Indie laughed at the look on Sam's face. "Not the skies," she said. "She means a disguise."

"Yeah, the skies," Kenzie repeated.

Sam chuckled, and they finished up their lunch, then headed back to the motel. He felt like he should be doing something, but he didn't have any idea where to start looking for new leads. It seemed he was at a dead end until the pathologist finished his autopsies on Millie and Daisy, and he had no idea when that would be.

He spent the rest of the day lounging around the motel. It was one of those days, he said, that made him want to just chill out for a while. The motel had a good selection of movies on its pay-per-view system, so they ordered a pizza for dinner and relaxed with some movies.

The following morning, Sam called Detective Moore to ask if he'd heard anything from the pathologist, but there was no news yet. Moore promised to let him know as soon as he heard anything, and Sam thanked him.

With no new information, however, Sam couldn't just take off and leave his family. Instead, they went out for breakfast and spent the morning just looking around the countryside. The weather was a little cool, so they put jackets on and took another drive around Rend Lake. While they were doing that, they discovered that there were two other lakes close by and went to look them over, as well. It was a nice, relaxing way to spend the morning, and then they went out for lunch.

When that was over, though, Sam was starting to get antsy. Since it was just after one, he told Indie he just had to do something to try to make some kind of progress on the case, dropped his family off at the motel, and headed back toward Thompsonville. The air had warmed up quite a bit by then, so Sam tossed his jacket into the back seat on the way. There was at least one person on his list of potential witnesses that he hadn't spoken to yet, and that was the man who had employed Ross.

Gary's Auto Repair was located just off Highway 34 near the middle of Thompsonville. Sam pulled in and parked, then climbed out of the truck and walked into the big open garage. Several men were working on a number of vehicles, and Sam stood just inside the entrance until one of them had a moment to look his way.

"Help you?" the fellow asked, and Sam held out his ID.

"My name is Sam Prichard," he said. "I'm a private eye. Is Gary Burgess around?"

The man raised one eyebrow. "That's me," he said. "What can I do for you?"

A big air compressor started running, and Sam winced at the loud noise. "Is there somewhere quieter we could talk?"

Gary grinned and motioned for Sam to follow him into an office that was attached to the side of the building. The sound vanished as soon as the door was closed. "Extra soundproofing," Gary said. "Sometimes I just have to get away from the racket myself. Have a seat."

Gary sat down behind a battered desk, and Sam took the chair opposite. "I'm working for the family of Millie Cameron," he said. "I understand Ross used to work for you?"

Gary looked at him for a moment before answering, then nodded slowly. "You said you're working for her family? I'm assuming you mean Debbie?"

"Yes, but I was actually originally employed by a distant relative. He simply wanted to find some missing relations, but when I told him about Millie and Ross, he instructed me to do everything I could to ascertain the truth. A lot of people don't believe Ross killed his mother, and frankly, neither do I."

Gary grinned at him then. "God, it's good to hear someone say that. That boy couldn't have hurt anybody, let alone his own mama. And now, we've got another woman killed the same exact way from what I hear. I'm guessing there's a connection?"

"I certainly think so, and so does Detective Moore at the sheriff's office. Earlier today I arranged to have Millie's body exhumed and sent to a forensic pathologist down in Carbondale. Daisy Willis, the woman who was murdered on Saturday, will be examined by the same doctor. With any luck, he'll be able to tell us that there is a reasonable certainty that both women were killed by the same person."

Gary nodded, leaning back in his chair and putting his feet up on the corner of his desk. "I reckon that ought to clear Ross," he said. "How can I help you?"

"Well, I'm wondering if you might have any suspicions as to who might have actually killed Millie. From what I've heard about you, you probably know everybody in this little town, and both Moore and I have come to the conclusion that the killer most likely lives here."

Gary's eyebrows shot upward. "Here? In Thompsonville?"

Sam nodded. "Or at least close by," he said. "I came down here Saturday morning to get my first look at Millie's house, and a woman who looked a lot like Daisy Willis showed up while I was there. She had the keys to the house and asked me if I wanted to take a look inside, so I did. When I came out, though, she was gone and I didn't know where to find her. That afternoon, I found out that it might have been Daisy and went looking for her, but someone had dragged her out of her trailer and hustled her into a car sometime before that. A couple hours later, her body was found out north of town. That strikes me as a pretty big coincidence, wouldn't you think? If she was killed because someone saw her talking to me, and that someone is probably the killer, it would be quite a coincidence if he just happened to be passing through town at the time."

Gary nodded slowly and stared at him for several seconds. "Damn big coincidence," he said. "Sounds to me like your killer had some idea you were coming."

14

Sam shrugged. "I feel the same way, but I can't think of any way he could have known. Can you?"

A laugh that sounded almost like a bark came out of Gary Burgess. "Hell, man, I knew you were coming. I mean, I didn't know a lot about you, but I heard over at Jim's that there was a private detective digging into the case."

"At Jim's?" Sam asked, but then his eyes opened wide. "Let me guess," he said. "Marcy Elimon?"

"Yep. She said there was a private detective stopped in there the other day asking questions and she sent him up to Debbie, and then Debbie called to say he was coming back and wanted to try to prove Ross didn't do it. I'd imagine that was all over town by Saturday."

Sam chewed on his cheek for a second. "I should've thought of that," he said. "I knew that Debbie and Marcy were friends, but I never considered that Debbie might have called her. Any idea how many other people were in there at the time?"

Gary shrugged. "Maybe a dozen of us at the time, but Marcy would've been telling everybody all day long. See, she's always been sort of a cheerleader for Ross, insisting he couldn't possibly have done it, the same way I do. Hell, anybody who knew that boy didn't believe it, but there's some people in this town that are so stupid they just naturally accept whatever ends up in the newspaper. By the time they got Ross to jail that day, every paper around here was already saying he was guilty. That's why Debbie and her family ended up moving away."

Sam nodded his head. "Yeah, so I heard. Listen, I was told that there were a lot of local boys who used to try to pick on Ross, but that he never lost his temper with anyone. Does that sound true to you?"

"It not only sounds true, it is true. You know how kids are—anything they don't understand is something to poke a stick at. Ross was different, so a lot of those little lunkheads would try to pick on him. They call him names, or take something from him and play keep-away, but he never, ever got mad. To be perfectly honest, he laughed right along with them."

"Then you never heard of him ever hurting anyone?"

Gary frowned. "I didn't quite say that," he said. "Back when Ross was a kid, and bear in mind this was before my time so I only heard about it, he apparently used to play with kids who were younger than him. I guess a few times, what he considered simple playing around might have banged up a kid here and there, and for a long time people wouldn't trust him at all. By the time he got into his late teens, though, he had figured out that he had to be more careful, and a lot of that died off. It was just some of the folks around his age around here, kids who got hurt back then, who never really cared for him. Hell, most of the kids that picked on him were their kids."

"Things like that are understandable. Ross is autistic, and autistic children don't have the normal social skills of other kids. He probably never meant to do any harm, but accidents happen."

Gary grinned and pointed at Sam. "Give that man a cigar," he said. "From everything I heard, that's exactly how it was. Anyway, I started this place up about twenty years ago, and Ross used to just hang around. He didn't bother anybody and he never got in the way, so I never objected. Then one day, when I was busy doing something else, an old man came in who was just passing through. His car was making a funny noise and he saw the shop and figured he'd ask us to check it out, but he saw Ross standing outside and started talking to him. I didn't think anything of it until a few minutes later when Ross raised the hood on his car and leaned in over the engine. Well, I figured I'd better go rescue that poor man's car, so I hurried out there just in time to hear the engine go from spitting and sputtering to purring like a kitten. The distributor cap had popped loose on one side, not enough to kill the engine but enough to make it run rough. Ross took one look under that hood and solved the problem, then just reached in and fixed it."

Sam grinned. "I was told he had a knack for mechanical things."

"I'll say. After that, I started trying him out on different little jobs, and he turned out to be a whiz at them. I've been doing this more than thirty years, but Ross could listen to an engine with a misfire and tell you exactly which cylinder wasn't firing, and whether it was because of a foul spark plug or a stuck valve. I've never known anyone else who can do that, so after a couple weeks of watching him, I asked him if he wanted a job. He saved me probably half a dozen hours every week trying to figure out what the problem was because he could literally just listen to a car or ride in it and tell me what was wrong with it. In the twelve years he worked here, I don't think he was ever wrong once."

"How did your customers feel about him?" Sam asked.

Gary rolled his eyes with a grin. "I let Ross do simple jobs by himself, like oil changes and tune-ups and stuff like that, you know? I don't know how many people told me their cars ran better after he did something to it than it ever did when I worked on it. I think some of them were just saying it to make Ross feel good, but I had a few people that didn't want anyone but him putting in their spark plugs or changing their oil. And the kids around here, the younger ones in particular, they show up here with their bicycle chains broken or a tire gone flat, and Ross would drop whatever he was doing to help them. He probably patched a hundred bike tires over the years for free, because the kids didn't have any money. I never complained about it because their parents would come down later and offer to pay, or they were just good customers and I figure I made plenty of money off of them to throw in a free tire patch, you know?"

"Sure, little things like that bring a shop like yours a lot of goodwill."

"Yeah, exactly." Gary put his feet down and sat forward, leaning his elbows on the desk. "So, tell me the truth. Is there really a chance Ross could get out of prison?"

"The truth? The truth is I'm not going to stop until that's exactly what happens."

"I'm damn glad to hear it. I think most folks in this town would welcome him back, now. Between Marcy and me, I don't think there's too many left to still believe he was guilty, anyway. Maybe Debbie would move back here, and Ross could come back and work for me again. I'd like that."

Sam smiled at him. "Maybe," he said. "But listen, you never answered what I asked a while ago. Do you have any idea who the killer might be?"

"Me? Now, I wouldn't even be able to make a guess.

As far as I know, everybody around here is just your normal Illinois hillbilly. You got any ideas?"

Sam's smile turned into a grimace. "I had a couple of suspects in mind," he said, "but Daisy's death has pretty well cleared them. Do you know Jason Garrity?"

"Sure, I know him. Little bastard ever breaks into my shop again, I'm going to break both of his arms. He broke in about five years ago and sprayed paint all over three of my customers' cars. Cost me better than two grand to make that right, and all he got was six months of probation."

"I'd heard he's been in some trouble," Sam said. "The thing is, he's the only actual witness who saw anything, and he's convinced that the killer was a woman. His logic and coming to that conclusion is pretty sound, I think, but it turns out there've been several other killings just like these scattered all around southern Illinois and parts of Missouri, Indiana, and Kentucky. Millie seems to have been the first victim, but we're pretty certain that we're looking at a serial killer. If I remember correctly, Daisy would be the tenth victim."

Gary whistled, his eyes big and round. "Are you serious? Holy cow," he said. "And you think Garrity is right, that it's a woman?"

"I think he's convinced that the person he saw leaving Millie's place was a woman, and another witness says it was a woman who pushed Daisy into a car and drove off with her on Saturday. It looks for all the world like all of these killings were done by the same perpetrator. While female serial killers are rare, there have been a number of them in America, so it's not impossible."

"Man, that'd make it even harder to guess who it could be. I mean, we've got a few crazy ladies in town—every place does—but I can't imagine any of them being capable of doing something like what happened to Millie Cameron." He was still sitting with his elbows on the desk, and now he propped his chin on his clasped hands. "You know, I'm just at a loss for words. The thought that we got somebody here in this town who's capable of doing that sort of thing, and then it seems like it's a woman? Makes you wonder who you can trust at all, doesn't it?"

"Yeah, it does. I've seen far too much of what people are actually capable of, and what scares me the most is that many of the people who turn out to be killers seem like normal, everyday folks until they get caught." He took one of his business cards out of his pocket and passed it over to Gary. "I appreciate your time," he said, "and I'd appreciate it even more if you give me a call if you think of anything that might help. I've been asked to consult on Daisy's murder, so I'm probably going to be around here for a while."

Gary got to his feet and extended a hand, and Sam shook with him. "I'll be glad to help any way I can. Ross was a little strange, but he ain't no killer. If I think of anything at all that might help, I'll be calling."

Sam thanked him and got to his feet, then limped his way out to the truck. He started up and backed out, then headed back toward Benton, but the sight of Jim's Fresh Stop made him turn in and park once more. He walked into the place and was instantly greeted by Crystal, the waitress who had served them a few days before.

"Mr. Prichard," the girl said. "I'm so glad you're here. Everybody is so upset about what happened to Crazy Daisy, and there's a lot of rumors flying around that it might have been the same person who killed old Mrs. Cameron. Do you know anything about it?"

There were half a dozen people sitting around the dining room, and all of them were staring at Sam. "Well, the sheriff's office thinks it's possible that it's the work of the same person, and I tend to agree. Is Marcy around?"

Crystal nodded. "Yeah, she's in the back. You want anything?"

Sam pulled a chair out from a table and sat down. "How about some coffee?"

"Coming right up," the girl said. "I'll tell Marcy you're here." She disappeared into the back for a moment, then came back and poured a cup of coffee and brought it to Sam. "Here you go, and Marcy says she'll be right out."

Sam picked up the sugar bowl and held it over the cup for a few seconds, then used the spoon Crystal had given him to stir it while he waited. By the time he was finished, Marcy was coming out of the kitchen, wiping her hands on a towel as she approached him. She sat down in the chair across the table and looked at him with a worried expression.

"So it's true, then? The same killer got Daisy?"

"We can't say for certain, but it looks that way. Marcy, I was just talking to Gary Burgess, and he said that you told him on Friday that I was coming back to town. I'm guessing Debbie called you?"

"Yeah," Marcy said, nodding. "Man, I haven't heard her so excited in years. She says you feel pretty good about the chances of getting Ross out of prison?"

"I do," Sam said. "And as sad as it is, Daisy's murder makes it even more likely. We've got a forensic pathologist examining both the bodies, Daisy and Millie's, to see if the injuries appear to match. If they do, then it's a safe bet that the same person killed both of them."

Marcy shook her head sadly. "I was hoping you'd find something to help Ross," she said, "but I sure wish it had been something like this. Why in the world would anybody want to hurt Daisy? Sure, she was a little odd, but pretty much everybody in town liked her."

"That's kind of what I wanted to talk to you about," Sam said. "I went to Millie's old house on Saturday morning, and a woman I think was Daisy showed up there and said she had the keys if I wanted to look inside. I took them and went in, but by the time I came out she was gone. Now, the funny thing is that she told me her name was Marie, and I understand that Marie was the name of the woman that Debbie gave the keys to when she left town, but that she died sometime back. What strikes me as odd is that it was only probably an hour or so later that someone saw a woman drive up to Daisy's place and make her get into a car, then drive off with her. Three hours after that, her body was found out north of town. That makes me think the killer had to have been watching the house, expecting me to show up there, and got worried that Daisy might have told me something I wasn't intended to know."

Marcy's eyes went wide. "Oh, my God," she said. "You think the killer was in here and heard me talking about you coming back?"

Sam nodded. "I'm afraid that's exactly what I'm thinking. What I'm wondering is if there was anyone in here that might have heard it that you'd be suspicious of?"

"No, not really. Just local folk, that's all." Her mouth stopped halfway to the next word, and she stared at him. "Holy geez, you think the killer is somebody who lives here?"

"That's exactly what we're thinking. The chance that the same killer just happened to be passing through and saw me talking to Daisy at the house is just too big a stretch for the imagination. It almost had to be someone who heard I was coming, whether they heard it from you or from someone else who repeated what you told them.

I don't suppose it would be possible you could tell me the names of everyone who was here on Friday, would it?"

"Oh, Lordy, probably not. I mean, I could probably make a list of some of them, but there's times I don't even come out of the kitchen for hours. Bound to have been different ones in and out that day, and I know Crystal was telling people about it, too."

"If the two of you could put your heads together and try to make a list, it might be very helpful. I'm not saying the killer was actually here, but it might give us a place to start in trying to figure out who all knew I was coming."

Marcy frowned. "Mr. Prichard, this is a small town. Even if Crystal never told anybody, just the fact I mentioned it a couple of times while folks were in here would mean the whole town would know it by that night. I'd be surprised if you could find someone who hadn't heard, to be honest."

Sam sighed heavily. "Well, that might explain how Daisy happened to show up there that morning. If she had heard I was coming, she might've been watching the place herself, especially since she really did have the keys. Debbie thinks that Marie must have given them to her before she died." He took a sip of his coffee. "The problem is that now we think the killer must've been watching, too. Whoever it was saw me talking to Daisy probably started worrying about whether she knew anything that could lead back to them. It was pretty bold, though, to show up at her place in broad daylight and drag her into a car. Unfortunately, the few people who saw it didn't recognize the car or the woman who was driving it."

Marcy narrowed her eyes. "But they saw it was a woman?"

Sam nodded. "Yes, and I found out from Jason Garrity that the person he saw leaving Millie's backyard the day she was killed was probably also a woman. We're probably talking about someone who lives here and is well-known, a woman who you'd never suspect of being capable of murder, but we've got evidence that potentially connects her to at least eight more killings scattered across this part of the country."

"A woman," Marcy said softly. "That seems so strange. I mean, the way Millie died and now Daisy, it just doesn't seem like something a woman would do, you know?"

"Under normal circumstances, I would agree with you. On the other hand, there have been some pretty brutal and bloody female murderers in the past."

"Yeah, I watch all them crime shows, so I know that. The thing is, I don't think I've ever heard of a woman who would beat someone to death this way. Have you?"

"No, I confess I haven't," Sam said. "Most female serial killers use poison or a gun, rather than blunt force trauma. Unfortunately, everything I've got so far indicates that this one is the exception."

Marcy chewed on her bottom lip for a moment. "Thing about this place, there's not a lot of women who come in here unless it's with the husband. This is farm country, so most of our business comes from the farmers and the people that work for them. Mornings especially, we see probably a couple dozen men but hardly ever a woman. They don't tend to come in until it's close to lunchtime, and then there's only a handful who ever come in here alone. Betty Donner, Nancy Jeffries—oh, and Royce Garrity, she comes in now and then." She narrowed her eyes for a moment. "You know, Royce and Millie never did get along very well. Don't know what it was about, but you get them two in a room together and sparks were gonna fly."

Sam nodded again. "I heard about that, but Mrs. Garrity had a pretty good alibi for when Millie died. She was actually in the hospital having surgery, the kind of surgery that means you're not going to be up moving around much for a while. She was still in the hospital when it happened and apparently didn't get out for a couple of days after."

Marcy nodded. "Yeah, I remember that now. Funny how you forget things like that, isn't it? A woman, a woman—I'll talk to Crystal, and we'll see about putting together a list for you. Probably won't be ready before tomorrow, though."

"I'd really appreciate it," Sam said. "It will mean a lot of work, but at least it would give me someplace to start looking."

"No problem," Marcy said. "Anything I can do to help, I'm willing."

She got up and headed back into the kitchen, and Sam finished his coffee. He got up and went to the register, but Crystal told him not to worry about it. "Somebody else already paid for your coffee, Mr. Prichard. You have a great day."

Sam looked around at the other people who were smiling and nodding in his direction, then gave a wave and walked out the door. They seemed like a nice bunch of folks, but Sam couldn't help wondering if one of them actually knew exactly who the murderer might be.

He got back into the Ridgeline and started up, but then he decided to go back to Millie's house one more time. It was only a couple of minutes' drive from Jim's, but this time he looked around as he drove along the street. As far as he could tell, there was no one paying any attention to him at all, but he wouldn't have bet his life on it.

He parked on the street in front of the house again and then reached into the console and withdrew his pistol. He snapped its holster onto his belt and stepped out of the truck, carefully looking around once more before approaching the house. He fished the keys out of his pocket and unlocked the front door, then looked carefully inside before stepping across the threshold and closing it behind him.

The house still felt spooky to him, but he didn't see

or hear anything unusual. He walked past the bloodied chair and into the kitchen, then set aside to make sure he was out of the line of sight from the big living room window. He crouched down a bit and poked his head slightly out into the doorway so that he could look through that window himself.

He stayed there for several minutes, until his hip began to complain about the position, but there was no sign of anyone approaching the house. He stretched into a standing position again, balancing on his good leg for a moment to let his hip relax, then turned and looked around the kitchen one more time. He didn't expect to find anything new, but it was something to do while waiting for the pain to let up a bit.

There wasn't anything new to see, so he turned back toward the living room. He was limping as he crossed it, and a sharp twinge made him wish he had brought his cane. He stopped in the middle of the room and shifted his weight to the other leg again, instinctively leaning out and putting a hand on the back of one of the chairs to balance himself.

He stood there for a moment and then let go of the chair, but a whiff of something unusual made him stand where he was. The odor seemed slightly familiar, and he sniffed the air, trying to find its source. After a second he lifted his hand to his face, and that's when he realized that the odor was coming from his palm. He sniffed again and realized that what he was smelling was the scent of a pine cleaner.

Sam rubbed his fingers together and realized that his hand was greasy. He reached out with his other hand and touched the chair, and it came away greasy as well.

He stepped around that chair to get to the other one, the one Millie had died in, and felt the back of it. There was no greasy feeling, and the pine cleaner aroma was only coming from the other chair. He stood there for a couple of minutes, wondering why in the world someone would have sprayed pine cleaner on one chair but not on the other. He filed it away as an interesting side note on this already unusual case and turned toward the door once again.

Sam heard the sound of breaking glass a split second before he heard the gunshot, and then he registered pain on his left arm. Instinctively, he dropped to the floor and snatched the Glock from its holster, then rolled across the floor until he was beside its back wall. Carefully, he raised his head slightly to look through the shattered window, but he saw nothing.

This is a dumb place to be when someone is trying to shoot me, he thought. Quickly, he rose to a crouch and hurried across the room until he was just beside the broken window, then leaned his head out for just a second to try to look around. There was no one in sight, but there were so many trees in every direction that he could easily be in somebody's crosshairs already.

Carefully, trying not to expose himself to the unknown shooter, Sam looked down at his arm. Blood was slowly running down the outer side of his upper arm, and he tugged at his sleeve enough to see that the bullet had apparently just grazed him. He had been lucky, he knew. A split-second earlier, before he turned toward the door, that bullet would probably have struck him in the center of his back.

He considered trying to make a run for the truck, but that would put him right out in plain sight. If he remained where he was, however, all the shooter had to do was start punching bullets through the wall. The house was an old frame structure, and Sam knew that the flimsy walls wouldn't offer any true protection. He crawled on all fours until he got to the door that led into the hallway going back to Ross's room, then jumped up and hurried as quickly as his bad hip allowed. He stepped into Ross's old bedroom and leaned against the wall, then took out his phone.

He found Detective Moore's number in his recent call list and tapped it twice. The phone dialed the number automatically, and Sam was delighted when the detective answered on the first ring.

"It's Sam Prichard," he said quickly. "I'm in Millie Cameron's old house, and someone just took a shot at me through the window."

"Holy crap," Moore said, "are you okay?"

"Yeah, the bullet just grazed my arm. The problem is that I can't see the shooter, so I'm kind of trapped. Got anybody out my way?"

"Dale Miller is out there somewhere," Moore said. "You stay put—I'm sending him your way now."

The phone went dead, and Sam put it back into his pocket, then listened intently for any sign that someone was trying to enter the house. It was less than a minute later when he heard a siren, and only forty seconds after that when a squad car screeched to a halt behind his truck.

"Mr. Prichard?" Sam looked out and down the hall to see a deputy standing in the yard. "Mr. Prichard, I'm Deputy Miller from the sheriff's office. Are you all right?"

15

"Yeah," Sam yelled. "Watch yourself. Somebody in the woods fired a shot through that window." He stepped into the hallway and moved slowly along it until he got back to the living room, then crouched again as he ran past the window to the front door. He popped up long enough to look through the door window and then yanked the door open.

"Doesn't seem to be anyone out here now," the deputy said, and Sam leaned around the doorpost for a second. No shots rang out, and a few seconds later he stepped out and shook hands with Deputy Miller.

"I appreciate you coming," Sam said. "I think the siren must've scared the shooter off."

"Hey, that's what we're here for," Miller said. "Johnny says to tell you he's on the way and to do your best not to get shot. He doesn't want to have to do the paperwork."

242

"Well, I promise you I'll do my best to save him from having to fill it all out." A sound from down the street caught his ear, and Sam turned to see a couple of men standing in the street and staring in their direction. "Looks like we've drawn a lot of attention. Maybe the shot made enough noise that somebody actually got a look at whoever was leaving in a hurry."

Miller looked around. "I'll stay here with you for the moment," he said. "When Johnny and the others get here, I'll go talk to those folks and see if they saw or heard anything that might help."

Another siren could be heard coming from a distance, and it was only a couple of minutes before another deputy arrived. Miller, whose insignia said he was a sergeant, told the new arrival to go and interview the men in the street.

Detective Moore showed up ten minutes later with Sheriff Jim McCollum right behind him, and two more deputies and an ambulance arrived just after them. Sam explained what had happened while a paramedic wrapped a bandage around his arm, and one of the deputies went into the house and found where the slug had lodged in the doorpost. Using a knife and a pair of needle-nose pliers, he was able to retrieve it.

"It's mangled," McCollum said, "but from the size of it I'd say we're looking at a 9 mm. That's a popular round with a lot of the hunters around here; they buy these little carbines that look like miniature assault rifles and then wonder why the deer they shoot run off into the woods. I will say they're accurate little suckers, though. If the shooter was any good with it at all, you'd probably be dead."

"I almost was," Sam said. "The shot came just as I was turning away from where I've been standing for a minute or more. If I had moved a split second later, that would've hit me center mass."

"Johnny's told me who you are," the sheriff said. "We're going to find out who did this, because I'm not having a national freaking hero killed in my county."

"I appreciate that," Sam said with a grin. "I suspect if we find out who took a shot at me, we'll also find the person who murdered Millie Cameron and Daisy Willis."

"About that," Moore said, "I got a call from Havelock about five minutes before you called me. He said there's no doubt in his mind that both women were killed in the exact same manner, and the injuries appear to be inflicted by the same weapon based on the types and shapes of the fractures in their skulls. He's willing to state that he's more than ninety percent certain both women were murdered by the same perpetrator. Oh, and he said the weapon is a heavy metal object with a rounded end about the size of a golf ball. Mrs. Cameron had over fifty impacts to her skull, and Daisy had a few more than that. The ironic thing is that any one of the blows would have almost certainly been fatal, he said."

"Well, that shoots down the theory that Ross beat his mother to death with his fists," Sam said, "and if somebody like Havelock thinks it's the same killer, then it probably is."

"I agree," said Sheriff McCollum. "Johnny explained to me over the weekend about what you're trying to do, and I'm going to back you. I wasn't around here when this case happened, but from everything Johnny has told me it sounds like that poor man was hustled. I might not have been sheriff at the time, but that looks bad for my office."

Sam smiled at him. "Sheriff, I certainly appreciate your support. In the meanwhile, though, we've got a killer on the loose." He turned back to Moore. "I don't suppose you got anything back on the hat yet, did you?"

"No, not yet," Moore replied. "That lab is pretty quick, though, so I expect we'll hear something shortly."

"That would be good. We may not learn much, but every little bit helps." The paramedic finished with Sam's arm, and then he and Moore walked over to the Ridgeline. Sam opened the door and sat down in the driver's seat but left it open so they could talk. The sheriff was busy supervising his deputies, sending them in different directions to interview potential witnesses, and into the woods to look for footprints or shell casings.

"I figured out how the killer knew I was going to be here," Sam said. "Debbie Jenkins called her friend Marcy Elimon after I left her last week and told her I was coming down here to start looking around. Marcy told some people at the diner, and the word probably just spread all over town from that. I'm guessing the killer heard about it and must have figured I'd want to come by the house. All she had to do then was sit out there in the woods and watch. Probably just wanted to see who I was, but when she saw me talking to Daisy, she must've started worrying about whether Daisy knew anything that might lead back to her."

"Makes sense," Moore said. "And you're right— there's a joke in Thompsonville that whatever Marcy knows, everybody knows. She's been working there for years, and I think it's more about being the local gossip queen that it is about her paycheck. If she said the sun turned blue, half the people in this town would swear they could see it."

Sam nodded. "She and Crystal are going to try to make a list of the people they told," he said, "and I'll try to talk to as many as I can. It might not help, but at this point I'll take any leads I can get."

"Sure you want to stick around? I mean, you got enough evidence already to clear Ross Cameron, but now it looks like the killer has taken a personal interest in you. This might not be the safest place for you to hang out."

Sam gave him an evil grin. "I've been a target before," he said. "I look at it this way. If the killer is trying to come after me, I'm going to do everything I can to make it as difficult for her as it can be. But at least, while she's trying to get me, it might keep her from hurting anyone else."

Moore grinned, but he shook his head. "Man, you got some brass ones. I doubt I could be that cocky after someone took a shot at me like this."

"Like I said," Sam replied, "this ain't my first rodeo. And just for the record, it's not the first time I've dealt with a female serial killer. Believe me, they can be even more deadly and ruthless than men."

Moore started to speak, but his phone rang at that moment. He pulled it out of the holder on his belt and glanced at it, then answered it quickly on speaker.

"Detective Moore," he said, holding it out so Sam could hear as well.

"Hey, Johnny, this is Jay down at the lab. I just ran your after processing and found a couple things I thought you'd want to know right away."

"Thanks, Jay," Moore said, "I really appreciate it. What have you got?"

"Well, first," Jay continued, "you were right in suspecting that those are bloodstains on it, because they are. They're also pretty old, which you also suspected. I can't give you an exact age, but based on RNA decomposition testing, I can tell you they are definitely more than two years old, and probably more than five."

Johnny looked at Sam and nodded. "Okay, that helps some. What else?"

"Well, it's about those hairs you saw. We put them under the microscope and got quite a surprise. Those aren't human hairs at all—they're the kind of synthetic fibers used in cheap wigs."

Both Moore and Sam lowered their eyebrows. "Fake hair?" Moore asked. "They weren't real?"

"Nope. Polyester fibers, basically plastic that's been strung out into fine strands and made to look like hair. Whoever wore this hat didn't want anyone seeing whatever hair they naturally have on their heads."

"Okay, got that. Was there anything else?" Moore asked.

Jay hesitated. "Well, maybe, but I don't know if it'll be any help. The hat still had a tag in it, tucked in under the lining. The print was really badly faded on it, but we put it under a camera and used the computers to enhance it. This hat was made by Johnson Millinery out of Bloomington, and there was a style number. The company went out of business fifteen years ago, but I punched it into the internet and found out that this type of hat was actually made for a specific customer, a direct sales company that sent workers door-to-door selling cosmetics. The name of the company was Olde Naturelle, but they went out of business just about the same time Johnson did. From what I found out, the only way to get one of these hats new was to sign up to be one of their distributors. The hat and the feather were actually part of their company logo."

Moore frowned and shrugged. "If the company is out of business," he said, "then it probably doesn't help much, and if the person who had it was into selling cosmetics, then a wig might have been just part of her vanity. You know, there are a lot of women who wear wigs just because it's easier to keep them styled."

"Yeah, I know," Jay said. "Anyway, that's what we got. If we come up with anything else, I'll let you know, but I don't know what other tests to run on it."

Moore thanked him and ended the call, shoving the phone back into its holster. "Would have been nice if it was real hair," he said. "At least we might have had some DNA to compare to when we finally come up with a suspect."

One side of Sam's mouth twisted downward. "I don't know," he said. "I'm actually more interested in this direct sales company. If they went out of business around fifteen years ago, there might be some way to find out who around here might have been working for them. I'll have my wife see what she can find out about that and let you know."

Sam looked around for a moment at where deputies were examining the scene. "Can I get someone to board up that window?" he asked. "Probably shouldn't leave it open like that."

Moore looked at the sky and then turned back to Sam. "Doesn't really look like rain," he said. "I'll call Bob Hankey, he's a local handyman. Probably won't get out here until tomorrow morning, but with the reputation this place has for being haunted, nobody's going to climb in the window tonight. Get with me tomorrow afternoon sometime, and I'll have the bill ready for you."

Sam nodded. "Sounds good," he said. "Let me know if anything else comes up."

"Ha!" Moore said. "The way this case is going, you'll be the one to let me know. Keep your head low, Sam Prichard. I don't want to see anything happen to it, or to the rest of you either."

Sam chuckled and closed his door, then started up the Ridgeline and made a U-turn. As he headed off down the street, he saw Moore grinning at him.

Sam watched carefully along the sides of the street until he got back out to the highway, then relaxed a bit. It was always possible the killer would be waiting along the side of the road somewhere, but it's a lot harder to hit someone in a moving vehicle than most people would think. He set the cruise control so he could relax his leg and took out his phone.

"Hey, babe," Indie said when she answered his call. "How's it going?"

Sam glanced down at the torn sleeve and the bandage over his left bicep and mentally cringed. "It's going," he said. "I went out and talked to Gary Burgess—he's the guy Ross used to work for, who told me that the whole town knew we were coming back here. Debbie called her friend Marcy, the one at the diner in Thompsonville, and I guess she was talking about it there all day Friday. That tells me how the killer must have gotten the idea of watching the house. I'm sure she figured I'd want to at least check it out."

"Good point. You know, we should've thought of that."

"Yeah, we should've. Anyway, I stopped by to talk to Marcy to see how many people might have heard her mention me that day, and I guess there were an awful lot of folks. According to her and Detective Moore, letting Marcy know something is like taking out a billboard ad. Whatever Marcy knows, the whole town knows."

Indie chuckled at him. "Sounds like your mother," she said. "I love her, but she couldn't keep a secret to save her life."

Sam grinned. "That's very true. So, after that I went back to Millie's house to see if I might spot someone watching it. I went inside and kind of hit, just so I could see out the main front window, but nobody showed themselves. I was coming out when I lost my balance—stupid hip of mine, you know—and leaned against the chair Ross had sat in when he found his mother dead, and noticed something strange. It's got like some kind of pine oil all over it, like somebody sprayed it down with the stuff a long time ago. It isn't wet, exactly, but it's sort of greasy if you know what I mean."

"Wow, that's weird. What about the other chair, was

it sprayed down as well?"

"Not that I could tell. Anyway, I stood there and thought about that for a few seconds and then went to leave, and that's when somebody fired a shot through the window at me."

"They did what?" Indie shrieked. "Sam, are you all right?"

"I'm fine, I'm fine," he said. "It's sort of nicked me on the side of my left arm, but that was all. I ducked down and waited for another shot to come, but it never did, so I called Moore and he sent a deputy who was close by. I guess the sirens scared off the shooter, but Moore and the sheriff showed up a few minutes later with an ambulance, and the paramedics patched up my arm. Tore hell out of the sleeve on one of my favorite shirts, though."

"Oh, Sam," Indie said. "Shirts can be replaced—you can't. God, I don't know what I'd do if anything actually happened to you."

"Well, don't start planning for it yet," Sam said, forcing humor into his voice. "I'm not ready to let this scumbag take me out. Hey, I got something I want you to look into."

"Nice segue," she said sarcastically. "I know you're just trying to change the subject. Okay, what is it?"

"The lab that was examining that had called while we were there, and there are a couple of interesting things about it. First, the blood on it is pretty old, so it very well could be the hat Ross saw. Second, I don't know if I mentioned it before, but there were a couple of hairs inside it. They turned out to be fake, from a wig of some sort. But third, and this is the one that piqued my interest, they found a tag inside the hat that let them identify the manufacturer. This particular hat was only made for a certain company, one of those door-to-door cosmetic sales outfits. The name of the company was Olde Naturelle, with an e-l-l-e on the end, and they went out of business somewhere around fifteen years ago. Do you think Herman could find any way to identify who their sales agents in this area might have been?"

"Fifteen years? That might be asking a lot of him, but I'll give it a try. Are you on the way back here?"

"I'm headed toward Benton," Sam said, "but I think there's one more stop I want to make before I call it a day. Call me if you find anything, or else I'll see you in an hour or so."

"Okay. Just don't get yourself shot at anymore, okay? I really hate it when you get shot at."

"Yeah, well I'd rather be shot at and missed than shot and hit. Talk to you in a bit, babe. Love you."

"I love you more," Indie said, and then the line went dead.

It took Sam another fourteen minutes to get to the west side of Benton, where the police department was located. He turned left onto South Pope Street and then made a right into the parking lot.

He glanced down at his sleeve again and considered how it looked, then reached into the back seat to grab the light jacket he had tossed there earlier in the afternoon. He slipped it on and then got out of the truck and walked into the police station.

The dispatcher, a young man, was sitting just inside, and Sam asked if the chief might be in.

"Yes, sir," the dispatcher said. "Is he expecting you?"

"It wouldn't surprise me if he is," Sam said. "My name is Sam Prichard."

The young man, who was wearing a name tag that said Jarvis, picked up a phone and pushed the button. "Chief? There's a Sam Prichard here to talk to you." He listened for a second, then hung up and pointed down the hallway. "Third door on the left," he said, and then he seemed to dismiss Sam from his awareness.

Sam went down the hall, leaning on his cane, and tapped on the glass in the door. He heard Weimer call out for him to enter and stepped inside, shutting the door behind him. He sat down in a chair in front of Weimer's desk without being invited.

"Prichard," Weimer said. "To what do I owe the pleasure?" There didn't seem to be any pleasure in his voice.

"I just wanted to share some new information with you," Sam said. "Dr. Havelock, the forensic pathologist, says he is almost certain that Daisy Willis was killed by the same person who killed Millie Cameron eight years ago. With that, and with the backing of the sheriff's office, I'm going to be hiring an attorney to file a motion to vacate Ross's conviction and expunge it from his record."

Weimer sat behind his desk, leaning back in his chair with his hands folded over his stomach, and simply looked at Sam. When he said nothing for almost a minute, Sam started to rise.

"Sit down, sit down," Weimer said. "Listen, I know you think I bungled the case..."

Sam dropped back into his chair and leaned toward the police chief. "No, sir," he said. "I am absolutely certain you bungled the case back then. You didn't care about the truth; all you cared about was an easy solution and a quick conviction. I've known cops like you for years, and all you ever care about is building your own reputation. Well, the fact that you lost the election for sheriff tells me that you haven't fooled everyone around here, but I can't imagine why the city ever agreed to hire you as their chief of police. Weimer, you bullied a man of limited mental capacity into confessing to a crime he did not commit. I don't care how you try to justify it—that is the fact." Sam took a moment to get himself under control, because he could feel the anger rising and trying to leap out of him.

Weimer seized upon the break. "Who the hell do you think you are, Prichard? You come in here and start making noises about how we didn't do our jobs right, and act like you're some kind of hero. Well, I don't care what your pathologist says, I know damn well I arrested the right man for that crime. I..."

"You really are an idiot, aren't you?" Sam asked incredulously. "Weimer, I was shot at forty-five minutes ago by someone who doesn't want me digging into this case. Now, can you imagine anyone other than the actual killer who would really care whether I clear Ross's name or not?"

Weimer glared at him but said nothing.

"So, here's how it's going to go. I'm going to retain an attorney and get this motion filed. What you're going to do is testify during the hearing that you've come to believe that new evidence indicates the wrong man was implicated in this crime. And before you insist that you're not going to do that, let me ask you how you're going to feel when I turn the whole story over to Rob Girardi. Something tells me he'd love to get a story like that about you, but I'm wondering how the people of this town would take knowing their police chief would stoop to such underhanded tactics just to make a name for himself. I'm wondering how long it would be before somebody started asking questions about more recent cases, and if there's one thing I know about cops like you, it's that this sort of thing becomes a pattern. Ross won't be the only one you bullied or coerced into a confession, and if people start asking the right questions, sooner or later the answers are going to come out. I can't help wondering how long you'd keep your job if those questions start being asked. Care to guess?"

Weimer continued to glare but still sat there in stony silence. Sam rose again and walked out of his office, leaving the door open on his way. He was halfway back to the door when he heard Weimer call his name, and forced himself to turn around and go back to the doorway.

"What?"

Weimer looked at him for a moment, but there was something in his gaze that seemed softer. "Pathologist really said he thinks it's the same killer?"

Sam nodded. "He did. He said he would state on record that he is ninety percent certain of it."

Weimer motioned for him to step back inside and shut the door, and Sam complied. He settled back into the same chair and looked at the police chief, who seemed to be wrestling with himself over something.

"You're right," Weimer said at last, his eyes on his desk. "I just wanted a quick and easy solution, and I convinced myself that the son did it. I didn't even bother to look for any other explanation." He raised his eyes to meet Sam's. "But that's not the kind of cop I wanted to be. To be honest, I've always known that case was going to blow up in my face sooner or later, but the truth is that it always made me dig deeper to find out what really happened in cases after that one. I mean, every cop has cases that he's not a hundred percent certain about, and I'll admit I've got a few of those, but I really wanted to be the kind of cop that made a difference."

Sam relaxed his jaw a bit, taking some of the sternness out of his expression. "It's not too late," he said. "Stand up for Ross on this, and let yourself learn from it. If you got other cases you think you should own up about, then do so." He leaned forward, resting his hands on his cane. "You testify for Ross, and I'll forget about that reporter. Deal?"

Weimer gave him a reluctant grin. "Deal," he said. "But you're right, there are a few other cases I need to go back over. Maybe it's not too late to help somebody else get their life back on track. I hope Mr. Cameron can."

Weimer stood and reached out a hand, and Sam got to his feet and shook with him. When he turned and walked out this time, it was with a little less weight on his shoulders.

16

The motel was only a few blocks away, so Sam was back within a matter of minutes. He walked into the room and was immediately attacked by Kenzie, who threw both arms around his neck and kissed him on both cheeks.

"Daddy," she said, "Mommy said you got shot again."

"Not really," Sam said, rolling his eyes at Indie. "I really only got a scratch on my arm. It stings a little bit, but I'm okay."

Sufficiently reassured, the little girl gave him another hug and kiss, then kicked to be put down. Sam tossed her gently onto one of the beds and sat down in the chair at the table beside his wife.

"So," Indie said, but then she looked at him and sort of deflated, shrugging her shoulders. "Look, she overheard me getting frantic and wanted to know why.

We always agreed that we won't lie to her, so I told her the truth. Okay?"

Sam leaned forward and gave her a kiss. "Okay," he said. "Now, what was the 'so' about?"

"It's about Olde Naturelle. The company didn't actually go out of business; it was taken over by one of its creditors because it couldn't pay its debts. The new management changed the name and shut down all the direct sales stuff, but they don't have any of those old records anymore." She frowned and shrugged. "I tried, babe."

Sam frowned. "Thanks, sweetheart," he said. "That hat very likely belonged to one of their agents from around here. If we could have gotten a list of them, we might have found a lead on our killer."

Indie nodded. "I saw a picture of the hat online, and it's actually kinda cute. Not something somebody my age would wear, but I can imagine some of the ladies who used to sell those cosmetics might still like the way it looked. Have you thought about running a picture of it in the newspaper? Maybe somebody around here would remember a woman who continued to wear it after the company went out of business."

Sam's eyes opened wide. "No, but that's an excellent idea," he said. "I just need to run it by Detective Moore first."

He took out his phone and punched Moore's number. The detective answered on the second ring.

"Sam? Everything okay?"

"Yeah, but remember I said I was going to have my wife check on the company that was connected to those hats? Well, she found out they didn't actually go out of business, they just got taken over by somebody else and stopped using salespeople. Unfortunately, they don't have any of the old records from that time, but my wife came up with an idea. What if I were to run something in the newspaper, like an ad, asking people if they know anyone who used to wear one of those hats? It might give us a lead, don't you think?"

Moore seemed to think about it for a moment, then said, "That's actually a pretty sharp idea. And it might be smart to run it that way, rather than putting it in a news story. That way, we might not give away the fact that we have that particular hat."

"All right," Sam said, "then I'm going to do it. I'll let you know if anything comes of it."

He ended the call, looked at the time in the lower right of the computer's screen, then googled the number for the local paper. It came up instantly, and he hit the button to place the call, putting the phone on speaker.

"*Benton Evening News*," the receptionist answered. "How may I direct your call?"

"Display advertising, please," Sam replied.

"One moment." Sam listened to some mild country music for a moment, and then another voice came on the line.

"This is Jennifer Daley in Display," said a young woman. "How can I help you today?"

"Hi, Jennifer," Sam said. "I'm calling about placing an ad in your newspaper. I want to put in a photograph of a hat and see if anyone might remember someone who might have worn it about eight or ten years ago."

"Really? Wow, never had anything like that before. Can I ask why?"

"My name is Sam Prichard, and I'm a private investigator looking into an old murder case. This particular hat was worn by the person we believe is responsible for the murder, as well as the one that happened in Thompsonville over the weekend. I'm hoping that someone might recognize the hat and give us an idea of who it might have belonged to."

"Oh, my gosh," Jennifer said, "that was so awful. I didn't know the lady who died Saturday personally, but my sister did. She lives over there."

"I'm sorry. Were they friends?"

"I don't know if they were really friends, but she said she knew her pretty well." Jennifer was quiet for a moment, then said, "Listen, sir, I think maybe you've got the wrong department. Can you hold for just a moment?"

Sam sighed but agreed. He knew what was coming and had hoped to avoid it, but it was probably too late now.

The music ended again, and a man's voice came on.

"Mr. Prichard? This is Rob Girardi, we met yesterday. Jenny said something about you wanting to run a picture of a hat in the paper?"

"Yes, Rob. There was a hat that was discovered in the home of Millie Cameron, and it seems to be the same one Ross Cameron says he saw someone drop in the woods behind the house the day his mother was killed. There's a pretty good chance that the killer wore that hat and tossed it away because it had Millie's blood on it at the time. The crime lab has examined it and says the bloodstains are definitely old, so I'm trying to think of a way to ask the public if they might remember who the hat may have belonged to back then. I had thought of running it as a display ad with the question, because I'm not ready to release a lot of information about the case just yet."

"Hmm," Girardi said. "Is there something special about this hat? I mean, it's apparently not your average, run-of-the-mill derby hat, right?"

"No, as it happens, this hat was only available to people who worked for a particular company that went out of business sometime back. What we're thinking is that the killer might have worked with that company at one time, and simply continued wearing the hat because she liked it."

"She? You think the killer is a woman?" Girardi didn't miss much, Sam realized.

"It's a definite possibility, yes."

"This hat, I'm guessing this is the new evidence that Johnny was talking about?"

"Yes, but again, I'm trying not to give away too much information at this time. I'd really like to just run this as an ad, like maybe I'm just trying to track down someone I knew a long time ago, that sort of thing."

There was a sucking sound that came through the phone, as if Girardi were sucking on his bottom lip. "I'll tell you what," he said after a moment. "I'll help you set up the ad and we'll run it, but I'm hoping you'll call me first when you're ready to go public with this information. Would that work?"

"You got a deal," Sam said.

"Okay, cool. What do you want the ad to say?"

"Well, I need an email address so I can send you a picture of the hat. Then let's put this with it: Reward for information about a woman in this area who once wore a hat like this one. Call 303-555-7968."

"Oh, no," Girardi said. "If you want to get a response from this, you've got to make it more appealing. How about this? 'Did you wear a hat like this a few years ago? You came to my door and our eyes met, and I have always wished I had gotten your name and gotten to know you. There was some kind of electricity, and I know you felt it, too. If that was you, or if you know who it might have been, please call 303-555-7968. Perhaps it's not too late for us to connect.' There, that'll do it."

Sam's eyebrows were trying to crawl over the top of

his head. "Are you sure about this? That sounds like I'm trying to find a girlfriend."

"Yeah, but it gives a reason for trying to find the woman who used to wear the stupid hat. Other women around here, if they knew someone who wore one like it, they'll call just to try playing Cupid. Trust me, this is how you get to the people around this area."

Sam shook his head, not entirely convinced. "O-kay, if you say so. What's your email address?" Girardi gave it to him and Sam repeated it so that Indie could send him the picture. "Okay, now how much do I owe you?"

"Nada, zip. You already promised me the first call, remember? That's enough. Let me go—if I hustle I can get this in this evening's edition."

The phone went dead, and Sam shook his head once more. "I think I'm going to let you answer my phone tonight," Sam said. "Girardi just made me sound like some kind of Casanova trying to find his lost love. I'm almost afraid of who might call."

Indie smiled sweetly at him. "Don't worry, Sam," she said. "I'll protect you."

Sam called the front desk of the motel and found out that, yes, they did receive copies of the newspaper every day, and that they were usually delivered between six and six thirty. It was just a little after five, though, so there was not much to do but wait.

Unfortunately, Kenzie had been cooped up in a motel room for most of the day and had had her fill of it.

She didn't want to watch TV as much as she just wanted to go run and play, so Sam googled local parks and found that there was one just a few blocks away.

"Sam, let us take her," Grace said. "After what you've been through today, you need to stay here and just rest and recuperate." Both Sam and Indie had to stifle a laugh as Grace's eyebrows bounced up and down pointedly. "I think you two need some alone time, anyway. Kim and I can take Kenzie, and we'll bring back sandwiches or something later."

Sam grinned and started to toss her the keys to the truck, but she waved them away. "Keep those. We need the exercise anyway. We'll see you kids later."

She took hold of Kenzie's hand and started toward the door, and Kim grabbed her purse to follow. A moment later, Sam and Indie were alone. They looked at each other for a few seconds, each of them with a slowly spreading grin, and then Sam got up and put the Do Not Disturb sign on the door before locking the dead bolt.

* * * * *

The park turned out to be farther away than it had appeared on the computer screen. Grace and Kim walked slowly, each of them holding on to one of little Kenzie's hands and delightedly answering her questions about trees and birds and the occasional flower that was still visible this late in the year. Both ladies enjoyed their time with the little girl, and Kenzie adored her grandmothers.

Both ladies, however, wished they had even a fraction of the child's energy. By the time they made it to the park, they were carefully pretending not to be as out of breath as they were and silently vowing to themselves that they would make a point of getting a lot more exercise in the future.

The road that led to the park was long and meandering, winding through trees and man-made hills. They finally arrived at the playground more than thirty minutes after they had left the motel, and happily plopped themselves onto a bench while Kenzie leapt onto a spring-mounted horse and rocked it to the point that both tail and nose occasionally touched the ground.

They weren't in that bad of condition, though, not really. By the time Kenzie was ready to get on the swings, they were rested enough to get up and take turns pushing her. Accompanied by cries of "Higher," and "Look at me, way up here," the two ladies laughed and enjoyed the child's antics.

A number of families were there, and it didn't take long before Kenzie found some playmates. As long as she stayed within eyesight, her grandmothers were content to sit on the bench and let her play.

Ninety minutes later, they were still watching. They had long ago mastered the skill of keeping at least one eye on the little girl while chatting between themselves, and they exercised it that afternoon. They had to lean close to each other, though, because the area was ringing with the sounds of children's laughter and squeaky playground equipment.

"So," Grace said after a lull in the conversation, "we haven't heard much out of Beauregard the last couple of days. Is he saying anything lately?"

"Not a lot," Kim said. While she knew that Grace occasionally thought she was a bit on the loony side, she was comfortable enough with her friend to just speak honestly. "I think he's a little bit worried, though. He's been a lot more quiet than usual. He gets that way sometimes, when he's trying to figure something out and his visions or whatever don't seem to be coming through."

"Well, he's got a pretty impressive track record. I mean, we really did find his descendants, and at least some of them really are in trouble. Any new information on who this woman is that's supposed to be in danger?"

Kim shook her head. "He said yesterday he still couldn't get anything more on that. I just hope that Sam can figure it out before anything bad happens."

"He will," Grace said with conviction. "It's what he does. Sometimes it takes him a little while, but he always gets to the truth before he's done."

"That's true, he always does." She focused both eyes on Kenzie for a moment, but the child was having a blast on the seesaw with another little girl her age. Kim turned back to Grace. "I think—I think maybe I'm beginning to believe that Sam is right."

Grace looked at her and raised one eyebrow. "Right about what?"

Kim gave her a sad smile. "About Beauregard maybe not being a real ghost. About maybe it's really me that gets these flashes of insight, you know?"

Grace focused on her. "And what's bringing this change of opinion about?"

Kim shrugged and looked down at the ground for a moment. "Ever since Beauregard first came into my life, he's always been there. It's not like being with a human friend, because sometimes you're still alone. Your friends go home, or even like you and me, you go in your room and I go in mine. There are sometimes when you're not with another person. With Beauregard, though, I've always been able to feel him with me. To be honest, it was a little embarrassing at first, because he was even there when I was taking a bath or changing clothes, but—well, I got used to it, I guess. I stopped worrying about it. I mean, it's not like having an actual man in the room, right?"

Grace chuckled, despite herself. "I suppose not," she said. "But has something changed lately?"

Kim looked over to check on Kenzie and then turned back to her friend. "Yeah, sort of. Ever since we knew that Sam had actually found Henry Beauregard's descendants, he's been more distant. It's like sometimes he actually goes away, and he's never done that before."

"I see," Grace said. "And have you asked him where he's going at those times?"

Kim sighed and shook her head. "I've tried, but he just ignores the question. To be honest, I haven't felt them at all since about dinnertime yesterday."

"Okay, and what about those flashes of insight? Have you had any?"

Kim bit her bottom lip for a moment, then shrugged. "I think—maybe I did."

Suddenly she had Grace's undivided attention. "Really? Like what?"

"Well," Kim began slowly, "there's this phrase that just keeps running through my mind, and I'm not sure what it means. It goes, 'The killer is not as old as you think, but far more ruthless than you can ever imagine.' Does that make any sense?"

Grace stared at her for a few seconds. "Wait. 'Not as old as you think, but more ruthless than you imagine.' That's what you said, right?"

Kim nodded. "Yeah, that's what keeps going through my mind. I don't know what it means—it doesn't seem like it really means anything."

"Kim, when did this start?"

"Last night," Kim said. "I woke up, it was about midnight, and that phrase just kept running through my mind. It took me a little while to get back to sleep, but it was still there when I got up this morning. I tried to ask Beauregard about it, but there was no sign of him today."

She closed her eyes for a second, then opened them again. "There still isn't. He's just gone."

Grace glanced over at Kenzie to make sure she was safe, then looked at Kim again. "Why haven't you told Sam about this? It's not any weirder than some of the stuff Beauregard has made you tell him."

Kim shrugged again. "I don't know," she said. "It just seems weird to me, saying that I'm thinking of something like this. It's always been Beauregard who came up with all this stuff, not me."

"Except that what you're saying is that you are starting to believe it really was you all along. Kim, some of those strange things Beauregard told you to tell Sam actually ended up saving his life. Remember when you had to tell him to watch out for the man with the red eye? That not only helped save Sam's life, it helped him save a lot of other people's lives."

"I know, I know," Kim said. "And you're right, I should tell him." She sat there and looked at Kenzie for a few more seconds, then turned back to Grace. "Listen, can you watch Kenzie for a few minutes by yourself? I'm going to give Sam a call. I think maybe I should tell him about this right now, don't you?"

Grace nodded. "I think maybe that would be a good idea," she said. She looked around for a moment. "It's awful noisy right here, though. Maybe if you go over behind the little bathroom building, it might be quieter there. I've got Kenzie, don't worry."

Kim gave her a sheepish grin and got up from the bench, walking in the direction Grace had indicated. The bathrooms were housed in a small brick building, and she nodded at a short, stocky woman who was leaning against the building as she walked past the entrance to the ladies' room. The noise level was definitely lower when she stepped behind the little structure, she noticed.

She took out her phone and found Sam's number in her contacts.

* * * * *

It was nearly ten minutes later when Grace realized that Kim had never come back. She looked toward the bathrooms but saw no sign of her friend. A brief moment of worry passed through her mind, but she brushed it off and went back to watching Kenzie running with four other children, apparently playing tag. The sight was delightful, and Grace found herself smiling as she forgot all about Kim.

After five more minutes, however, the worry was back. Grace rose to her feet and took a few steps toward the bathrooms, but her need to keep an eye on Kenzie was too great to let her walk away. She turned back toward the child and started to call her name, but then she saw the parents of two of the other children sitting on another bench nearby.

"Excuse me," she said as she approached them. "That's my granddaughter over there," she said, pointing at Kenzie. "I need to run over to the bathroom for a moment—would you mind just watching her for a few seconds? I'll be right back, I promise."

The young couple smiled at her and agreed, and Grace turned quickly to hurry off toward the bathroom building. She stepped around behind it, where she had seen Kim go to make a phone call, but there was no sign of her. Now starting to be genuinely concerned, she ducked into the ladies' room and called out, but there was no one inside.

She came out and looked frantically around, but there was no sign of her friend anywhere. Grace pulled her phone out of her purse as she walked quickly back toward the playground, and hit the speed dial button that would connect her directly to Sam.

"Hey, Mom," Sam answered, but she cut him off before he could say anything else.

"Sam! It's Kim—she's vanished. Did she call you?"

"Call me? No, my phone hasn't rung until just now. Where did she go?"

Indie, lying beside him on the bed, suddenly raised up on her elbow and stared at Sam. "Kenzie?" she asked, but Sam shook his head.

"Your mother," he said. "Mom says she disappeared." He put the phone on speaker so Indie could hear.

"She walked away to find a quiet spot to call you, Sam," Grace went on. "That was like twenty minutes ago, and I can't find her anywhere. Do you think she might have just started walking back toward the motel without telling me?"

"No, she wouldn't do that," Indie said. "Did you check the bathrooms? Maybe she had to..."

"She's not there. There's only one bathroom close by, and I checked, she's not there. Sam, I'm really worried."

In the motel room, Sam was already getting into his clothes. "Mom, we'll be right there. If she is walking back, we should probably spot her on the way. Just stay put, but close to the road so I can find you."

"All right, Sam. Kenzie and I are at the first playground you come to, you can't miss it. And Sam? Hurry."

"I will," Sam said. He cut off the call and shoved his feet into his shoes while Indie was struggling into her jeans. They were both mostly dressed within a minute and hurried down to the elevator.

They got into the truck and left the parking lot of the motel, then went east for a couple of blocks before turning south. The park was about eight blocks down that street, but it turned into a winding road at that point and weaved around the park itself. The speed limit there was only ten miles per hour, so it was almost four minutes before they spotted Grace and Kenzie standing beside the roadway.

Sam pulled up and came to a stop, and Grace

yanked open the back door. She picked Kenzie up and sat her inside, and the child quickly got into her car seat. Grace climbed in beside her and buckled her up, then put on her own seat belt, chattering the entire time.

"I kept looking, Sam, but there's no sign of her around here. It's like she just vanished into thin air."

"But where could she have gone?" Indie asked. Both she and Sam were frantically searching the area with their eyes, but Kim was nowhere to be found. "Why did she walk away from you?"

"She was telling me that she's starting to think you've been right about Beauregard all along, Sam. She said she hasn't heard from Beauregard since last night, but she woke up in the middle of the night with something going through her mind and it was still doing it this morning. It's the kind of thing Beauregard always says, something crazy that doesn't make any sense but might give you a clue, you know? I told her maybe it was important and she should've told you, so she went to call you and that's when she disappeared."

"But why did she walk away from you?" Indie asked. "That's what I don't understand."

"The noise," Grace said. "It was so loud around the playground that she went over behind the bathroom building so it would be quieter. Oh, dear Lord, I actually suggested that to her. We could barely hear each other while we were sitting on the bench, because of all the kids playing and laughing and the noisy swings and everything, so I told her maybe she could go behind that building so she could hear you better."

"Well, we didn't pass her on the way," Sam said. "This is a one-way street, so if she got confused and headed out the other direction, we'll find her on the way out. Everybody keep looking, okay?"

"I am, I am," Indie said. "Grace? What was it she wanted to tell Sam, do you know?"

"It was about the case, I think. She said she woke up in the middle of the night and this phrase was going through her head, and it was still doing it when she got up this morning. She said it goes, 'the killer is younger than you think but more ruthless than you can imagine.' Does that make any sense to you, Sam?"

"Younger than I think but more ruthless than I can imagine? I don't have a clue; it could mean a dozen things, but I don't know what. Younger than I think? Wait a minute. Those fake hairs in the hat were gray. Maybe it means the killer is posing as..." Sam's face went pale, and he shook his head. "No, that can't be. It wouldn't make any sense..."

It was at that moment that Sam's phone rang, and he snatched it out in the hope that it was Kim calling, but it wasn't. The number on the caller ID was a local one, though, and he answered it quickly.

"Sam Prichard," he said. "Yes, go ahead." He listened for a moment, and then his eyes went wide. When they got back to the main street where the motel was, he turned right instead of left, actually running a red light. He stayed on the phone for more than five minutes, occasionally asking things like, "What? Are you sure?" The more he listened, the more a dark and dangerous expression came across his face. "Thank you very much," he said. "I really appreciate it." He ended the call and dropped the phone back into his pocket, then looked over at his wife while he continued driving east out of town.

"I know who the killer is," he said. "And I know why she took your mother."

17

Indie stared at him, her eyes wide. "Sam? Tell me."

"The lady on the phone saw the ad I put in the paper," he said, "and she was calling to tell me who used to wear that hat around here. It's a woman we've actually met, someone I never would've suspected until now, but after what this lady just told me, it all starts to make sense."

"Oh, for God's sake, Samuel," Grace yelled, "tell us what's going on!"

"Remember Beauregard said he was worried about one of his descendants being in danger, a woman? Well, that was a woman named Betty, from Thompsonville. She just told me that the only person around here who ever wore a hat like that was Marcy Elimon, but it was back before she got married and divorced. Back then, when she was selling cosmetics, her name was Marcy Perkins. She was the daughter of a man named Bill

Perkins, except that he had somehow or other changed his last name years ago. Get this: it was originally Parkinson."

Indie shook her head in confusion. "Wait, Bill Parkinson changed his name to Perkins? That's my maiden name..."

"Yep, and Betty told me that he moved back here to a little town called Ewing in the north part of Franklin County after he got out of prison. Care to guess what he was imprisoned for? Never mind, I'll just tell you. It was for vehicular manslaughter. His wife had lost her mind to dementia a year or two earlier, even though she was really too young for it, and he started drinking a lot. He had a bad wreck and got in trouble over it. His daughter, Kimberly, was taken away by the state and he lost track of her, so when he got out of prison he came back here to Illinois. He'd changed his name back when he and Lynette got married, but Betty said she and a few other people around here knew who he really was. He and Betty are about the same age, and she even dated him in high school way back when."

"But what does all this have to do with my mom?"

"Everything. After Bill returned to this area, he settled in Benton and got married again. I guess he was still into younger women, because his new wife was only in her early twenties. They had a daughter named Marcy, and that's the Marcy we met at Jim's Fresh Stop there in Thompsonville, the one who was so happy to tell me all about Millie and Ross and Debbie."

Her head still shaking, Indie stared at him. "My God, Sam," he said, "that means Bill and Lynette, this Bill and Lynette we're talking about, those are my *grandparents*?"

"They have to be," he said. "Indie, this is way too much to be any kind of coincidence. Beauregard said he was worried about a female descendant being in danger, right? He was talking about your mother, Kim, even if he didn't know it."

"Oh, my God," Indie said again, "oh, my—Sam, you said you know who the killer is. Who?"

"It's Marcy," Sam replied. "Betty said she ran into Bill and Marcy together one time at Walmart, and asked if they'd ever gone to see Millie. She said Bill just looked at the floor, but Marcy flew into a rage and told her that they wanted nothing to do with her because Millie's daughter, Lynette, had ruined her father's life. Take all of that together with the fact that Marcy is probably the only person associated with Millie at all who would ever have worn a hat like that one, and it approaches certainty that she's the one Jason Garrity saw leaving the backyard that day, the one Ross saw throw down the hat and hurry away."

"Okay, I can see that," Indie said, "but why would she want to take Mom?"

"Think about it, babe. Marcy blamed Lynette, your grandmother, for somehow ruining her dad's life. She couldn't get to Lynette, so she attacked the only other person she could reach, Millie. But then, here we come along years later, and we introduced ourselves to her. Remember how she kept looking at your mom? She reacted when I told her your mother's name, and I'd just about bet you Marcy spotted a family resemblance or something. However it came about, she's apparently decided that trying to kill your mother is another shot of revenge against Lynette."

"Oh, God, Sam," Indie said with tears starting to stream down her cheeks. "Sam, what are we going to do? We can't let anything happen to my mom!"

"I don't intend to," Sam replied. He yanked his phone out of his pocket and quickly called Detective Moore. "It's Sam Prichard, and I'm pretty sure I know who the killer is, but I need your help. My mother-in-law has disappeared, and I'm just dead certain she's gonna be the next victim if we don't find her fast."

Moore sputtered. "Wait, what? If you know who it is, tell me."

"Remember we talked about Bill Parkinson and didn't know what happened to him? He's living right here in the area, and Marcy Elimon is his youngest daughter. I'll explain it all to you later, but Marcy killed Millie because she blames Lynette for somehow ruining Bill's life. Now, in an even stranger twist of fate, it turns out my mother-in-law is Bill and Lynette's daughter. If Marcy hated Lynette enough to kill Millie, her mother, imagine what she'll do to Lynette's daughter."

"Holy geez," Moore said. "But that would mean your mother-in-law is Marcy's half sister. Geez, this is like some damn soap opera, but I think you're right. About two years ago, Marcy got stopped in the middle of the night by one of the city officers, I think it was a taillight out or something. Anyway, the officer that stopped her knew her, but he said she was all dressed up like some old bag lady or something." Sam could hear him shouting something off to the side, as if he had put his hand over the mouthpiece. A second later he came back. "Marcy's car is a white Chevy Malibu, about five years old. That's just about as nondescript a car as you could possibly drive, because there are probably a few hundred of them around here. Remember Rosie saw Crazy Daisy get shoved into a white car? I've got our dispatcher putting in an APB out right now. She's out there somewhere, Sam, and we're going to find her."

"Keep me posted," Sam said. "I'm on the way to Thompsonville now, but I'm just hoping to spot them along the way."

* * * * *

Kim had been just about to place the call when the woman she had nodded to came around the building. She looked up with a smile, but the expression on the woman's face made it fade away quickly. The snub-nosed .38 in her hand sent a shiver of fear down Kim's spine.

"I need you to come with me, dear," she said. Her

voice was high, Kim noticed, and cracked a bit, but Kim wasn't about to criticize. Besides, there was something about those yellowed teeth that was almost more frightening than the gun.

"I—I need to make a phone call," she said, but the phone was suddenly snatched out of her hand. It went into the left pocket of a jacket the woman was wearing while the gun went into the right, and a quick motion of her head told Kim to start walking into the woods.

"There won't be any phone calls, I'm afraid," she said. "Just start walking that way. We're going to my car, and I don't want any trouble out of you."

Kim had never liked confrontation. Her childhood had been full of them, especially after her mother's Alzheimer's began to make its presence known. Her mother would get it in her head to go for a walk, or try to take the car for a drive, but even at ten years old Kim knew that she couldn't leave her mother unsupervised. There were many arguments, many confrontations, and she had grown weary of them by the time her father was taken away to jail and her mother had to go into a nursing home.

Then there were the foster homes. She learned quickly not to argue about anything, because all it would do was get her a beating, or something even worse. By the time became a teenager, she had reached the point of just going along with what anyone wanted. It kept her from the beatings, but it also led her to getting pregnant just after her sixteenth birthday. Suddenly she had to grow up, and she had never learned to properly deal with confrontation.

Confrontation on its own was bad enough, but a confrontation with someone holding a gun could be suicidal. Kim turned and started walking in the direction she was told to go. The terror-driven adrenaline that was racing through her made her walk quickly, but despite looking old and somewhat decrepit, the woman behind her was having no trouble keeping up.

There was a path in the woods, and Kim followed it instinctively. It came out a few minutes later onto the roadway that wound through the park, and the woman came up beside her and pointed at a white sedan. "That's my car," she said. She opened the passenger door and held it while Kim got in, then shut it. Keeping her eyes on Kim through the windshield, she walked around the front and got behind the wheel.

"Where are we going?" Kim asked, but the other woman simply barked at her to shut up. Kim huddled into herself and leaned against the car door as the woman started the car and put it in gear.

"If you're thinking about trying to jump out," she said to Kim, "don't. I prefer not to shoot you, especially in the middle of this park, but I will if I have to."

Kim only nodded. She didn't trust herself to say anything at that point. She looked out the window at the trees going past and suddenly realized that she was looking at the playground where Grace was still watching Kenzie running and playing tag with other children. She tried mightily to send a telepathic message to her friend to look toward the car, but Grace kept her eyes on her granddaughter and never noticed Kim riding past.

Within a couple of minutes, they were moving through the backstreets of the town and then turned onto one of the main streets. Kim watched through the window as buildings rolled past, and then they emerged onto the square. They headed east, and she began to suspect that her life was coming to its end.

"Would you at least tell me why?" Kim asked. "I'd really like to know, before you kill me."

The driver glanced over at her but said nothing. A second later she returned her attention to the road.

Kim waited a minute or so, then turned in her seat so that she was facing the woman who had abducted her. There was something familiar about her, but Kim couldn't quite put her finger on it. "I don't know who you are," she said, "but I know you're not who you pretend to be. You want people to look at you and see this old woman, but you're really much younger, aren't you?"

"You think you're so smart? You figure out why, then."

Kim stared at her for another moment, but then a familiar sensation began somewhere in the back of her skull. Something stirred back there, and she felt a sense of relief that now, in the final moments of her life, Beauregard was going to be back at her side. At least he'd be there to comfort her in her final moments, and she felt a sense of gratitude even as she waited for darkness to come.

It didn't come, though. Instead, a sense of peace came over her, just the way it always did when Beauregard began to speak.

I'm here, she heard in her mind. *I'm with you, and I'm going to help you. Kimberly, it's time for us to do what must be done. It's time for you to remember the things you chose not to remember.*

What things? she asked. *Beauregard, what am I supposed remember?*

I have found what I was seeking, Kimberly. Just open your mind and think back to when you were a little girl. Think about the stories your mother used to tell you at bedtime. Let yourself remember, and it will all become clear.

Bedtime stories? I remember Mother telling me stories, yes, but that was a long time ago. I'm sure they were the usual ones, like Cinderella *and* Sleeping Beauty *and the all those old stories. Weren't they?*

Remember, Kimberly. You must let yourself remember; you must not hide from it any longer. Just remember.

Marcy turned to look at her for a second, then looked back at the road ahead. "You think staring at me is going to make me nervous or something? Just turn around and look out the window again."

"I remember," Kim said. "Oh, my God, I remember."

"What are you, crazy? What the hell are you talking about?"

"It was so long ago," Kim said. "I was maybe four or five, I guess, and my mother used to tell me stories. They were all about our family, stories that were passed down from generation to generation, and she said it was important for me to know them."

The woman behind the wheel was bouncing her attention between the road and her passenger, and her eyes were quite wide. "What? Oh, my God, you're some kind of loony."

"Oh, I don't think so. I just haven't thought about these things in so many years, I had them buried so deeply. Have you ever buried something so deeply that you couldn't even remember it?"

"Oh, good Lord," Marcy said. "I always figured you must have been a weakling, but I never would've guessed you were just plain crazy."

Kim smiled at her, a sense of calm settling into place. "I don't think I'm weak," she said. "My life has dealt me some pretty bad cards, but I've always done whatever I had to do to survive. That isn't weakness; I think it's exactly the opposite. I think it's a kind of strength."

"Oh, God, knock it off! You think you got it all

figured out, don't you? You want to know why I'm going to kill you? It's because it was all your mother's fault!"

Kim cocked her head to one side, staring at the strange woman who was driving. "My mother? What was my mother's fault?"

Marcy looked over at her captive for a second, then cut her eyes back to the road. "My dad," she said, her words dripping with rage. "No, *our* dad. Your mother couldn't keep her own mind together, and it just about destroyed him. Even now, after all these years she's been gone, he still talks about her when he drinks, and he's always drinking. Mom got him dried out a dozen times, but he always goes back to it because he says it's the only way he can cope with knowing *your* mother is gone. I was only thirteen when Mom decided she'd had enough and walked out on us."

Kim stared at her, confused, but then something about the woman's eyes sent a shock of recognition through her. "Oh, my gosh," she said softly. "You're the lady from the diner. Marcy, that's your name, right?"

"Oh, you decide to start catching on?" Marcy asked her, snapping her attention back to the road ahead. "Don't you have any idea who I am?"

Kim shrugged and shook her head. "I remember your name, because we just met the other day. Other than that, how am I supposed to know anything about you?"

Marcy suddenly reached across and slapped her

across the face with the back of her hand. "I'm your freaking *sister*," she yelled. "Can't you see the resemblance? We both have our father's eyes, but you've got more of his chin than I do, and I've got more of his nose than you."

Kim was holding a hand to her stricken face, her mouth open and her eyes wide. "My sister? But I don't have any sisters."

Marcy shook her head, a derisive laugh coming from her. "That you knew of," she said. "We share the same father. Bill Perkins? Do you remember him at all?"

Kim was openly staring, now. Her hand was still on her cheek, but she had managed to close her mouth. "Of course I remember my father," she said. "But I haven't seen him in many, many years. The last time I saw him was the day the judge sent him to prison, but then they took me away and I was never able to find him after that. If you're my sister, then tell me, where has he been all this time?"

Marcy sneered at her. "He's been trying to drink himself to death, mooning over that crazy woman that gave birth to you. You know, the one who ended up in the loony bin? Your mother, who forgot who you even were?"

Kim lowered her hand and folded both of them together in her lap. "That wasn't her fault," she said. "It was Alzheimer's disease. They don't know why, but some people can develop it when they're still very young.

My mother just happened to be one of those unlucky souls."

"Unlucky? You're saying she was unlucky? My father was the unlucky one, because he loved her and all she did was destroy him. Back when I was a kid, I used to feel sorry for her when Daddy would talk about what happened, but the more I grew up, the more I came to hate her." She spun her head to face Kim. "And I hate *you*," she suddenly screamed. "You want to know what I grew up with? I grew up with a father who could hardly even stand to let me sit on his lap because it made him remember the daughter he couldn't find. Every time he started thinking about you, then he started thinking about her, and that would start another bout of drinking. He'd drink and drink until he either puked or passed out, and guess who had to clean up after him when that happened. Guess who had to help get him into bed, help take his clothes off. Me, that's who. Where the hell were you? You should've been there to help take care of him —it was all your mother's fault, anyway."

Kim looked at her, and there was pity in her face. "Oh, Marcy, I'm so sorry. I loved my father, I truly did. When Mom started getting bad, I felt like my whole world had come to an end, but I didn't even understand what that concept really meant. I didn't find that out until they took my daddy away from me, too." She took a deep breath. "But Marcy, Daddy's drinking wasn't my mother's fault. It was his. He was the one who decided to hide from all the pain in a bottle, not my mother.

What happened to her was beyond her control; she had no choice in it at all. But Daddy? Daddy chose to drink, and all of that has to be on him."

"*Shut up!*" Marcy screamed. "Don't you dare try to put this on him. *She's* the one who went crazy, she's the one who had to be put into a nuthouse. He didn't know how to cope with it—that's why he started drinking—but then everything went to hell. He got sent to prison, and you ran out on him, too. And me, I came along after he got out and had to be the one he couldn't hold, the one he couldn't love the way he loved you. God, how I hate you!"

"So that's why you're going to kill me?" Kim asked. "Because our father made you jealous? How many people have you killed, Marcy, trying to punish the world for the pain you felt growing up?"

What am I doing? Kim suddenly asked herself. *Am I trying to force her to shoot me? This is insane—I shouldn't be trying to argue with her.*

Just be calm, Kimberly, Beauregard's voice said in her mind. *Sam is coming, but we must delay her until he can arrive.*

Marcy clamped her jaw shut and gripped the wheel, then pressed her foot down on the accelerator. The car shot forward.

"It doesn't matter," Marcy said suddenly. "The only ones that matter are you and your grandmother. She gave birth to your mother, and your mother gave birth to you. You were the reasons Daddy couldn't go on with his life; you were the reasons he couldn't love me the way he should have. Well, I took care of your grandmother, and now I'm going to take care of you."

A four-way stop loomed ahead, and Marcy used the brakes to slow, but not to stop. The car roared around the corner. This was the Akin-Thompsonville Road, a strip of blacktop that Marcy knew well. The woods along both sides were so dense in spots that even hunters rarely bothered to go into them.

Any one of them would be a perfect place to leave a body, but Marcy knew one that was even better. It was just a matter of getting to it without being seen, but she knew exactly how to accomplish that, as well.

* * * * *

"Damn," Sam said, "where the hell is Beauregard when I really need him?"

The Ridgeline was doing close to a hundred miles an hour, but Sam knew that Marcy had at least a thirty-minute head start on him. He was racking his brain, trying to figure out just where she would take Kim to finish what she had started, but the only thing he could think of was the spot where Daisy had been found. He remembered how to get there and was pushing the truck for all it was worth.

A sign loomed on the side of the road, announcing that Thompsonville was only two miles farther ahead. He backed off the accelerator and let the truck begin to slow, but he was still doing nearly seventy as he rolled into town. His eyes were scanning for the turn that would take him north, back toward the wooded pond where Daisy had died.

"Sam!" Indie screamed suddenly. "Sam, watch out!"

Someone had stepped into the road ahead of him, and Sam stood on the brakes as he prayed that he could avoid hitting the person. The antilock brakes did their job, and he brought it to a stop mere inches from the old man who had been trying to cross the highway. They were just in front of the trailer park where Daisy had lived.

The old fellow didn't even seem to notice and continued plodding along. Sam was just about to cut around behind him when a voice called out, "Mr. Prichard?"

Sam looked to the right and saw Jason Garrity standing beside the passenger door. He hit the button to power down the window and looked at the young man. "Jason," he said quickly, "Marcy Elimon is the killer. Bill Parkinson is her father, but he changed his name years ago, and now he's a drunk. Marcy killed Millie because she blames Lynette for her father's condition, but we just found out that my mother-in-law is Bill and Lynette's daughter. Marcy has her and is taking her somewhere to kill her."

The boy gripped the window, looking past Indie into Sam's frantic face. "Marcy? Good Lord, I never even thought about her. Are you sure?"

"I'm sure," Sam said, "but I don't have time to explain. Think fast—where do you think she'd take Lynette's daughter to kill her?"

Jason was staring at him, but Sam could see the wheels spinning inside the boy's head. "I don't—wait a minute, she's Lynette's daughter? Then that means Marcy would be her sister, right? And if she hates Lynette so much she's trying to kill off that whole side of the family, then there's only one place I can think of."

Sam's eyes shot wide. "Of course," he said. "Millie's place!" He started to take his foot off the brake, but Jason reached into the truck, holding up a hand to tell him to wait.

"Hold on," the young man said. "I can help..."

18

Marcy kept her foot on the accelerator until they got within a mile of Thompsonville, then pumped the brakes to slow down. She had to come to a stop when they got to the main highway, but then it was just a matter of driving slowly through the backstreets of the little town, cutting from one to another until she came to its southwest edge. South Street met Highway 149 there, but she was lucky. There was no traffic around, so a quick right and an almost immediate left took her through the empty back parking lot of the Church of God. From there, it was a simple matter to hide the car in the trees.

No one had seen them, she knew. She lifted the pistol that had been lying in her lap and pointed it at Kim.

"Get out of the car," she said, "but don't be stupid enough to try to run. Believe me, I won't hesitate to just blow your head off."

She got out of the driver's side and kept the pistol pointed at Kim as she also stepped out. Marcy raised the gun and held it over the top of the car as she walked around, then grabbed Kim by the back of the neck. "Start walking," she said and guided her by the tight grip.

"You know, I hadn't actually planned to kill your grandmother that day, but things don't always go the way you plan. All I really wanted to do was track you down, and I'd actually spent months trying to figure out how to get the old biz to help me find you. I asked her a few times, when me and Debbie were hanging out together, but the old battleax never answered. She'd just sniff and look away, like I wasn't good enough to know the answers."

"Maybe she didn't know," Kim said. "My mother wouldn't ever have anything to do with her family. She may not have even known I existed."

"Of course she did," Marcy said. "She shipped her own daughter off for getting knocked up. She had to have known you were born, right? But then that Garrity kid gave me an idea. See, I went to the high school play with Debbie and her husband that year, and it was all the rage how Jason Garrity managed to transform himself completely into an old woman with some padding, a little makeup, and a wig. Up until the third act of the play, nobody even realized he was playing both parts—the guy called James and this old woman named Miss

Lydia—but then he actually sat right there on the stage and put on the makeup and wig and dress, and that's when I figured it out."

Kim turned her head slightly to look over her shoulder. "Figured what out?"

"Well, hell, if a teenage boy could do it, then so could I. I went out and bought a gray wig, a pair of those costume eyeglasses with just plain old glass in them, some oversized clothes that I added padding to, and an oversized bra I could stuff with toilet paper, and then I watched some videos about how to use theatrical makeup online." She chuckled. "It took me a few weeks to get it down right, but one day I looked into the mirror and knew that nobody would recognize me. Especially not that old bag—she could barely even see."

Kim almost stumbled as some vines tried to catch at her ankles. "But what was the point? Why even bother?"

"Why bother? Do you have any idea how long I dreamed of tracking you down, of making you feel just as miserable as I did? I used to daydream about it, back in school. Sometimes I'd get so into those daydreams that it was like they came to life. I'd tell you just how much misery you caused me, and in my fantasies you would break down and cry and beg me to forgive you, but I never would."

"I guess I can understand that," Kim said. "But it's a long way from daydreaming about yelling at someone and then committing murder."

"I told you, I didn't mean to kill her at first. If you want to know the truth, the only one I really ever thought about killing before that was you. All those fantasies? Just making you miserable wasn't enough, not after a while. I started fantasizing about beating you, using a horse whip on you or something, and then one day the fantasy just sort of took on a life of its own. It was so real —I couldn't believe how real it was—but it was like I suddenly got my hands on you and I just wouldn't stop hitting you." She laughed, an evil laugh that echoed slightly off the trees around them. "I could even see all the blood, because I fantasized about picking up a stick and just beating you in the head with it."

Millie's old house was the last one on the left, just before the little curve to the left that brought the road to an end. It was a good four hundred yards through the woods, and they had to duck around clearings to stay in the deep cover, but Marcy's luck held. The few people who lived on Fifth Street were paying no attention to the woods behind their homes, so it was only about twenty minutes of stumbling through the tangled brush before they came to the backyard of the house where Marcy had finally, truly become a killer.

"And then one day I got all dressed up in my costume and went to see her. I remember I was wearing a yellow blouse with red piping and a pair of brown slacks that went well with it, and I stood in front of the mirror and put on the wig, but it just didn't seem right. I don't know why, it just didn't look right, and then I spotted that hat I used to wear when I was selling makeup a few years before. I picked it up and put it on, and it just looked perfect. I looked for all the world like just another little old lady."

They were standing just inside the trees at the back of the yard where Millie had died. Looking at the house, Marcy suddenly found herself transported back eight years, to the moment when she had first stood in that exact spot. She had cut through the trees because she didn't want neighbors seeing her, just in case one of them might have better eyesight than Millie and realized who she was. She didn't want them ever telling the old woman that it was her, so cutting through the woods had avoided that problem. Then all she had to do was slip across the backyard and walk around to the front door to knock.

Millie had answered it herself. "Yes? What do you want?"

"Mrs. Cameron?" Marcy had asked in the high, elderly sounding voice she had practiced. "I'm Ethel Summers, from Social Services. Could I speak with you for a few minutes?"

"Social Services?" Millie had echoed as she opened the door wider to allow her visitor inside. "What do you want with me? I don't get no state check or anything."

Marcy stepped inside and closed the door behind herself, while Millie sat down in her usual chair. She took the one beside it and set her bulky purse on her knees. There was actually nothing in it, but it was part of the costume. "I know that, ma'am," Marcy said. "I actually have some questions about your granddaughter, Kimberly. It turns out that because of your husband's death, she may be entitled to certain benefits. I simply need to know how to find her."

"Granddaughter? I don't know what the hell you're talking about," Millie had said. "I ain't got no granddaughter named Kimberly. All I got is Mindy and Kaylee and a couple grandsons. Don't know where you got your information, but it's wrong."

Marcy cocked her head and looked at the old woman. Was it possible she actually didn't know?

"But, Mrs. Cameron, you had a daughter named Lynette, right? Well, she gave birth to a girl back in the seventies, and her name was Kimberly. Are you sure you don't have any idea where she might be?"

Millie's eyes were wide. "Was that her name?" she asked softly. "I never knew. Bill used to come over here all the time and ask if we heard anything, but we never did. I finally told him where we sent her, and he was supposed to let me know about the baby, but he never did."

Cheated! Marcy had thought to herself at that moment. *I've been cheated out of getting my hands on that brat. This old bat didn't even know Kimberly existed.*

The thought of never being able to take her revenge

on Lynette's daughter caused the sudden rage that seemed to burst through Marcy's mind. For years, ever since she had been old enough to understand that the Kimberly her father spoke of was another daughter from years before, she had been jealous and daydreamed of somehow making the girl pay for her father's pain and suffering, but that jealousy had evolved over time to an all-consuming desire to make her suffer.

But on that day, when the anger suddenly built up inside her, a daydream simply wasn't going to be enough. Millie wasn't going to tell her where to find her malevolent half sister, and so it was Millie who became the object of the rage that suddenly was flaring inside her. Marcy sat there and simply stared at the old woman for a moment, and then the rage boiled over.

There was a small table between the two chairs, and Marcy's gaze was suddenly drawn to an object sitting on it. It was a metal rod with a rounded knob on one end, about ten inches long, and Marcy realized that it was some sort of car part, but she didn't know what kind. All she knew was that it would be heavy, but that was enough. Without even thinking about what she was doing, she reached out and grabbed it, and then rose to her feet.

Millie looked up at her, her eyes wide in surprise. Ethel had looked like an old woman, but she jumped up out of that chair so fast that Millie was shocked. The look on Ethel's face was also shocking, as Millie realized that, for whatever reason, this woman was enraged.

And then Millie looked at the object in Ethel's hand. It was something Ross had brought home from work, some car part that he had taken a fancy to that was going to be tossed into the scrap pile. He had cleaned it up and brought it home, and would occasionally hold it and feel the smoothness of the ball-like knob on its end. The finely machined piece of metal fascinated him, and Millie had smiled many times as she watched him hold it close to his face and stare at it.

But now Ethel had it, and she was raising it up high, and in that moment Millie knew without any doubt that she was about to die. Her final thought was that she was glad Ross was not home, so that he would not also be injured, and then the big metal ball struck her in the temple.

Marcy had raised and dropped that bar with its ball on the end more times than she could count, and finally it was the exhaustion in her arm that made her stop. That was when she suddenly realized what she had done, and the thing that surprised her the most was that she felt not the slightest bit of remorse. Millie was dead, and Marcy was actually glad.

Of course, Millie was also Debbie's mother, and Debbie was her friend. Without giving it any thought, Marcy shoved the bloody metal bar into the pocket of the pants she was wearing and started toward the front door. She was reaching for the doorknob, but when she saw the blood on her hand and sleeve, she took a good look at the rest of her body. Blood had splattered everywhere, and she could suddenly feel it on her face, as well. She thought for a split second about trying to clean herself up in the bathroom, but a part of her mind told her to just get out, get away.

She turned away from the front door and went to the kitchen. That was where the back door was, she knew, and she found a piece of paper that she used to grab the doorknob. It wasn't locked and swung open easily, and then she was out the door and moving as quickly as she dared across the backyard. She needed to get away, to get as far away as possible at that moment. She entered the woods behind the house and began moving even more quickly, and then she felt the wig begin to slip. She reached up to hold it in place and accidentally knocked the hat off her head.

She didn't realize it at first, and when she did it was too late to go back for it. She had to keep moving, had to get away. She needed to get somewhere to clean up and make sure she had an alibi.

And yet...

And yet there was a part of her that was feeling such an intense thrill that it was almost terrifying. She had *killed* that old woman, she had *taken a life*, and there was something about it that filled her with a sense of power and energy, with a sense of being alive so intense that she couldn't imagine anything else ever feeling so good. Even her limited repertoire of orgasms paled in comparison.

She made it to where she had left her car, down by the church parking lot, and started to get in. She froze, as her eyes rested on an incinerator behind the church. It was where they burned their trash, and it was burning at the time. Someone must have come by while she was at Millie's and taken out the trash, then lit the fire.

There were no cars in the parking lot, so whoever had done it was gone. Marcy hurried over to the incinerator, opened the door on the side, and snatched the wig off her head, tossing it into the flames. She pulled the blouse off and wiped her face as clean as she could, then did the same with it. The overstuffed bra followed, and then she took off the slacks. The metal rod caught her attention, and something about it made her want to keep it, maybe like a souvenir. She wiped it off on the slacks before tossing them into the fire with everything else.

Underneath the costume clothing, she had been wearing a simple tank top and a pair of shorts, so she was still decent as she hurried back to her car. She got in and drove away, and it wasn't until two days later that she realized she had left that handbag on the living room floor in Millie's house.

She didn't worry much about that, though. There was nothing in it but paper, crumpled up paper that made it appear to be full and heavy. And those bungling deputies had already arrested Ross for the killing, so there was probably no chance in the world that anyone would ever connect that purse to her.

"Let's go." Marcy shook off the reverie and pushed Kim into the backyard of the house. Kim was walking as slowly as she could, dragging her feet and trying to delay the inevitable, but she knew it was coming. Marcy dug into a pocket and produced a set of keys, duplicates to the ones Crazy Daisy had given to Sam only a few days earlier. Debbie had given them to her after old Marie had passed away.

No one had known that Marie had given Daisy the spare set. If only the old witch had kept her nose out of things, it might not have been necessary for her to die.

When Debbie had called and told Marcy that Sam was coming back, she knew she needed to keep an eye on the situation. After she had googled Sam Prichard and learned who he was, she began to worry that he just might be capable of figuring out the truth. She had spread the word about his return on Friday morning, but Friday afternoon she had complained of stomach cramps and taken the rest of the day off. She called in sick on Saturday, as well, because she couldn't watch Millie's house from the woods if she was slaving away in the kitchen.

That's how she had seen Daisy talking to Sam, and the stress began to build. That afternoon, wearing Ms. Ethel, she had smeared mud on her license plates to prevent anyone getting the number and gone after Daisy. The crazy old woman had told her everything that had happened, including about how she had found that stupid hat a few weeks after the murder and hidden it inside the house. She somehow knew, she had said, that the hat was important, that it had belonged to the killer, and she even cackled a bit as she bragged about how she had rigged up the cabinet. Sooner or later, she knew, somebody would go into that house. She had watched it like a hawk, waiting for an opportunity to expose the hat without exposing herself.

Marcy questioned her until she got it all, and then she reached into her pocket and pulled out that same metal rod. Her anger at Daisy for helping the private eye was extreme, and she used all of it in beating Crazy Daisy to death.

That rod was her favorite method of killing, and it always gave her that thrill. As dangerous as it might have been to keep it, she had never been able to bring herself to get rid of it. Despite the small number of cases Indie had discovered, Marcy had used that rod over the years to claim more than two dozen victims. Many of them had just never been found, or weren't important enough to make the news.

She unlocked the door with one hand while holding the gun on Kim with the other. "Inside," she ordered, and Kim stepped over the threshold.

I am still with you, she heard Beauregard say in her mind. *I am here to help, but I shall need you with me.*

Kim nodded slightly, knowing that Beauregard would understand. She was willing to do whatever was necessary, but it was going to be up to him to decide what that might be.

They went through the kitchen into the living room, and Kim saw the gaping hole where the front window had been. She turned and looked at Marcy, and her own eyes were wide. "This is where you tried to kill Sam," she said, "isn't it?"

"Damn near did, too," Marcy said. "I had a perfect bead on him, but he moved at the last second. If he had just stood up, I could've finished the job."

Ask her why she tried to shoot him, rather than bludgeon him, Beauregard said.

"I thought you liked to beat people to death," Kim said. "Why cheat and use a gun on Sam?"

Marcy sneered. "Yeah, well, he looked like he might be big enough to give me a problem with that. You want to know something cute? The gun I used was our daddy's gun. I took it away from him a couple years ago, when he was threatening to kill himself, and I've had it in the trunk of my car all this time. Never even thought about it until I needed to try to get rid of your son-in-law."

Kim shook her head. "I feel so sorry for you," she said. "You must be so terribly miserable."

Tell her about me, Beauregard said.

Kim looked surprised, but she was smart enough to do as Beauregard told her. "I'm not alone, you know," she said.

"Not alone?" Marcy asked. "What is that supposed

to mean?"

"It's true," Kim said. "His name is Beauregard, and he is a ghost. He has been my constant companion for well over twenty years, now. He was a Confederate soldier during the Civil War, and after he died his spirit seemed to be unable to move on. He waited for many, many years before he found me, the only person he knows who can hear him, and he has been with me ever since. He's with me right now."

Something about the conviction in Kim's words made Marcy nervous, and she found herself looking around. She cursed herself for a fool and turned her eyes back to Kim. "Yeah, right," she said. "You don't have any ghost with you."

"Oh, but I do," Kim said, allowing a small smile onto her face. "He just told me to tell you that he knows about the little boy. He knows about the little boy that you killed, because you wanted to see if killing a child would give you a bigger thrill." She cocked her head slightly to the right and looked into Marcy's eyes. "Did it?"

Marcy's eyes were suddenly wide. Nobody knew about that, nobody. It had been about five years ago, when the bloodlust was building up in her. She had learned with Millie that killing someone gave you a fantastic sense of power, that it was actually even erotic in some ways, and every victim after that had given her another burst of that incredible, powerful energy. She craved it, had to have it, and then one day she had been driving through the back roads down around Creal Springs.

The ten-year-old boy who was walking along the road in the middle of nowhere had suddenly struck her as potentially giving her more of that power than anyone else ever had. She stopped the car just ahead of him and got out, and stood there smiling, the metal rod hidden behind her back, as she waited for him to catch up. When he walked up to her, smiling and friendly, she had grabbed him and dragged him into the brush nearby. She held her hand over his mouth, just in case anyone might be within earshot, but he never made a sound before the first blow silenced him forever.

"I never killed any little boy," Marcy said, but the tremor in her voice made it sound like the lie that it was.

"Yes, you did," Kim said. "Beauregard told me about it. You see, he has this ability to see things. Sometimes they don't make a lot of sense until we really look closely, but in all the years I've known him, he's never been wrong. Not even once."

"Shut up," Marcy said suddenly. "You're just crazy, that's all. I told you I never did that, so just shut up about it."

Sam is coming, Beauregard said in her mind. *He's getting close.*

Marcy reached out and grabbed Kim by her arm and pushed her toward the chair where Millie had died. "Sit down," she commanded, but Kim only looked at the chair for a moment and then turned back to face Marcy.

The woman was holding a steel rod with a round ball on its end. Kim glanced at it, then raised her eyes back to meet Marcy's own.

"Is that what you have in mind?" Kim asked her. "You want to kill me in the same place where you killed my grandmother?"

"That's kind of fitting, isn't it? I think so. Maybe your ghost friend can go on ahead and tell her you're coming. Maybe she will be waiting for you."

Refuse, Beauregard said. *Do not cooperate. She has killed many people, but almost all of them have done what she said because they feared her. Do not be afraid, Kimberly.*

"I'm not afraid," Kim said aloud. The instant look of surprise that crossed Marcy's face only reinforced her courage. "I'm not afraid of you, Marcy. And I'm not going to sit down in that chair."

The expression of surprise turned to one of disbelief. How dare this evil half sister of hers show courage at this moment? How dare she? Marcy stood there, staring at her, and for the very first time since she had murdered Millie, she couldn't quite figure out what to do.

The sound of screeching tires invaded the moment, as Sam's truck came flying around the corner from Division Street, a few hundred feet south. Seconds later, it slid to a stop in front of the house.

Marcy reached out and grabbed Kim's arm once again, yanking hard to drag her between herself and the open window. Sam was getting out of the truck, and he had a pistol in his hand. Marcy wrapped her left arm, with the rod in its hand, around Kim's throat and pressed her own pistol against the side of her head.

"Marcy!" Sam yelled. "I know you're in there, and I know you have Kim. The police are on the way, and you can't escape. Let her go, and this can end without anyone else getting hurt."

Marcy dragged Kim slightly to the left so that she could see clearly through the shattered window, then pointed the pistol at Sam and pulled the trigger. The explosion was so loud that Kim reeled for a second, but Marcy held her upright.

Snub-nosed pistols, especially those with very short barrels, can still hit the bull's-eye at two hundred yards if the shooter holding it truly knows what he or she is doing. The problem is that the lighter a gun is relative to the ammunition it uses, the more it will amplify any error in stance or aim. Like many women from the country, Marcy was incredibly accurate with a rifle, but she had never done a lot of shooting with a pistol. This one had actually come from one of her victims, an old man in New Harmony, Indiana. It had been in his pocket when Marcy decided, on the spur of the moment, that she wanted to kill him, and he actually tried to pull it out when he realized that she was raising a weapon. He was a bit too slow, but Marcy had decided to take it with her when she was finished.

Unfortunately, she had never fired it before. The bullet passed wide to Sam's right and punched a hole in his left front fender, but it still had the desired effect. Sam ran around the truck as quickly as he could and crouched down behind it, his Glock leveled across the hood.

"Marcy, there is no hope," he shouted. "You can't get away. I see you in there, so I know you can hear me. Let Kim come out, and let's end this peacefully."

Inside the house, Marcy was trembling with rage. It was all going to hell; it was all falling apart. With Prichard sitting outside, and there was no doubt he was telling the truth when he said the police were coming, all of her plans and dreams of revenge against Lynette's daughter were being wrenched away from her.

"I'm going to end it," Marcy screamed out at him. "This bitch has caused me all the pain and suffering she's ever going to. I can't let her get away now!"

Sam saw motion, but the lowering sun was casting its light onto the back of the house, now, rather than the front. He couldn't quite make out what Marcy was doing, but there was a sense of dread inside him. He had listened to what Jason had to say, then told Indie and his mother to take Kenzie and get out of the truck. They were waiting out by the highway, waiting to see if Sam could bring Kim out alive and unhurt.

The thought of failing to do so was simply

unbearable to him.

"Marcy, wait," he called out. He took the chance that she was watching him and laid his pistol on the hood of the truck, then raised his hands into the air and stepped out from behind it. "Let me come in and talk to you. Maybe we can work this out; maybe there's a way you can actually come out of this."

Another shot rang out from inside the house, and the windshield of the truck disintegrated. Sam fought the instinct to duck, standing his ground. He knew that Kim probably had only seconds to live, but he was praying for a miracle.

19

Marcy pulled Kim back toward the kitchen door, desperately trying to think of something, trying to find some way to get out of this without losing everything. She backed through the doorway and shook her head, tears starting to run down her face as she realized that no matter what happened, her own life was basically over. Once she was arrested, she knew it would be only a matter of time before they came up with enough evidence to convict her, and then someone would realize that at least a few of those other victims had to have been hers, as well.

She'd never see her father again, never be back in the diner, never feel that fantastic, wonderful thrill that came from bashing someone's brain into jelly again. A sob escaped her, but at least she could finish getting her revenge. She pulled the pistol back and cocked it, then stepped back away from Kim and pointed it at her.

"Turn around," she commanded, and Kim turned slowly. She looked past the gaping maw of the gun and focused on Marcy's eyes.

"I forgive you," Kim said.

Marcy's eyes went wide as she stared at her half sister, but then she shook her head. "Well, I don't forgive you," she spat. She adjusted her aim slightly and started to squeeze the trigger, but at that moment a sound in the hallway to her left made her glance in that direction. Her finger instinctively relaxed, and then her eyes went even whiter and her mouth opened as far as it could as she screamed in absolute terror.

She turned her arm and aimed the gun down the hallway, squeezing the trigger over and over. Four shots in rapid succession, all aimed at the apparition that was coming toward her, its arms stretched out and reaching, its face wearing that maniacal grin...

And then the figure rushed forward. It collided with her, slamming her back into the kitchen cabinets behind her as she continued to scream. This horrible, spectral image had come from nowhere, and now it had hold of her and...

"I've got her," yelled a voice that was almost in her ear, and she managed to focus her eyes on another figure, the one behind the one that attacked her. There was a young man there, and he had hold of her as well. The other figure, that horrible grinning one, was trapped between them.

Kim stood in the doorway, her own eyes wide as she stared at the tableau in front of her, but then the front door burst open and Sam rushed in. He had his gun in his hand again, and he pushed past Kim to get into the kitchen, but Jason already had things under control.

Sam held on to her for a moment so Jason could get the manikin out of the way. The terrifying visage that Marcy had seen was Ross's old manikin coming down the hall toward her. Jason had bent its arms so they were reaching forward, and for that brief few seconds she honestly thought that the ghost of Donald Cameron—Millie's husband and Kimberly's grandfather—was coming for her.

Sirens sounded in the distance, but they were coming closer in a hurry. Two minutes later, the first of the deputies' cars arrived, and Detective Johnny Moore showed up before the second one. Sam called out to let them know that everything was under control, and then the house was suddenly full of men and women in uniform. Marcy was taken into custody and stuffed into the back of a squad car, while Moore looked at Sam and Jason Garrity.

"Somebody want to tell me just what the hell happened here?" Moore asked.

"Well, I had thought Marcy might be taking Kim out to where she left Daisy," Sam said, "but just as I got into town, here, some old man was in the road and I had to stop. Jason happened to be right there, and I naturally asked him if he had any idea where Marcy might go, and it hit both of us at the same time. Since Kim is Lynette's daughter, she'd almost certainly want to kill her in Millie's house. I was just going to come racing over here, but Jason came up with an idea."

Moore turned and looked at the young man he'd arrested at least half a dozen times. "What?"

Jason grinned at him. "Back when I was still in high school," he said, "me and a bunch of other boys used to dare each other to sneak into this house. You know how everyone said it was haunted? Well, we used to challenge each other about who could sneak in here at night and manage to stay the longest. We rigged the window in Ross's old bedroom so that we could unlatch it from outside—that's how we got in and out. I told Mr. Prichard that I could cut through the woods and get here in a hurry, and get inside the house if he could keep Marcy busy for a minute."

"So I," Sam said, taking up the story, "left my family out on the highway and out of the line of fire while I raced on over here, and then started yelling at Marcy to get her attention. She took a couple wild shots at me, but I'm happy to say she wasn't a very good shot."

"And I came through the woods," Jason continued, "at a dead run and crawled in through the window. I could hear Marcy and the other lady talking, and I suddenly got the idea of using that old manikin to try to distract her so Mr. Prichard could get in here. I grabbed it and was planning to just throw it into the kitchen, but then Marcy backed right up in there and turned and saw it, so I just ducked down low and kept pushing it that way. I guess Marcy thought it was a ghost or something, because she screamed and started shooting at it." The manikin was leaning against the wall, and Jason pointed at the holes Marcy's bullets had punched all the way through it. "Good thing I ducked, huh? I knew that little gun only held six shots, and she already shot at Mr. Prichard a couple times, so when I counted four more shots I just slammed it right into her."

Moore's eyes bounced from one to the other a couple of times, and then he just shook his head.

"Jason," he said, "as much as I hate to admit this, that was pretty good thinking." He turned to Sam. "And you —I want to know how in the world you figured out that it was her."

Sam grinned at him. "Remember that ad I put in the paper today? Your buddy Girardi managed to get it in today's issue, and it paid off. I think the only woman in the county who is a bigger gossip than Marcy herself was the one who called me. She was the one who knew that Marcy's father, who went by the name of Perkins, was really Bill Parkinson. Bill and Lynette Perkins were Kim's parents. It didn't take too long to figure out that we were in the middle of the biggest freaking coincidence in history."

Kim had been standing off to the side, quietly

listening as the men talked, but now she stepped forward.

"Sam, it wasn't a coincidence," she said. "You did exactly what Beauregard wanted you to do. You found his descendants."

Moore looked at Kim, then turned back to Sam. "Beauregard? Who is Beauregard?"

Sam started to say something, but Kim cut him off. "He's not anybody," she said. "He's a figment of my imagination, but he's saved our lives on many occasions."

Moore stared her for a moment, then looked at Sam. The expression on his face seemed to indicate that he was attempting to offer some sort of sympathy.

Sam sighed. "She's telling you the truth," he said. "Kim has this uncanny ability to see little bits and pieces of the future, sometimes, but I guess the ability frightened her. Somewhere along the line, she came up with the notion that this old Civil War ghost named Beauregard was the one who was telling her these things. It was Beauregard who wanted me to track these folks down, because he—actually, because Kim subconsciously knew that they were related and that someone in the family needed help."

Detective Moore's mouth was hanging slightly open. He stood there like that for a few seconds, then rolled his eyes. "I can't say I haven't heard stranger things," he said.

* * * * *

It had been a busy week, Sam thought. He and his family had stayed in Benton after Marcy's capture, and Sam had retained the services of an attorney to file the motion overturning Ross's conviction. With the sheriff, the chief of police and even the prosecutor all in agreement, Judge Middleton had been delighted to do so. The paperwork was done up in a hurry, and it took less than twenty-four hours for Ross to be released.

Debbie, Ross, and the children had all loaded into Debbie's Chrysler minivan and driven down. They all wanted to thank Sam personally, but he told them over and over that he was simply doing his job.

But then they all got to hear the rest of the story, and Debbie realized that Kim was actually her niece. She threw her arms around Kim and pulled her close, grateful to finally get to know the daughter of the sister she had never even met.

Ross didn't seem all that surprised. He looked at Kim closely for about two full minutes, then said, "You look like Lynette."

Royce Garrity was shocked to find out her father was back in the area, but once she knew the whole story about Kim and Marcy, she decided it was time to be forgiving. She had spent several hours at her father's place in Ewing the day after Marcy's arrest, and Kim had gone with her. Both women admitted later that they burst into tears when they saw their father again, each of them for the first time in many years. Bill was in his late eighties, but his mind was still in fairly decent shape despite all the alcohol. He was able to recall many moments from both of their childhoods, and both Royce and Kim came away from the experience happy. They promised to keep in touch with each other, and to try to be the sisters they had never gotten to be.

On the second day of their visit, Sam had taken everyone involved out to dinner. He even called up Detective Moore and Jason Garrity to invite them along, and was pleasantly surprised when they showed up together in Moore's car.

"Well, hell," Moore said when Sam grinned at him, "you wanted me to give the kid a chance, right? After what he did to help you on this case, I figured he might be worth trying to salvage. We spent half the afternoon with the sheriff, and he's agreed to hire this punk. He's going to be stuck in dispatch for quite a while, but it turns out the office has a little money for educating and training new deputies."

Sam congratulated Jason, and they all went into the restaurant to eat.

At dinner, with a dozen people in his party, Sam felt like he had actually accomplished something. It was a wonderful evening, and by the time it was over, Sam realized that there was only one loose end left that he needed to tie up.

"So, I've got to know," he said during a lull in the

table conversation. "When Moore asked us who Beauregard was, you actually said he was just a figment of your imagination, this time. I'm still trying to figure out what I believe, but I want to know why you said that."

Everyone in the party had finally been told that Sam's mysterious client had hired him to track down the descendants of an old Civil War soldier named Henry Thomas Beauregard. When Sam asked that question, they all turned and looked at him expectantly.

Kim sat there for a moment, as if gathering her thoughts. She looked at Sam, then looked at Indie and smiled. She looked at Grace and the smile got a little wider, and then she looked at her granddaughter and it spread completely across her face. Then she looked at all of the others sitting there, and the smile turned into something thoughtful.

"I said it," she began, "because it's true. When Marcy grabbed me, I hadn't heard Beauregard in more than a day. I was actually afraid he was gone forever, but it turned out he wasn't. He had been digging around in my memories and found some that I had apparently suppressed a long time ago. I guess it was because I watched my mother lose so many of her own memories. I saw her go from this vibrant, happy woman to someone who couldn't even remember the way to the grocery store, and it was only three blocks down the street. I guess that hurt, and so for some reason I started burying a lot of the memories I had of her."

She looked at all of their guests. "You see, for many years I was convinced that Beauregard was a ghost that had somehow attached himself to me. At first it kind of scared me, but then I learned that he could often tell me things that were going to happen, or he could give me answers to questions I didn't even know needed to be asked. Once, when Indie and I were struggling just to survive, he told me to go into this old abandoned house, because there was something there that would help us out. In that house, that seemingly belonged to no one, we discovered a box of silver dishes and such, very old and very valuable. We lived on that money for quite a while.

"Anyway, just about everyone else who knew me thought I was a bit on the crazy side, and I guess that's understandable. What they couldn't deny, though, was that whatever Beauregard told me always seemed to be true. When Sam and Indie got married, Beauregard started helping him out a bit, telling him things about his cases that made it possible for him to solve them, or to save lives. Sometimes it even saved Sam's life."

"That's absolutely true," Sam said. "More than once."

"Well, anyway, when Marcy had me and I was so scared, Beauregard came back. This time, though, he told me to just sit quietly and try to remember some things. And do you know, suddenly a lot of those old memories began to come back. I remembered when I was a very little girl, and my mother would pull me up onto her lap and tell me these wonderful stories. They were stories that her mother had told her, she said, stories that were passed down from generation to generation in our family."

She took a deep breath. "Some of the most important stories she told me were about my great-great-great-I don't know how many greats-great-grandfather. And his name—his name was Henry Thomas Beauregard. He had served in the Confederate Army during the Civil War, and he had never come home, but he had such a rich and powerful personality that he was incredibly well respected by everyone who knew him. I don't remember everything she told me about him, but I do know that I probably heard those stories over and over throughout my early childhood. It wasn't until Mom's mind started really going that she stopped telling me about him, and that's probably when I started to suppress those memories. I guess I missed those moments, and because it was painful to think about them, I simply put them away."

She reached out and touched her daughter's face. "Then one day, right after Indie and I had moved into this terrible old house, I suddenly knew that if I didn't take her out of her playpen, something bad was going to happen. I hurried into the room where she was at and snatched her up, and it was only seconds later a big part of the ceiling fell in and landed right where she had been. Well, I'd always been taught that anything supernatural was probably evil, so some part of me subconsciously wanted to blame my supernatural knowledge on something even more supernatural. And I guess that's why, when I had to come up with something, those buried memories of Henry Thomas Beauregard surfaced a bit."

She looked around the table again, smiling at each person. "They say that when someone suffers a great trauma, they sometimes create a whole new personality to deal with it. Abuse victims do that, prisoners of war have been known to do that, and I'm sure there are other examples, but I don't know them. Well, I guess that's what I did. Beauregard became a part of me that could handle knowing the future, because I couldn't. Now, though, since I finally know the truth, I'm no longer afraid of this gift. If it continues, then I'll simply accept it. But that's why I say Beauregard is not a real ghost, that he is nothing but a part of myself that was created when I needed him."

Everyone sat there in silence for a moment, just looking at her, and then Sam cleared his throat.

"Is he gone?"

Kim looked at him for a moment, then closed her eyes. She opened them a moment later and smiled.

"He says not to worry, Sam," she said. "You're not quite free of him yet."

What'd You Think?

Thank you for reading *Fact or Fiction.* I had a blast writing it, and I hope you had fun reading it.

If you enjoyed the book, please consider telling your friends, or posting a short review. Word of mouth is an author's best friend and is much appreciated.

All the best,

David Archer

Full List Of My Books Can Be Found At

www.davidarcherbooks.com

Made in the USA
Coppell, TX
09 February 2023

12465396R00192